THE RUBBER BAND

Also Available in Large Print
by Rex Stout:

The Red Box
Fer-De-Lance
The League of Frightened Men

Nero Wolfe

THE RUBBER BAND

By Rex Stout

G.K. HALL & CO.

Boston, Massachusetts

1981

Library of Congress Cataloging in Publication Data

Stout, Rex, 1886-1975.
The rubber band.

At head of title: Nero Wolfe.
Large print ed.
Reprint of the ed. published by Jove/HBJ, New York.
1. Large type books. I. Title: Nero Wolfe,
The rubber band.
[PS3537.T733R8 1981]   813'.52   80-29550
ISBN 0-8161-3224-0

Published in Large Print by arrangement
with the estate of Rex Stout

Set in Compugraphic 18 pt English Times
by Adhanet Elias

THE RUBBER BAND

1

I threw down the magazine section of the Sunday *Times* and yawned. I looked at Nero Wolfe and yawned again. "Is this bird, S. J. Woolf, any relation of yours?"

Wolfe, letting fly with a dart and getting a king of clubs, paid no attention to me. I went on:

"I suppose not, since he spells it different. The reason I ask, an idea just raced madly into my bean. Why wouldn't it be good for business if this S. J. Woolf did a picture of you and an article for the *Times?* God knows you're full of material." I took time out to grin, considering Wolfe's size in the gross or physical aspect, and left the grin on as Wolfe grunted, stooping to pick up a dart he had dropped.

I resumed. "You couldn't beat it for

publicity, and as for class it's Mount Everest. This guy Woolf only hits the high spots. I've been reading his pieces for years, and there's been Einstein and the Prince of Wales and Babe Ruth and three Presidents of the United States (O say, can you see very little in the White House) and the King of Siam and similar grandeur. His idea seems to be, champions only. That seems to let you in, and strange as it may appear, I'm not kidding, I really mean it. Among our extended circle there must be a couple of eminent gazabos that know him and would slip him the notion."

Wolfe still paid no attention to me. As a matter of fact, I didn't expect him to, since he was busy taking exercise. He had recently got the impression that he weighed too much — which was about the same as if the Atlantic Ocean formed the opinion that it was too wet — and so had added a new item to his daily routine. Since he only went outdoors for things like earthquakes and holocausts, he was rarely guilty of movement except when he was up on the roof with Horstmann and the orchids, from nine to eleven in the morning and four to six in the afternoon, and there was no provision there for pole vaulting. Hence the new apparatus for a daily workout, which was a beaut. It was scheduled from 3:45 to 4:00 P.M. There was a board about two feet square, faced with cork, with a large circle marked on it, and 26 radii and a smaller inner circle, outlined with fine wire, divided the circle's area into 52 sections. Each section had its symbol painted on it, and together they made up a deck of cards; the bull's-eye, a small disk in the corner, was the Joker. There was also a supply of darts, cute little things about four inches long and weighing a couple of ounces, made of wood and feathers with a metal needle-point. The idea was to hang the board up on the wall, stand off 10 or 15 feet, hurl five darts at it and make a poker hand, with the Joker wild. Then you went and pulled the darts out, and hurled them over again. Then you went and pulled . . .

Obviously, it was pretty darned exciting. When I mean to convey is, it would have been a swell game for a little girls' kindergarten class; no self-respecting boy over six months of age would have wasted much time with it. Since my only excuse for writing this is to relate the facts of one of Nero Wolfe's cases, and since I take that trouble only where murder was involved, it may be supposed that I tell about that poker-dart game because later on one of the darts was dipped in poison and used to pink a guy with. Nothing doing. No one ever suffered any injury from those darts that I know of, except me. Over a period of two months Nero Wolfe nicked me for a little worse than eighty-five bucks, playing draw with the Joker and deuces wild, at two bits a go. There was no chance of getting any real accuracy with it, it was mostly luck.

Anyhow, when Wolfe decided he weighed too much, that was what he got. He called the darts javelins. When I found my losses were approaching the century point I decided to stop humoring him, and quit the thing cold, telling him that my doctor had warned me against athlete's heart. Wolfe kept on with his exercise, and by now, this Sunday I'm telling about, he had got so he could stick the Joker twice out of five shots.

I said, "It would be a good number. You rate it. You admit yourself that you're a genius. It would get us a lot of new clients. We could take on a permanent staff —"

One of the darts slipped out of Wolfe's handful, dropped to the floor, and rolled to my feet. Wolfe stood and looked at me. I knew what he wanted, I knew he hated to stoop, but stooping was the only really violent part of that game and I figured he needed the exercise. I sat tight. Wolfe opened his eyes at me:

"I have noticed Mr. Woolf's drawings. They are technically excellent."

The son of a gun was trying to bribe me to pick up his dart by pretending to be interested in what I had said. I thought to myself, all right, but you'll pay for it, let's just see how long you'll stand there and stay interested. I picked up the magazine section and opened it to the article, and observed briskly:

"This is one of his best. Have you seen it? It's about some Englishman that's

over here on a government mission —
wait — it tells here —''

I found it and read aloud: *"It is not
known whether the Marquis of Clivers is
empowered to discuss military and naval
arrangements in the Far East; all that has
been disclosed is his intention to make a
final disposition of the question of spheres
of economic influence. That is why, after
a week of conferences in Washington with
the Departments of State and Commerce,
he has come to New York for an
indefinite stay to consult with financial
and industrial leaders. More and more
clearly it is being realized in government
circles that the only satisfactory and
permanent basis for peace in the Orient is
the removal of the present causes of
economic friction."*

I nodded at Wolfe. "You get it?
Spheres of economic influence. The same
thing that bothered Al Capone and Dutch
Schultz. Look where economic friction
landed them."

Wolfe nodded back. "Thank you,
Archie. Thank you very much for
explaining it to me. Now if you —"

I hurried in: "Wait, it gets lots more interesting than that." I glanced down the page. "In the picture he looks like a ruler of men — you know, like a master barber or a head waiter, you know the type. It goes on to tell how much he knows about spheres and influences, and his record in the war — he commanded a brigade and he got decorated four times — a noble lord and all prettied up with decorations like a store front — I say three cheers and let us drink to the King, gentlemen! You understand, sir, I'm just summarizing."

"Yes, Archie. Thank you."

Wolfe sounded grim. I took a breath. "Don't mention it. But the really interesting part is where it tells about his character and his private life. He's a great gardener. He prunes his own roses! At least it says so, but it's almost too much to swallow. Then it goes on, new paragraph: *While it would be an exaggeration to call the marquis an eccentric, in many ways he fails to conform to the conventional conception of a British peer, probably due in some measure to the fact that in his younger* days — he is now 64 — he spent many years, in various activities, in Australia, South America, and the western part of the United States. He is a nephew of the ninth marquis, and succeeded to the title in 1905, when his uncle and two cousins perished in the sinking of the Rotania off the African coast. But under any circumstances he would be an extraordinary person, and his idiosyncrasies, as he is pleased to call them, are definitely his own.

"He never shoots animals or birds, though he owns some of the best shooting in Scotland — yet he is a famous expert with a pistol and always carries one. Owning a fine stable, he has not been on a horse for fifteen years. He never eats anything between luncheon and dinner, which in England barely misses the aspect of treason. He has never seen a cricket match. Possessing more than a dozen automobiles, he does not know how to drive one. He is an excellent poker player and has popularized the game among a circle of his friends. He is passionately fond of croquet, derides golf as a

8

'corrupter of social decency,' and keeps an American cook at the manor of Pokendam for the purpose of making pumpkin pie. On his frequent trips to the Continent he never fails to take with him —"

There was no point in going on, so I stopped. I had lost my audience. As he stood facing me Wolfe's eyes had gradually narrowed into slits; and of a sudden he opened his hand and turned it palm down to let the remaining darts fall to the floor, where they rolled in all directions; and Wolfe walked from the room without a word. I heard him in the hall, in the elevator, getting in and banging the door to. Of course he had the excuse that it was four o'clock, his regular time for going to the plant-rooms.

I could have left the darts for Fritz to pick up later, but there was no sense in me getting childish just because Wolfe did. So I tore off the sheet of the magazine section I had been reading from, with the picture of the Marquis of Clivers in the center, fastened it to the corkboard with a couple of thumbtacks, gathered up the darts, stood off 15 feet and let fly. One of the darts got the marquis in the nose, another in his left eye, two of them in his neck, and the last one missed him by an inch. He was well pinned. Pretty good shooting, I thought, as I went for my hat to venture out to a movie, not knowing then that before he left our city the marquis would treat us to an exhibition of much better shooting with a quite different weapon, nor that on that sheet of newspaper which I had pinned to the corkboard was a bit of information that would prove to be fairly useful in Nero Wolfe's professional consideration of a sudden and violent death.

2

For the next day, Monday, October 7th, my memo pad showed two appointments. Neither displayed any promise of being either lucrative or exciting. The first one, down for 3:30 in the afternoon, was with a guy named Anthony D. Perry. He was a tycoon, a director of the Metropolitan Trust Company, the bank we did business with, and president of the Seaboard Products Corporation — one of those vague firms occupying six floors of a big skyscraper and selling annually a billion dollars' worth of something nobody ever actually saw, like soy beans or powdered cocoanut shells or dried llama's hoofs. As I say, Perry was a tycoon; he presided at meetings and was appointed on Mayor's Committees and that king of hooey. Wolfe had handled a couple of investigations for him in previous years — nothing of any importance. We didn't know what was on his mind this time; he had telephoned for an appointment.

The second appointment was for 6:00 P.M. It was a funny one, but we often had funny ones. Saturday morning, October 5th, a female voice had phoned that she wanted to see Nero Wolfe. I said okay. She said, yes, but she wanted to bring someone with her who would not arrive in New York until Monday morning, and she would be busy all day, so could they come at 5:30. I said, no, but they could come at six, picking up a pencil to put down her name. But she wasn't divulging it; she said she would bring her name along with her, and they would arrive at six sharp, and it was very important. It wasn't much of a date, but I put it on the memo pad and hoped she would turn up, for she had the kind of voice that makes you want to observe it in the flesh.

Anthony D. Perry was there on the dot at three-thirty. Fritz answered the door and brought him to the office. Wolfe was at his desk drinking beer. I sat in my corner and scowled at the probability that Perry was going to ask us to follow the scent of some competitor suspected of unfair trade practices, as he had before, and I did not regard that as a treat. But this time he had a different kind of difficulty, though it was nothing to make your blood run cold. He asked after our health, including me because he was democratic, inquired politely regarding the orchids, and then hitched his chair up and smiled at Wolfe as one man of affairs to another.

"I came to see you, Mr. Wolfe, instead of asking you to call on me, for two reasons. First, because I know you refuse to leave your home to call on anyone whatever, and, second, because the errand I want you to undertake is private and confidential."

Wolfe nodded. "Either would have sufficed, sir. And the errand?"

"Is, as I say, confidential." Perry cleared his throat, glancing at me as I opened up my notebook. "I suppose Mr. . . ."

13

"Goodwin." Wolfe poured a glass of beer. "Mr. Goodwin's discretion reaches to infinity. Anything too confidential for him would find me deaf."

"Very well. I want to engage you for a delicate investigation, one that will require most careful handling. It is in connection with an unfortunate situation that has arisen in our executive offices." Perry cleared his throat again. "I fear that a young woman, one of our employees, is going to suffer an injustice — a victim of circumstances — unless something is done about it."

He paused. Wolfe said, "But, Mr. Perry. Surely, as the directing head of your corporation, you are its fount of justice — or its opposite?"

Perry smile. "Not absolutely. At best, a constitutional monarch. Let me explain. Our executive offices are on the thirty-second floor of our building — the Seaboard Building. We have some thirty private offices on the floor, officers of the corporation, department heads and so on. Last Friday one of the officers had in his desk a sum of money in currency, a fairly large sum, which disappeared under circumstances which led him to suspect that it had been taken by — by the employee I spoke of. It was not reported to me until Saturday morning. The officer requested immediate action, but I could not bring myself to believe the employee guilty. She has been — that is, she has always seemed to merit the most complete confidence. In spite of appearances . . .''

He halted. Wolfe asked, ''And you wish us to learn the truth of the matter?''

''Yes. Of course. That's what I want.'' Perry cleared his throat. ''But I also want you to consider her record of probity and faithful service. And I would like to ask you, in discussing the affair with Mr. Muir, to give him to understand that you have been engaged to handle it as you would any investigation of a similar nature. In addition, I wish your reports to be made to me personally.''

''I see.'' Wolfe's eyes were half closed. ''It seems a little complex. I would like to avoid any possibility of misunderstanding. Let us make it clear. You are not asking us to discover an arrangement of evidence that will demonstrate the employee's guilt. Nor are you engaging us to devise satisfactory proof of her innocence. You merely want us to find the truth."

"Yes," Perry smiled. "But I hope and believe that the truth will be her innocence."

"As it may be. And who is to be our client, you or the Seaboard Products Corporation?"

"Why . . . that hadn't occurred to me. The corporation, I should think. That would be best."

"Good." Wolfe looked at me. "If you please, Archie." He leaned back in his chair, twined his fingers at the peak of his middle mound, and closed his eyes.

I whirled on my swivel, with my notebook. "First the money, Mr. Perry. How much?"

"Thirty thousand dollars. In hundred-dollar bills."

"Egad. Payroll?"

"No." He hesitated. "Well, call it payroll."

"It would be better if we knew about it."

"Is it necessary?"

"Not necessary. Just better. The more we know the less we have to find out."

"Well . . . since it is understood this is strictly confidential . . . you know of course that in connection with our business we need certain privileges in certain foreign countries. In our dealings with the representatives of those countries we sometimes need to employ cash sums."

"Okay. This Mr. Muir you mentioned, he's the paymaster?"

"Mr. Ramsey Muir is the senior vice-president of the corporation. He usually handles such contacts. On this occasion, last Friday, he had a luncheon appointment with a gentleman from Washington. The gentleman missed his train and telephoned that he would come on a later one, arriving at our office at five-thirty. He did so. When the moment arrived for Mr. Muir to open the drawer of his desk, the money was gone. He was of course greatly embarrassed."

"Yeah. When had he put it there?"

An interruption came from Wolfe. He

moved to get upright in his chair, then to arise from it. He looked down at Perry:

"You will excuse me, sir. It is the hour for my prescribed exercise and, following that, attention to my plants. If it would amuse you, when you have finished with Mr. Goodwin, to come to the roof and look at them, I would be pleased to have you." He moved halfway to the door, and turned. "It would be advisable, I think, for Mr. Goodwin to make a preliminary investigation before we definitely undertake the commission you offer us. It appears to present complexities. Good day, sir." He went on out. The poker-dart board had been moved to his bedroom that morning, it being a business day with appointments.

"A cautious man." Perry smiled at me. "Of course his exceptional ability permits him to afford it."

I saw Perry was sore by the color above his cheekbones. I said, "Yeah. When had he put it there?"

"What? Oh, to be sure. The money had been brought from the bank and placed in Mr. Muir's desk that morning, but he

18

had looked in the drawer when he returned from lunch, around three o'clock, and saw it intact. At five-thirty it was gone."

"Was he there all the time?"

"Oh, no. He was in and out. He was with me in my office for twenty minutes or so. He went once to the toilet. For over half an hour, from four to until about four-forty, he was in the directors' room, conferring with other officers and Mr. Savage, our public relations counsel."

"Was the drawer locked?"

"No."

"Then anyone might have lifted it."

Perry shook his head. "The executive reception clerk is at a desk with a view of the entire corridor; that's her job, to know where everyone is all the time, to facilitate interviews. She knows who went in Muir's room, and when."

"Who did?"

"Five people. An office boy with correspondence, another vice-president of the company, Muir's stenographer, Clara Fox, and myself."

"Let's eliminate. I suppose you

3/1998

didn't take it?"

"No. I almost wish I had. When the office boy was there, Muir was there too. The vice-president, Mr. Arbuthnot, is out of the question. As for Muir's stenographer, she was still there when the loss was discovered — most of the others had gone home — and she insisted that Muir search her belongings. She has a little room next to Muir's, and had not been out of it except to enter his room. Besides, he has had her for eleven years, and trusts her."

"Which leaves Clara Fox."

"Yes." Perry cleared his throat. "Clara Fox is our cable clerk — a most responsible position. She translates and decodes all cables and telegrams. She went to Muir's office around a quarter after four, during his absence, with a decoded message, and waited there while Muir's stenographer went to her own room to type a copy of it."

"Has she been with you long?"

"Three years. A little over."

"Did she know the money was there?"

"She probably knew it was in Muir's

office. Two days previously she had handled a cablegram giving instructions for the payment.''

''But you think she didn't take it.''

Perry opened his mouth and closed it again. I put the eye on him. He didn't look as if he was really undecided; it seemed rather that he was hunting for the right words. I waited and looked him over. He had clever, careful, blue-gray eyes, a good jaw but a little too square for comfort, hair no grayer than it should be considering he must have been over sixty, a high forehead with a mole on the right temple, and a well-kept healthy skin. Not a layout that you would ordinarily regard as hideous, but at that moment I wasn't observing it with great favor, because it seemed likely that there was something phony about the pie he was inviting me to stick my finger into; and I give low marks to a guy that asks you to help him work a puzzle and then holds out one of the pieces on you. I don't mind looking for the fly in a client's ointment, but why throw in a bunch of hornets?

Perry finally spoke. ''In spite of

appearances, I am personally of the opinion that Clara Fox did not take that money. It would be a great shock to me to know that she did, and the proof would have to be unassailable."

"What does she say about it?"

"She hasn't been asked. Nothing has been said, except to Arbuthnot, Miss Vawter — the executive reception clerk — and Muir's stenographer. I may as well tell you, Muir wanted to send for the police this morning, and I restrained him."

"Maybe Miss Vawter took it."

"She has been with us eighteen years. I would sooner suspect myself. Besides, someone is constantly passing in the corridor. If she left her desk even for a minute it would be noticed."

"How old is Clara Fox?"

"Twenty-six."

"Oh. A bit junior, huh? For such a responsible position. Married?"

"No. She is a remarkably competent person."

"Do you know anything of her habits? Does she collect diamonds or frolic with the geegees?"

Perry stared at me. I said, "Does she bet on horse races?"

He frowned. "Not that I know of. I am not personally intimate with her, and I have not had her spied on."

"How much does she get and how do you suppose she spends it?"

"Her salary is thirty-six hundred. So far as I know, she lives sensibly and respectably. She has a small flat somewhere, I believe, and she has a little car — I have seen her driving it. She — I understand she enjoys the theater."

"Uh-huh." I flipped back a page of my notebook and ran my eye over it. "And this Mr. Muir who leaves his drawer unlocked with thirty grand inside — might he have been caught personally with his financial pants down and made use of the money himself?"

Perry smiled and shook his head. "Muir owns some twenty-eight thousand shares of the stock of our corporation, worth over two million dollars at the present market, besides other properties. It was quite usual for him to leave the drawer

23

unlocked under those circumstances.''

I glanced at my notebook again, and lifted my shoulders a shade and let them drop negligently, which meant that I was mildly provoked. The thing looked like a mess, possibly a little nasty, with nothing much to be expected in the way of action or profit. The first step, of course, after what Wolfe had said, was for me to go take a look at the 32nd floor of the Seaboard Building and enter into conversation. But the clock on the wall said 4:20. At six the attractive telephone voice with her out-of-town friend was expected to arrive; I wanted to be there, and I probably wouldn't be if I once got started chasing that thirty grand. I said to Perry:

''Okay. I suppose you'll be at your office in the morning? I'll be there at nine sharp to look things over. I'll want to see most of —''

''Tomorrow morning?'' Perry was frowning. ''Why not now?''

''I have another appointment.''

''Cancel it.'' The color topped his cheekbones again. ''This is urgent. I am one of Wolfe's oldest clients. I took the trouble to come here personally . . ."

"Sorry, Mr. Perry. Won't tomorrow do? My appointment can't very well be postponed."

"Send someone else."

"There's no one available who could handle it."

"This is outrageous!" Perry jerked up in his chair. "I insist on seeing Wolfe!"

I shook my head. "You know you can't. You know darned well he's eccentric." But then I thought, after all, I've seen worse guys, and he's a client, and maybe he can't help it if he gets on Mayor's Committees, perhaps they nag him. So I got out of my chair and said, "I'll go upstairs and put it up to Wolfe, he's the boss. If he says —"

The door of the office opened. I turned. Fritz came in, walking formal as he always did to announce a caller. But he didn't get to announce this one. The caller came right along, two steps behind Fritz, and I grinned when I saw he was stepping so soft that Fritz didn't know he was there.

Fritz started, "A gentleman to —"

"Yeah, I see him. Okay."

Fritz turned and saw he had been stalked, blinked, and beat it. I went on observing the caller, because he was a specimen. He was about six feet three inches tall, wearing an old blue serge suit with no vest and the sleeves a mile short, carrying a cream-colored ten-gallon hat, with a face that looked as if it had been left out on the fire escape for over half a century, and walking like a combination of a rodeo cowboy and a panther in the zoo.

He announced in a smooth low voice, "My name's Harlan Scovil." He went up to Anthony D. Perry and stared at him with half-shut eyes. Perry moved in his chair and looked annoyed. The caller said, "Are you Mr. Nero Wolfe?"

I butted in, suavely. "Mr. Wolfe is not here. I'm his assistant. I'm engaged with this gentleman. If you'll excuse us . . ."

The caller nodded, and turned to stare again at Perry. "Then who — you ain't Mike Walsh? Hell no, Mike was a runt." He gave Perry up, and glanced around the room, then looked at me. "What do I do now, sit down and hang my hat on my ear?"

I grinned. "Yeah. Try that leather one over there." He panthered for it, and I started for the door, throwing over my shoulder to Perry, "I won't keep you waiting long."

Upstairs, in the plant-rooms on the roof, glazed-in, where Wolfe kept his ten thousand orchids, I found him in the middle room turning some off-season Oncidiums that were about to bud, while Horstmann fussed around with a pot of charcoal and osmundine. Wolfe, of course, didn't look at me or halt operations; whenever I interrupted him in the plant-rooms he pretended he was Joe Louis in his training camp and I was a boy peeking through the fence.

I said, loud so he couldn't also pretend he didn't hear me, "That millionaire downstairs says I've got to go to his office right now and begin looking under the rugs for his thirty grand, and there's an appointment here for six o'clock. I expressed a preference to go tomorrow morning.''

Wolfe said, ''And if your pencil fell to the floor and you were presented with the alternative of either picking it up or leaving it there, would you also need to consult me about that?''

''He's exasperated.''

''So am I.''

''He says it's urgent, I'm outrageous, and he's an old client.''

''He is probably correct all around. I like particularly the second of his conclusions. Leave me.''

''Very well. Another caller just arrived. Name of Harlan Scovil. A weather-beaten plainsman who stared at Anthony D. Perry and said he wasn't Mike Walsh.''

Wolfe looked at me. ''You expect, I presume, to draw your salary at the end of the month.''

''Okay.'' I wanted to reach out and tip over one of the Oncidiums, but decided it wouldn't be diplomatic, so I faded.

When I got back downstairs Perry was standing in the door of the office with his hat on and his stick in his hand. I told him, ''Sorry to keep you waiting.''

"Well?"

"It'll have to be tomorrow, Mr. Perry. The appointment can't be postponed. Anyhow, the day's nearly gone, and I couldn't do much. Mr. Wolfe sincerely regrets —"

"All right," Perry snapped. "At nine o'clock, you said?"

"I'll be there on the dot."

"Come to my office."

"Right."

I went and opened the front door for him.

In the office Harlan Scovil sat in the leather chair over by the bookshelves. As, entering, I lamped him from the door, I saw that his head was drooping and he looked tired and old and all in; but at the sound of me he jerked up and I caught the bright points of his eyes. I went over and wheeled my chair around to face him.

"You want to see Nero Wolfe?"

He nodded. "That was my idea. Yes, sir."

"Mr. Wolfe will be engaged until six o'clock, and at that time he has another appointment. My name's Archie Goodwin. I'm Mr. Wolfe's confidential assistant. Maybe I could help you?"

"The hell you are." He certainly had a smooth soft voice for his age and bulk and his used-up face. He had his half-shut eyes on me. "Listen, sonny. What sort of a man is this Nero Wolfe?"

I grinned. "A fat man."

He shook his head in slow impatience. "It ain't to the point to tease a steer. You see the kind of man I am. I'm out of my country." His eyes twinkled a little. "Hell, I'm clear over the mountains. Who was that man that was in here when I came?"

"Just a man. A client of Mr. Wolfe's."

"What kind of a client? Anybody ever give him a name?"

"I expect so. Next time you see him, ask him. Is there anything I can do for you?"

"All right, sonny." He nodded. "Naturally I had my suspicions up, seeing any kind of a man here at this time, but you heard me remark that he wasn't Mike

Walsh. And God knows he wasn't Vic Lindquist's daughter. Thanks for leaving my ideas free. Could I have a piece of paper? Any kind."

I handed him a sheet of typewriter bond from my desk. He took it and held it in front of him spread on the palms of his hands, bent his head over it and opened his mouth, and out popped a chew of tobacco the size of a hen's egg. I'm fairly observant, but I hadn't suspected its existence. He wrapped the paper around it, clumsily but thoroughly, got up and took it to the wastebasket, and came back and sat down again. His eyes twinkled at me.

"There seems to be very little spittin' done east of the Mississippi. A swallower like me don't mind, but if John Orcutt was here he wouldn't tolerate it. But you was asking me if there's anything you can do for me. I wish to God I knew. I wish to God there was a man in this town you could let put your saddle on."

I grinned at him. "If you mean an honest man, Mr. Scovil, you must have got an idea from a movie or something.

There's just as many honest men here as the other side of the mountains. And just as few. I'm one. I'm so damn honest I often double-cross myself. Nero Wolfe is almost as bad. Go ahead. You must have come here to spill something besides that chew."

With his eyes still on me, he lifted his right hand and drew the back of it slowly across his nostrils from left to right, and then, after a pause, from right to left. He nodded. "I've traveled over two thousand miles, from Hiller County, Wyoming, to come here on an off chance. I sold thirty calves to get the money to come on, and for me nowadays that's a lot of calves. I didn't know till this morning I was going to see any kind of a man called Nero Wolfe. All that is to me is just a name and address on a piece of paper I've got in my pocket. All I knew was I was going to see Mike Walsh and Vic's daughter and Gil's daughter, and I was supposed to be going to see George Rowley, and by God if I see him and what they say is true I'll be able to fix up some fences this winter and get something besides lizards and coyotes inside of 'em. One thing you can tell me anyhow, did you ever hear of any kind of a man called a Marquis of Clivers?''

I nodded. "I've read in the paper about that kind of a man."

"Good for you. I don't read much. One reason, I'm so damn suspicious I don't believe it even if I do read it, so it don't seem worth the trouble. I'm here now because I'm suspicious. I was supposed to come here at six o'clock with the rest of those others, but I had my time on my hands anyhow, so I thought I might as well ride out and take a look. I want to see this Nero Wolfe man. You don't look to me like a man that goes out at night after lambs, but I want to see him. What really made me suspicious was the two daughters. God knows a man is bad enough when you don't know him, but I doubt if you ever could get to know a woman well enough to leave her loose around you. I never really tried, because it didn't ever seem to be worth the trouble." He stopped, and drew the back of his hand across his nostrils again, back and forth, slowly. His eyes twinkled at me. "Naturally, your opinion is that I talk a good deal. That's the truth. It won't hurt you any, and it may even do you good. Out in Wyoming I've been talking to myself like this for thirty years, and by God if I can stand it you can."

It appeared to me that I was going to stand it whether I wanted to or not, but something interfered. The phone rang. I turned to my desk and plucked the receiver, a female voice asked me to hold the wire, and then another voice came at me:

"Goodwin? Anthony D. Perry. I just got back to my office, and you must come here at once. Any appointments you have, cancel them, if there's any damage I'll pay it. The situation here has developed. A taxi will get you here in five minutes."

I love these guys that think the clock stops every time they sneeze. But by the tone of his voice it was a case either of aye, aye, sir, or a plain go to hell, and by nature I'm a courteous man. So I told him okay.

"You'll come at once?"

"I said okay."

I shoved the phone back and turned to the caller.

"I've got to leave you, Mr. Scovil. Urgent business. But if I heard you right, you've been invited here to the six o'clock party, so I'll see you again. Correct?"

He nodded. "But look here, sonny, I wanted to ask you —"

"Sorry, I've got to run." I was on my way. I looked back from the door. "Don't nurse any suspicions about any kind of a man named Nero Wolfe. He's as straight as he is fat. So-long."

I went to the kitchen, where Fritz had about nine kinds of herbs spread out on the shredding board all at once, and told him:

"I'm going out. Back at six. Leave the door open so you can see the hall. There's an object in the office waiting for a six o'clock appointment, and if you have any good deeds to spare like offering a man a drink and a plate of cookies, I assure you he is worthy. If Wolfe comes down before I get back, tell him he's there."

Fritz, nibbling a morsel of tarragon, nodded. I went to the hall and snared my hat and beat it.

3

I didn't fool with a taxi, and it wasn't worth while to take the roadster, which as usual was at the curb, and fight to park it. From Wolfe's house in West 35th Street, not far from the Hudson, where he had lived for over twenty years, and I had slept on the same floor with him for eight, it was only a hop, skip and jump to the new Seaboard Building, in the twenties, also near the river. I hoofed it, considering meanwhile the oddities of my errand. Why had Anthony D. Perry, president of the Seaboard Products Corporation, taken the trouble to come to our office to tell us about an ordinary good clean theft? As the Tel & Tel say in their ads, why not telephone? And if he felt so confident that Clara Fox hadn't done it, did he suspect she was being framed or what? And so on.

Having been in the Seaboard Building before, and even, if you would believe it, in the office of the president himself, I knew my way around. I remembered what the executive reception clerk on the 32nd floor looked like, and so was expecting no treat in that quarter, and got none. I now knew also that she was called Miss Vawter, and so addressed her, noting that her ears stuck out at about the same angle as three years previously. She was expecting me, and without bothering to pry her thin lips open she waved me to the end of the corridor.

In Perry's office, which was an enormous room furnished in The Office Beautiful style with four big windows giving a sweeping view of the river, there was a gathering waiting for me. I went in and shut the door behind me and looked them over. Perry was seated at his desk with his back to the windows, frowning at his cigar smoke. A bony-looking medium-sized man, with hair somewhat grayer than Perry's, brown eyes too close together, and pointed ears, sat near-by. A woman something over thirty, with a flat nose, who could have got a job as schoolteacher just on her looks, stood at a corner of Perry's desk. She looked as if she might have been doing some crying. In another chair, out a little, another woman sat with her back to me as I entered. On my way approaching Perry I caught a glimpse of her face as I went by, and saw that additional glimpses probably wouldn't hurt me any.

Perry grunted at me. He spoke to the others: "This is the man. Mr. Goodwin, from Nero Wolfe's office." He indicated with nods, in succession, the woman sitting, the one standing, and the man. "Miss Fox. Miss Barish. Mr. Muir."

I nodded around, and looked at Perry. "You said you've got some developments?"

"Yes." He knocked ashes from his cigar, looked at Muir, and then at me. "You know most of the facts, Goodwin. Let's come to the point. When I returned I found that Mr. Muir had called Miss Fox to his office, had accused her of stealing the money, and was questioning her in the presence of Miss Barish.

This was contrary to the instructions I had given. He now insists on calling in the police."

Muir spoke to me, smoothly. "You're in on a family quarrel, Mr. Goodwin." He leveled his eyes at Perry. "As I've said, Perry, I accept your instructions on all business matters. This is more personal than business. The money was taken from my desk. I was responsible for it. I know who stole it, I am prepared to swear out a warrant, and I intend to do so."

Perry stared back at him. "Nonsense. I've told you that my authority extends to all the affairs of this office." His tone could have been used to ice a highball. "You may be ready to swear out a warrant and expose yourself to the risk of being sued for false arrest, but I will not permit a vice-president of this corporation to take that risk. I went to the trouble of engaging the best man in New York City, Nero Wolfe, to investigate this. I even took pains that Miss Fox should not know she was suspected before the investigation. I admit that I do not believe she is a thief. That is my opinion. If evidence is uncovered to prove me wrong, then I'm wrong."

"Evidence?" Muir's jaw had tightened. "Uncovered? A clever man like Nero Wolfe might either cover or uncover. No? Depending on what you paid him for."

Perry smiled a controlled smile. "You're an ass, Muir, to say a thing like that. I'm the president of this company, and you're an ass to suggest I might betray its interests, either the most important or the most trivial. Mr. Goodwin heard my conversation with his employer. He can tell you what I engaged him to do."

"No doubt he could tell me what he has been instructed to tell me."

"I'd go easy, Muir." Perry was still smiling. "The kind of insinuations you're making might run into something serious. You shouldn't bark around without considering the chances of starting a real dogfight, and I shouldn't think you'd want a fight over a triviality like this."

"Triviality?" Muir started to tremble. I saw his hand on the chair-arm begin to shake, and he gripped the wood. He turned his eyes from Perry onto Clara Fox, sitting a few feet away, and the look in them made it plain why trivialities were out. Of course I didn't know whether he was hating her because she had lifted the thirty grand or because she had stepped on his toe, but from where I stood it looked like something much fancier than either of those. If looks could kill she would have been at least a darned sick woman.

Then he shifted from her to me, and he had to pinch his voice. "I won't ask you to report the conversation you heard, Mr. Goodwin. But of course you've had instructions and hints from Mr. Perry, so you might as well have some from me." He got up, walked around the desk, and stood in front of me. "I presume that an important part of your investigation will be to follow Miss Fox's movements, to learn if possible what she has done with the money. When you see her entering a theater or an expensive restaurant with Mr. Perry, don't suppose she is squandering the money that way. Mr. Perry will be paying. Or if you see Mr. Perry entering her apartment of an evening, it will not be to help her dispose of the evidence. His visit will be for another purpose."

He turned and left the room, neither slow nor fast. He shut the door behind him, softly. I didn't see him, I heard him; I was looking at the others. Miss Barish stared at Miss Fox and turned pale. Perry's only visible reaction was to drop his dead cigar into the ash tray and push the tray away. The first move came from Miss Fox. She stood up.

The idea occurred to me that on account of active emotions she was probably better looking at that moment than she ordinarily was, but even discounting for that there was plenty to go on. In my detached impersonal way, I warmed to her completely at exactly that moment, when she stood up and looked at Anthony D. Perry. She had brown hair, neither long nor boyish bob, just a swell lot of careless hair, and her eyes were brown too and you could see at a glance that they would never tell you anything except what she wanted them to.

She spoke. "May I go now, Mr. Perry?

It's past five o'clock, and I have an appointment."

Perry looked at her with no surprise. Evidently he knew her. He said. "Mr. Goodwin will want to talk with you."

"I know he will. Will the morning do? Am I to come to work tomorrow?"

"Of course. I refer you to Goodwin. He has charge of this now, and the responsibility is his."

I shook my head. "Excuse me, Mr. Perry. Mr. Wolfe said he would decide whether he'd handle this or not after my preliminary investigation. As far as Miss Fox is concerned, tomorrow will suit me fine." I looked at her. "Nine o'clock?"

She nodded. "Not that I have anything to tell you about that money, except that I didn't take it and never saw it. I have told Mr. Perry and Mr. Muir that. I may go then? Good night."

She was perfectly cool and sweet. From the way she was handling herself, no one would have supposed she had any notion that she was standing on a hot spot. She included all of us in her good-night glance, and turned and walked out as self-possessed as a young doe not knowing that there's a gun pointed at it and a finger on the trigger.

When the door was shut Perry turned to me briskly. "Where do you want to start, Goodwin? Would fingerprints around the drawer of Muir's desk do any good?"

I grinned at him and shook my head. "Only for practice, and I don't need any. I'd like to have a chat with Muir. He must know it won't do to have Miss Fox arrested just because she was in his room. Maybe he thinks he knows where the money is."

Perry said, "Miss Barish is Mr. Muir's secretary."

"Oh." I looked at the woman with the flat nose still standing there. I said to her, "It was you that typed the cablegram while Miss Fox waited in Muir's room. Did you notice —"

Perry horned in. "You can talk with Miss Barish later." He glanced at the clock on the wall, which said 5:20. "Or, if you prefer, you can talk with her here, now." He shoved his chair back and got up. "If you need me, I'll be in the directors' room, at the other end. I'm late now, for a conference. It won't take long. I'll ask Muir to stay, and Miss Vawter also, in case you want to see her." He had moved around to the front of his desk, and halted there. "One thing, Goodwin, about Muir. I advise you to forget his ridiculous outburst. He's jerky and nervous, and the truth is he's too old for the strain business puts on a man nowadays. Disregard his nonsense. Well?"

"Sure." I waved a hand. "Let him rave."

Perry frowned at me, nodded, and left the room.

The best chair in sight was the one Perry had just vacated, so I went around and took it. Miss Barish stood with her shoulders hanging, squeezing her handkerchief and looking straight at me. I said, friendly, "Move around and sit down — there, where Muir was. So you're Muir's secretary."

"Yes, sir." She got onto the edge of the chair.

"Been his secretary eleven years."

"Yes, sir."

"Cut out the sir. Okay? I'm not gray-headed. So Muir looked through your belongings last Friday and didn't find the money?"

Her eyes darkened. "Certainly he didn't find it."

"Right. Did he make a thorough search of your room?"

"I don't know. I don't care if he did."

"Now don't get sore. I don't care either. After you copied the cablegram and took the original back to Miss Fox in Muir's room, what was she carrying when she left there?"

"She was carrying the cablegram."

"But where did she have the thirty grand, down her sock? Didn't it show?"

Miss Barish compressed her lips to show that she was putting up with me. "I did not see Miss Fox carrying anything except the cablegram. I have told Mr. Muir and Mr. Perry that I did not see Miss Fox carrying anything except the cablegram."

I grinned at her. "And you are now telling Mr. Goodwin that you did not see Miss Fox carrying anything except the cablegram. Check. Are you a friend of Miss Fox's?"

"No. Not a real friend. I don't like her."

"Egad. Why don't you like her?"

"Because she is extremely attractive, and I am homely. Because she has been here only three years and she could be Mr. Perry's private secretary tomorrow if she wanted to, and that is the job I have wanted ever since I came here. Also because she is cleverer than I am."

I looked at Miss Barish, more interested at all the frankness. Deciding to see how far down the frankness went, I popped at her, "How long has Miss Fox been Perry's mistress?"

She went red as a beet. Her eyes dropped, and she shook her head. Finally she looked up at me again, but didn't say anything. I tried another one:

"Then tell me this. How long has Muir been trying to get her away from Perry?"

Her eyes got dark again, and the color stayed. She stared at me a minute, then all at once rose to her feet and stood there squeezing her handkerchief. Her voice trembled a little, but it didn't seem to bother her.

"I don't know whether that's any of your business, Mr. Goodwin, but it's none of mine. Don't you see . . . don't you see how this is a temptation to me? Couldn't I have said I saw her carrying something out of that room?" She squeezed the handkerchief harder. "Well . . . I didn't say it. Don't I have to keep my self-respect? I'll go out of my way too, I don't know anything about it, but I don't believe Clara Fox has ever been anybody's mistress. She wouldn't have to be, she's too clever. I don't know anything about that money either, but if you want to ask me questions to see if I do, go ahead."

I said, "School's out. Go on home. I may want you again in the morning, but I doubt it."

She turned pale as fast as she had turned red. She certainly was a creature of moods. I got up from Perry's chair and walked all the way across the room to open the door and stand and hold it. She went past, still squeezing the handkerchief and mumbling good night to me, and I shut the door.

Feeling for a cigarette and finding I didn't have any, I went back to the windows and stood surveying the view. As I had suspected, the thing wasn't a good clear theft at all, it was some kind of a mess. From the business standpoint, it was obvious that the thing to do was go back and tell Nero Wolfe it was a case of refusing to let the administrative heads of the Seaboard Products Corporation use our office for a washtub to dump their dirty linen in. But what reined me up on that was my professional curiosity about Clara Fox. If sneak thieves came as cool and sweet as that, it was about time I found it out. And if she wasn't one, my instinctive dislike of a frame-up made me hesitate about leaving her parked against a fireplug. I was fairly well disgusted, and got more disgusted, after gazing out of the window for a while, when I felt in my pockets again for a cigarette with no results.

I wandered around The Office Beautiful a little, sightseeing and cogitating, and then went out to the corridor. It was empty. Of course, it was after office hours. All its spacious width and length, there was no traffic, and it was dimmer than it had been when I entered, for no more lights were turned on and it was getting dark outdoors. There were doors along one side, and at the further end the double doors, closed, of the directors' room. I heard a cough, and turned, and saw Miss Vawter, the executive reception clerk, sitting in the corner under a light with a magazine.

She said in a vinegar voice, "I'm remaining after hours because Mr. Perry said you might want to speak to me."

She was a pain all around. I said, "Please continue remaining. Which is Muir's room?"

She pointed to one of the doors, and I headed for it. I was reaching out for the knob when she screeched at me, "You can't go in there like that! Mr. Muir is out."

I called to her, "Do tell. If you want to interrupt Mr. Perry in his conference, go to the directors' room and give the alarm. I'm investigating."

I went on in, shut the door, found the wall switch and turned on the lights. As I did so, a door in another wall opened, and Miss Barish appeared. She stood and looked without saying anything.

I observed, "I thought I told you to go home."

"I can't." Her color wasn't working either way. "When Mr. Muir is here I'm not supposed to go until he dismisses me. He is in conference."

"I see. That your room? May I come in?"

She stepped back and I entered. It was a small neat room with one window and the usual stenographic and filing equipment. I let the eyes rove, and then asked her, "Would you mind leaving me here for a minute with the door shut, while you go to Muir's desk and open and close a couple of the drawers? I'd like to see how much din it makes."

She said, "I was typing."

"So you were. All right, forget it. Come and show me which drawer the money was in."

She moved ahead of me, led the way to

Muir's desk, and pulled open one of the drawers, the second one from the top on the right. There was nothing in it but a stack of envelopes. I reached out and closed it, then opened and closed it again, grinning as I remembered Perry's suggestion about fingerprints. Then I left the desk and strolled around a little. It was a vice-president's office, smaller and modester than Perry's but still by no means a pigpen. I noticed one detail, or rather three, a little out of the ordinary. There was no portrait of Abraham Lincoln nor replica of the Declaration of Independence on the walls, but there were three different good-sized photographs of three different good-looking women, hanging framed. I turned to Miss Barish, who was still standing by the desk:

"Who are all the handsome ladies?"

"They are Mr. Muir's wives."

"No! Honest to God? Mostly dead?"

"I don't know. None of them is with him now."

"Too bad. It looks like he's sentimental."

She shook her head. "Mr. Muir is

a sensual man.''

She was having another frank spell. I glanced at my watch. It was a quarter to six, giving me another five minutes, so I thought I might as well use them on her. I opened up, friendly, but although she seemed to be willing to risk a little more chat with me, I didn't really get any facts. All I learned was what I already knew, that she had no reason to suppose that Clara Fox had lifted the jack, and that if there was a frame-up she wasn't in on it. When the five minutes was up I turned to go, and at that moment the door opened and Muir came in.

Seeing us, he stopped, then came on again, to his desk. ''You may go, Miss Barish. If you want to talk with me, Goodwin, sit down.''

Miss Barish disappeared into her room. I said, ''I won't keep you now, Mr. Muir. I suppose you'll be here in the morning?''

''Where else would I be?''

That kind of childishness never riles me. I grinned at the old goat, said, ''Okay,'' and left him.

Outside in the corridor, down a few

paces towards the directors' room, a group of four or five men stood talking. I saw Perry was among them, and approached. He saw me, and came to meet me.

I said, "Nothing more tonight, Mr. Perry. Let's let Mr. Muir have a chance to cool off. I'll report to Nero Wolfe."

Perry frowned. "He can phone me at my home any time this evening. It's in the book."

"Thanks. I'll tell him."

As I passed Miss Vawter on my way out, still sitting in the corner with her magazine, I said to her out of the side of my mouth, "See you at the Rainbow Room."

4

Down on the sidewalk the shades of night were not keeping the metropolitan bipeds from the swift completion of their appointed rounds. Striding north toward 35th Street, I let the brain skip from this to that and back again, and decided that the spot Clara Fox was standing on was probably worse than hot, it was sizzling. Had she lit the fire herself? I left that in unfinished business.

I got home just at six o'clock and, knowing that Wolfe wouldn't be down for a few minutes yet, I went to the office to see if the Wyoming wonder had thought of any new suspicions and if his colleagues had shown up. The office was empty. I went through to the front room to see if he had moved his base there, but it was empty too. I beat it to the kitchen. Fritz was there, sitting with his slippers off, reading that newspaper in French. I asked him:

"What did you do with him?"

"Qui? Ah, le monsieur —" Fritz giggled. "Excuse me, Archie. You mean the gentleman who was waiting."

"Yeah, him."

"He received a telephone call," Fritz leaned over and began pulling on his slippers. "Time already for Mr. Wolfe!"

"He got a phone call here?"

Fritz nodded. "About half an hour after you left. More maybe. Wait till I look." He went to the stand where the kitchen phone extension was kept, and glanced at his memo pad. "That's right. 5:26. Twenty-six minutes past five."

"Who was it?"

Fritz's brows went up. "Should I know, Archie?" He thought he was using slang. "A gentleman said he wished to speak to Mr. Scovil in case he was here, and I went to the office and asked if it was Mr. Scovil, and he talked from your desk, and then he got up and put on his hat and went out."

"Leave any message?"

"No. I had come back to the kitchen, closing the office door for his privacy but leaving this one open as you said, and he came out and went in a hurry. He said nothing at all."

I lifted the shoulders and let them drop. "He'll be back. He wants to see a kind of a man named Nero Wolfe. What's on the menu?"

Fritz told me, and let me take a sniff at the sauce steaming on the simmer-plate; then I heard the elevator and went back to the office. Wolfe entered, crossed to his chair and got himself lowered, rang for beer and took the opener out of the drawer, and then vouchsafed me a glance.

"Pleasant afternoon, Archie?"

"No, sir. Putrid. I went around to Perry's office."

"Indeed. A man of action must expect such vexations. Tell me about it."

"Well, Perry left here just after I came down, but about eight minutes after that he phoned and instructed me to come galloping. Having the best interests of

58

my employer in mind I went."

"Notwithstanding the physical law that the contents can be no larger than the container." Fritz arrived with two bottles of beer, Wolfe opened and poured one, and drank. "Go on."

"Yes, sir. I disregard your wit, because I'd like to show you this picture before the company arrives, and they're already ten minutes late. By the way, the company we already had has departed. He claimed to be part of the six o'clock appointment and said he would wait, but Fritz says he got a phone call and went in a hurry. Maybe the appointment is off. Anyhow, here's the Perry puzzle. . . ."

I laid it out for him, in the way that he always liked to get a crop of facts, no matter how trivial or how crucial. I told him what everybody looked like, and what they did, and what they said fairly verbatim. He finished the first bottle of beer meanwhile, and had the second well on its way when I got through. I rattled it off and then leaned back and took a sip from a glass of milk I had brought from the kitchen.

Wolfe pinched his nose. "Pfui! Hyenas. And your conclusions?"

"Maybe hyenas. Yeah." I took another sip. "On principle I don't like Perry, but it's possible he's just using all the decency he has left after a life of evil. You have forbidden me to use the word louse, so I would say that Muir is an insect. Clara Fox is the ideal of my dreams, but it wouldn't stun me to know that she lifted the roll, though I'd be surprised."

Wolfe nodded. "You may remember that four years ago Mr. Perry objected to our bill for an investigation of his competitors' trade practices. I presume that now he would like us to shovel the mud from his executive offices for twelve dollars a day. It is not practicable always to sneer at mud; there's too much of it. So it gives the greater pleasure to do so when we can afford it. At present our bank balance is agreeable to contemplate. Pfui!" He lifted his glass and emptied it and wiped his lips with his handkerchief.

"Okay," I agreed. "But there's something else to consider. Perry wants you to phone him this evening. If you take the case on we'll at least get expenses, and if you don't take it on Clara Fox may get five years for grand larceny and I'll have to move to Ossining so as to be near her and take her tidbits on visiting day. Balance the mud-shoveling against the loss of my services — but that sounds like visitors. I'll finish my appeal later."

I had heard the doorbell sending Fritz into the hall and down it to the door. I glanced at the clock: 6:30; they were half an hour late. I remembered the attractive telephone voice, and wondered if we were going to have another nymph, cool and sweet in distress, on our hands.

Fritz came in and shut the door behind him, and announced callers. Wolfe nodded. Fritz went out, and after a second in came a man and two women. The man and the second woman I was barely aware of, because I was busy looking at the one in front. It certainly was a nymph cool and sweet in distress. Evidently she knew enough about Nero Wolfe to recognize him, for with only a swift glance at me she came forward to Wolfe's desk and spoke.

"Mr. Wolfe? I telephoned on Saturday. I'm sorry to be late for the appointment. My name is Clara Fox." She turned. "This is Miss Hilda Lindquist and Mr. Michael Walsh."

Wolfe nodded at her and at them. "It is bulk, not boorishness, that keeps me in my chair." He wiggled a finger at me. "Mr. Archie Goodwin. Chairs, Archie?"

I obliged, while Clara Fox was saying, "I met Mr. Goodwin this afternoon, in Mr. Perry's office." I thought to myself, you did indeed, and for not recognizing your voice I'll let them lock me in the cell next to yours when you go up the river.

"Indeed." Wolfe had his eyes half closed, which meant he was missing nothing. "Mr. Walsh's chair to the right, please. Thank you."

Miss Fox was taking off her gloves. "First I'd like to explain why we're late. I said on the telephone that I couldn't make the appointment before Monday because I was expecting someone from out of town who had to be here. It was a man from out west named Harlan Scovil. He arrived this morning, and I saw him during the lunch hour, and arranged to meet him at a quarter past five, at his hotel, to bring him here. I went for him, but he wasn't there. I waited and . . . well, I tried to make some inquiries. Then I met Miss Lindquist and Mr. Walsh, as agreed, and we went back to Mr. Scovil's hotel again. We waited until a quarter past six, and decided it would be better to come on without him."

"Is his presence essential?"

"I wouldn't say essential. At least not at this moment. We left word, and he may join us here any second. He must see you too, before we can do anything. I should warn you, Mr. Wolfe, I have a very long story to tell."

She hadn't looked at me once. I decided to quit looking at her, and tried her companions. They were just barely people. Of course I remembered Harlan Scovil telling Anthony D. Perry that he wasn't Mike Walsh. Apparently this bird was. He was a scrawny little mick, built wiry, over sixty and maybe even seventy, dressed cheap but clean, sitting only half in his chair and keeping an ear palmed with his

63

right hand. The Lindquist dame, with a good square face and wearing a good brown dress, had size, though I wouldn't have called her massive, first because it would have been only a half-truth, and second because she might have socked me. I guess she was a fine woman, of the kind that would be more apt to be snapping a coffee cup in her fingers than a champagne glass. Remembering Harlan Scovil to boot, it looked to me as if, whatever game Miss Fox was training for, she was picking some odd numbers for her team.

Wolfe had told her that the longer the story the sooner it ought to begin, and she was saying:

"It began forty years ago, in Silver City, Nevada. But before I start it, Mr. Wolfe, I ought to tell you something that I hope will make you interested. I've found out all I could about you, and I understand that you have remarkable abilities and an equally remarkable opinion of their cash value to people you do things for."

Wolfe sighed. "Each of us must choose

his own brand of banditry, Miss Fox."

"Certainly. That is what I have done. If you agree to help us, and if we are successful, your fee will be one hundred thousand dollars."

Mike Walsh leaned forward and blurted, "Ten per cent! Fair enough?"

Hilda Lindquist frowned at him. Clara Fox paid no attention. Wolfe said, "The fee always depends. You couldn't hire me to hand you the moon."

She laughed at him, and although I had my notebook out I decided to look at her in the pauses. She said, "I won't need it. Is Mr. Goodwin to take down everything? With the understanding that if you decide not to help us his notes are to be given to me?"

Cagey Clara. The creases of Wolfe's cheeks unfolded a little. "By all means."

"All right." She brushed her hair back. "I said it began forty years ago, but I won't start there. I'll start when I was nine years old, in 1918, the year my father was killed in the war, in France. I don't remember my father much. He was killed in 1918, and he sent my mother a letter

65

which she didn't get until nearly a year later, because instead of trusting it to the army mail he gave it to another soldier to bring home. My mother read it then, but I never knew of it until seven years later, in 1926, when my mother gave it to me on her death-bed. I was seventeen years old. I loved my mother very dearly.''

She stopped. It would have been a good spot for a moist film over her eyes or a catch in her voice, but apparently she had just stopped to swallow. She swallowed twice. In the pause I was looking at her. She went on:

''I didn't read the letter until a month later. I knew it was a letter father had written to mother eight years before, and with mother gone it didn't seem to be of any importance to me. But on account of what mother had said, about a month after she died I read it. I have it with me. I'll have to read it to you.''

She opened her alligator-skin handbag and took out a folded paper. She jerked it open and glanced at it, and back at Wolfe. ''May I?''

''Do I see typewriting?''

She nodded. "This is a copy. The original is put away." She brushed her hair back with a hand up and dipping swift like a bird. "This isn't a complete copy. There is — this is — just the part to read.

"So, dearest Lola, since a man can't tell what is going to happen to him here, or when, I've decided to write you about a little incident that occurred last week, and make arrangements to be sure it gets to you, in case I never get home to tell you about it. I'll have to begin away back.

"I've told you a lot of wild tales about the old days in Nevada. I've told you this one too, but I'll repeat it here briefly. It was at Silver City, in 1895. I was 25 years old, so it was 10 years before I met you. I was broke, and so was the gang of youngsters I'm telling about. They were all youngsters but one. We weren't friends, there was no such thing as a friend around there. Most of the bunch of 2000 or so that inhabited Silver City camp that time were a good deal older than us, which was how we happened to get together — temporarily. Everything was temporary!

"The ringleader of our gang was a kid we called Rubber on account of the way he bounced back up when he got knocked down. His name was Coleman, but I never knew his first name, or if I did I can't remember it, though I've often tried. Because Rubber was our leader, someone cracked a joke one day that we should call ourselves The Rubber Band, and we did. Pretty soon most of Silver City was calling us that.

"One of the gang, a kid named George Rowley, shot a man and killed him. From what I heard — I didn't see it — he had as good a right to shoot as was usually needed around there, but the trouble was that the one he killed happened to be a member of the Vigilance Committee. It was at night, 24 hours after the shooting, that they decided to hang him. Rowley hadn't had sense enough to make a getaway, so they took him and shut him up in a shanty until daylight, with one of their number for a guard, an Irishman. As Harlan Scovil would say — I'll never forget Harlan — he was a kind of a man named Mike Walsh.

"Rowley went after his guard, Mike Walsh. I mean talking to him. Finally, around midnight, he persuaded Mike to send for Rubber Coleman. Rubber had a talk with him and Mike. Then there was a lot of conspiring, and Rubber did a lot of dickering with Rowley. We were gathered in the dark in the sagebrush out back of John's Palace, a shack out at the edge of the city —"

Clara Fox looked up. "My father underscored the word city."

Wolfe nodded. "Properly, no doubt."

She went on: " — and we had been drinking some and were having a swell time. Around two o'clock Rubber showed up again and lit matches to show us a paper George Rowley had signed, with him and Mike Walsh as witnesses. I've told you about it. I can't give it to you word for word, but this is exactly what it said. It said that his real name wasn't George Rowley, and that he wasn't giving his real name in writing, but that he had told it to Rubber Coleman. It said that he was from a wealthy family in England, and that if he got out of Silver City alive

69

he would go back there, and some day he would get a share of the family pile. It said it wouldn't be a major share because he wasn't an oldest son. Then it hereby agreed that whenever and whatever he got out of his family connections, he would give us half of it, provided we got him safe out of Silver City and safe from pursuit, before the time came to hang him.

"We were young, and thought we were adventurers, and we were half drunk or maybe more. I doubt if any of us had any idea that we could ever get hold of any of the noble English wealth, except possibly Rubber Coleman, but the idea of the night rescue of a member of our gang was all to the good. Rubber had another paper ready too, all written up. It was headed, PLEDGE OF THE RUBBER BAND, and we all signed it. It had already been signed by Mike Walsh. In it we agreed to an equal division of anything coming from George Rowley, no matter who got it or when.

"We were all broke except Vic Lindquist, who had a bag of gold dust.

It was Rubber's suggestion that we get Turtle-back in. Turtle-back was an old-timer who owned the fastest horse in Silver City. He had no use for that kind of a horse; he only happened to own it because he had won it in a poker game a few days before. I went with Rubber down to Turtle-back's shanty. We offered him Vic Lindquist's dust for the horse, but he said it wasn't enough. We had expected that. Then Rubber explained to him what was up, told him the whole story, and offered him an equal share with the rest of us, for the horse, and the dust to boot. Turtle-back was still half asleep. Finally, when he got the idea, he blinked at us, and then all of a sudden he slapped his knee and began to guffaw. He said that by God he always had wanted to own a part of England, and anyway he would probably lose the horse before he got a chance to ride it much. Rubber got out the PLEDGE OF THE RUBBER BAND, but Turtle-back wouldn't have his name added to it, saying he didn't like to have his name written down anywhere. He would trust us to see that he got his share.

Rubber scribbled out a bill of sale for the horse, but Turtle-back wouldn't sign that either; he said I was there as a witness, the horse was ours, and that was enough. He put on his boots and took us over to Johnson's corral, and we saddled the horse, a palamino with a white face, and led it around the long way, back of the shacks and tents and along a gully, to where the gang was.

"We rescued George Rowley all right. You've heard me tell about it, how we loosened a couple of boards and then set fire to the shanty where they had him, and how he busted out of the loose place in the excitement, and how Mike Walsh, who was known to be a dead shot, emptied two guns at him without hitting him. Rowley was in the saddle and away before anyone else realized it, and nobody bothered to chase him because they were too busy putting out the fire.

"The story came out later about our buying Turtle-back's horse, but by that time people's minds were on something else, and anyway our chief offense was that we had started the fire and it couldn't

be proved we had done that. It might have been different if the man we helped to escape had done something really criminal, like cheating at cards or stealing somebody's dust.

"So far as I know, none of us ever saw Rowley or heard of him since that night. You've heard me mention twenty times, when you and I were having hard going, that I'd like to find him and learn if he owed me anything, but you know I never did and of course I meant it more or less as a joke anyhow. But recently, here in France, two things have come up about it. The first one is a thought that's in my mind all the time, what if I do get mine over here, what kind of a fix am I leaving you and the kid in? My little daughter Clara — God how I'd love to see her. And you. To hell with that stuff when it's no use, but I'd gladly stand up and let the damn Germans shoot me tomorrow morning if I could see you two right this minute. The answer to my question, is, a hell of a fix. My life would end more useless than it started, leaving my wife and daughter without a single

solitary damn thing.

"The other thing that's come up is that I've seen George Rowley. It was one day last week. I may have told you that the lobe of his right ear was gone — he said he had it hacked off in Australia — but I don't think I really knew him by that. There probably is a mighty good print of his mug in my mind somewhere, and I just simply knew it was him. After twenty-three years! I was out with a survey detail about a mile back of the front trenches, laying out new communication lines, and a big car came along. British. The car stopped. It had four British officers in it, and one of them called to me and I went over and he asked for directions to our division headquarters. I gave them to him, and he looked at my insignia and asked if we Americans let our captains dig ditches. I had seen by his insignia that he was a brigade commander. I grinned at him and said that in our army everybody worked but the privates. He looked at me closer and said, 'By Gad, It's Gil Fox!' I said, 'Yes, sir. General Rowley?' He shook his head and laughed and told the driver to go on, and the car jumped forward, and he turned to wave his hand at me.

"So he's alive, or he was last week, and not in the poorhouse, or whatever they call it in England. I've made various efforts to find out who he was, but without success. Maybe I will soon. In the meantime, I'm writing this down and disposing of it, because although it may sound far-fetched and even a little batty, the fact is that this is the only thing resembling a legacy that I can leave to you and Clara. After all, I did risk my life that night in Silver City, on the strength of a bargain understood and recorded, and if that Englishman is rolling in it there's no reason why he shouldn't pay up. It is my hope and wish that you will make every effort to see that he does, not only for your sake but for our daughter's sake. That may sound melodramatic, but the things that are going on over here get you that way. As soon as I find out who he is I'll get this back and add that to it.

"Another thing. If you do find him and get a grubstake out of it, you must not use it to pay that $26,000 I owe those people out in California. You must promise me this. You must, dearest Lola. I'm bestowing this legacy on you and Clara, not them! I say this because I know that you know how much that debt has worried me for ten years. Though I wasn't really responsible for that tangle, it's true that it would give me more pleasure to straighten that out than anything in the world except to see you and Clara, but if I die that business can die with me. Of course, if you should get such a big pile of dough that you're embarrassed — but miracles like that don't happen.

"If something should come out of it, it must be split with the rest of the gang if you can find them. I don't know a thing about any of them except Harlan Scovil, and I haven't heard from him for several years. The last address I had for him is in the little red book in the drawer of my desk. One of the difficulties is that you haven't got the paper that George Rowley signed. Rubber Coleman, by agreement, kept both that and the PLEDGE OF THE RUBBER BAND. Maybe you can find Coleman. Or maybe Rowley is a decent *guy and will pay without any paper. Either sounds highly improbable. Hell, it's all a daydream. Anyhow, I have every intention of getting back to you safe and sound, and if I do you'll never see this unless I bring it along as a souvenir.*

"Here are the names of everybody that was in on it: George Rowley. Rubber Coleman (don't know his first name). Victor Lindquist. Harlan Scovil (you've met him, go after him first). Mike Walsh (he was a little older, maybe 32 at the time, not one of the Rubber Band). Turtle-back was a good deal older, probably dead now, and that's all the name I knew for him. And last but by no means least, yours truly, and how truly it would take a year to tell, Gilbert Fox, the writer of these presents."

Clara Fox stopped. She ran her eyes over the last sentence again, then placed that sheet at the back, folded them up, and returned them to her handbag. She put her hand up and brushed back her hair, and sat and looked at Wolfe. No one said anything.

Finally Wolfe sighed. He opened his

eyes at her. "Well, Miss Fox. It appears to be the moon that you want after all."

She shook her head. "I know who George Rowley is. He is now in New York."

"And this, I presume —" Wolfe nodded — "is Mr. Victor Lindquist's daughter." He nodded again. "And this gentleman is the Mr. Walsh who emptied two guns at Mr. Rowley without hitting him."

Mike Walsh blurted, "I could have hit him!"

"Granted, sir. And you, Miss Fox, would very much like to have $26,000, no doubt with accrued interest, to discharge debts of your dead father. In other words, you need something a little less than $30,000."

She stared at him. She glanced at me, then back at him, and asked coolly, "Am I here as your client, Mr. Wolfe, or as a suspected thief?"

He wiggled a finger at her. "Neither as yet. Please do not be so foolish as to be offended. If I show you my mind, it is only to save time and avoid irrelevancies.

Haven't I sat and listened patiently for ten minutes although I dislike being read aloud to?"

"That's irrelevant."

"Indeed. I believe it is. Let us proceed. Tell me about Mr. George Rowley."

But that had to be postponed. I had heard the doorbell, and Fritz going down the hall, and a murmur from outside. Now I shook my head at Clara Fox and showed her my palm to stop her, as the office door opened and Fritz came in and closed it behind him.

"A man to see you, sir. I told him you were engaged."

I bounced up. There were only two kinds of men Fritz didn't announce as gentlemen: one he suspected of wanting to sell something, and a policeman, uniform or not. He could smell one a mile off. So I bounced up and demanded:

"A cop?"

"Yes, sir."

I whirled to Wolfe. "Ever since I saw Muir looking at Miss Fox today I've been thinking she ought to have a lightning rod. Would you like to have her pinched in here, or out in the hall?"

Wolfe nodded and snapped, "Very well, Archie."

I crossed quick and got myself against the closed office door, and spoke not too loud to Fritz, pointing to the door that opened into the front room: "Go through that way and lock the door from the front room to the hall." He moved. I turned to the others: "Go in there and sit down, and if you don't talk any it won't disturb us." Walsh and Miss Lindquist stared at me. Clara Fox said to Wolfe:

"I'm not your client yet."

He said, "Nor yet a suspect. Here. Please humor Mr. Goodwin."

She got up and went and the others followed her, Fritz came back and I told him to shut that door and lock it and give me the key. Then I went back to my desk and sat down, while Fritz, at a nod from Wolfe, went to the hall for the visitor.

The cop came in, and I was surprised to see that it was a guy I knew. Surprised, because the last time I had heard of Slim Foltz he had been on the Homicide Squad, detailed to the District Attorney's office.

"Hello, Slim."

"Hi, Goodwin." He had his own clothes on. He came on across with his hat in his hand. "Hello, Mr. Wolfe. I'm Foltz, Homicide Squad."

"Good evening, sir. Be seated."

The dick put his hat on the desk and sat down, and reached in his pocket and pulled out a piece of paper. "There was a man shot down the street an hour or so ago. Shot plenty, five bullets in him. Killed. This piece of paper was in his pocket, with your name and address on it, Along with other names. Do you know anything about him?"

Wolfe shook his head. "Except that he's dead. Not, that is, at this moment. If I knew his name, perhaps . . ."

"Yeah. His name was on a hunting license, also in his pocket. State of Wyoming. Harlan Scovil."

"Indeed. It is possible Mr. Goodwin can help you out. Archie?"

I was thinking to myself, hell, he didn't come for her after all. But I was just as well pleased she wasn't in the room.

5

Slim Foltz was looking at me.

I said, "Harlan Scovil? Sure. He was here this afternoon."

Foltz got in his pocket again and fished out a little black memo book and a pencil stub. "What time?"

"He got here around 4:30, a little before maybe, and left at 5:26."

"What did he want?"

"He wanted to see Nero Wolfe."

"What about?"

I shook my head regretfully. "There you've got me, mister. I told him he'd have to wait until six o'clock, so he was waiting."

"He must have said something."

"Certainly he said something. He said he wanted to see Nero Wolfe."

"What else did he say?"

"He said there seemed to be very little spittin' done east of the Mississippi River, and he wanted to know if there were any honest men this side of the mountains. He didn't say specifically what he wanted to see Mr. Wolfe about. We'd never seen him or heard of him before. Oh yes, he said he just got to New York this morning, from Wyoming. By the way, just because that license was in his pocket — was he over six feet, around sixty, blue serge suit with sleeves too short and the lapel torn a little on the right side, with a leathery red face and a cowboy hat —"

"That's him," the dick grunted. "What did he come to New York for?"

"To see Nero Wolfe I guess." I grinned. "That's the kind of a rep we've got. If you mean, did he give any hint as to who might want to bump him off, he didn't."

"Did he see Wolfe?"

"No. I told you, he left at 5:26. Mr. Wolfe never comes down until six o'clock."

"Why didn't he wait?"

"Because he got a phone call."

83

"He got a phone call here?"

"Right here in this room. I wasn't here. I had gone out, leaving this bird here waiting for six o'clock. The phone was answered by Fritz Brenner, Mr. Wolfe's chef and household pride. Want to see him?"

"Yeah. If you don't mind."

Wolfe rang. Fritz came. Wolfe told him he was to answer the gentleman's questions, and Fritz said "Yes, sir" and stood up straight.

All Foltz got out of Fritz was the same as I had got. He had put down the time of the phone call, 5:26, in accordance with Wolfe's standing instructions for exactness in all details of the household and office. It was a man phoning, and he had not given his name and Fritz had not recognized his voice. Fritz had not overheard any of the conversation. Harlan Scovil had immediately left, without saying anything.

Fritz went back to the kitchen.

The dick frowned at the piece of paper. "I wasn't expecting to draw a blank here. I came here first. There's other names on this paper — Clara Fox, Michael Walsh, Michael spelled wrong, Hilda Lindquist, that's what it looks like, and a Marquis of Clivers. I don't suppose you —"

I horned in, shaking my head. "As I said, when this Harlan Scovil popped in here at half-past four today, I had never seen him before. Nor any of those others. Strangers to me. I'm sure Mr. Wolfe hadn't either. Had you, sir?"

"Seen them? No. But I believe I had heard of one of them. Wasn't it the Marquis of Clivers we were discussing yesterday?"

"Discussing? Yes, sir. When you dropped that javelin. That piece in the paper." I looked at Foltz helpfully. "There was an article in the *Times* yesterday, magazine section —"

He nodded. "I know all about that. The sergeant was telling me. This marquis seems to be something like a duke, he's immune by reason of a foreign power or something. It don't even have to be a friendly foreign power. The sergeant says this business might possibly be an international plot. Captain Devore is going to make arrangements to see this marquis and maybe warn him or protect him."

"Splendid." Wolfe nodded approvingly. "The police earn the gratitude of all of us. But for them, Mr. Foltz, we private investigators might sit and wait for clients in vain."

"Yeah." Foltz got up. "Much obliged for the compliment, even if that's all I get. I mean, I haven't got much information. Except that telephone call, that may lead to something. Scovil was shot only four blocks from here, on 31st Street, only nine minutes after he got that phone call, at 5:35. He was walking along the sidewalk and somebody going by in a car reached out and plugged him, filled him full. He was dead right then. It was pretty dark around there, but a man nearby saw the license, and the car's already been found, parked on Ninth Avenue. Nobody saw anyone get out of it."

"Well, that's something." I was hopeful. "That ought to get you somewhere."

"Probably stolen. They usually are."

The dick had his hat in his hand, "Gang stuff, it looks like. Much obliged to you folks anyhow."

"Don't mention it, Slim."

I went to the hall with him, and saw him out the front door, and shut it after him and slid the bolt. Before I returned to the office I stopped at the kitchen and told Fritz that I'd answer any doorbells that might ring for the rest of the evening.

I crossed to Wolfe's desk and grinned at him. "Ha ha. The damn police were here."

Wolfe looked at the clock, which said ten minutes past seven. He reached out and pushed the button, and when Fritz came, leaned back and sighed.

"Fritz."

"Yes, sir."

"A calamity. We cannot possibly dine at eight as usual. Not dine, that is. We can eat, and I suppose we shall have to. You have filets of beef with sauce Abano."

"Yes, sir."

Wolfe sighed again. "You will have to serve it in morsels, for five persons.

By adding some of the fresh stock you can have plenty of soup. Open Hungarian *petits poissons*. You have plenty of fruit? Fill in as you can. It is distressing, but there's no help for it."

"The sauce is a great success, sir. I could give the others canned chicken and mushrooms —"

"Confound it, no! If there are to be hardships, I must share them. That's all. Bring me some beer."

Fritz went, and Wolfe turned to me: "Bring Clara Fox."

I unlocked the door to the front room. Fritz hadn't turned on all the lights, and it was dim. The two women were side by side on the divan, and Mike Walsh was in a chair, blinking at me as if he had been asleep.

I said, "Mr. Wolfe would like to speak to Miss Fox."

Mike Walsh said, "I'm hungry."

Clara Fox said, "To all of us."

"First just you. Please. —There'll be some grub pretty soon, Mr. Walsh. If you'll wait in here."

Clara Fox hesitated, then got up and

preceded me. I shut the door, and she went back to her chair in front of Wolfe, the one the dick had sat in. Wolfe had emptied a glass and was filling it up again.

"Will you have some beer, Miss Fox?"

She shook her head. "Thank you. But I don't like to discuss this with you alone, Mr. Wolfe. The others are just as much —"

"To be sure. Permit me." He wiggled a finger at her. "They shall join us presently. The fact is, I wish to touch on something else for a moment. Did you take that money from Mr. Muir's desk?"

She looked at him steadily. "We shouldn't let things get confused. Are you acting now as the agent of the Seaboard Products Corporation?"

"I'm asking you a question. You came here to consult me because you thought I had abilities. I have; I'm using them. Either answer my question or find abilities elsewhere. Did you take that money?"

"No."

"Do you know who took it?"

"No."

"Do you know anything about it?"

"No. I have certain suspicions, but nothing specific about the money itself."

"Do you mean suspicions on account of the attitude of Mr. Perry and Mr. Muir toward you personally?"

"Yes. Chiefly Mr. Muir."

"Good. Now this: Did you kill anyone this evening between five and six o'clock?"

She stared at him. "Don't be an idiot."

He drank some beer, wiped his lips, and leaned back in his chair. "Miss Fox. The avoidance of idiocy should be the primary and constant concern of every intelligent person. It is mine. I am sometimes successful. Take, for instance, your statement that you did not steal that money. Do I believe it? As a philosopher, I believe nothing. As a detective, I believe it enough to leave it behind me, but am prepared to glance back over my shoulder. As a man, I believe it utterly. I assure you, my reason for the questions I am asking is not idiotic. For one thing, I am observing your face as you reply to them. Bear with me; we will be getting somewhere, I think. Did you kill anyone this evening between five and six o'clock?"

"No."

"Did Mr. Walsh or Miss Lindquist do so?"

"Kill anyone?"

"Yes."

She smiled at him. "As a philosopher, I don't know. I'm not a detective. As a woman, they didn't."

"If they did, you have no knowledge of it?"

"No."

"Good. Have you a dollar bill?"

"I suppose I have."

"Give me one."

She shook her head, not in refusal, but in resigned perplexity at senseless antics. She looked in her bag and got out a dollar bill and handed it to Wolfe. He took it and unfolded it and handed it across to me.

"Enter it, please, Archie. Retainer from Miss Clara Fox. And get Mr. Perry on the phone." He turned to her. "You are now my client."

She didn't smile. "With the understanding, I suppose, that I may —"

"May sever the connection?" His creases unfolded. "By all means. Without notice."

I found Perry's number and dialed it. After giving my fingerprints by television to some dumb kluck I finally got him on, and nodded to Wolfe to take it.

Wolfe was suave. "Mr. Perry? This is Nero Wolfe. I have Mr. Goodwin's report of his preliminary investigation. He was inclined to agree with your own attitude regarding the probable innocence of Clara Fox, and he thought we might therefore be able to render some real service to you. But by a curious chance Miss Fox called at our office this evening — she is here now, in fact — and asked us to represent her interests in the matter. . . . No, permit me, please. . . . Well, it seemed to be advisable to accept her retainer. . . . Really, sir, I see nothing unethical . . ."

Wolfe hated to argue on the telephone. He cut it as short as he could, and rang off, and washed it down with beer. He turned back to Clara Fox.

"Tell me about your personal relations with Mr. Perry and Mr. Muir."

She didn't answer right away. She was sitting there frowning at him. It was the first time I had seen her brow wrinkled, and I liked it better smoothed out. Finally she said, "I supposed you had already taken that case for Mr. Perry. I had gone to a lot of trouble deciding that you were the best man for us — Miss Lindquist and Mr. Walsh and Mr. Scovil and me — and I had already telephoned on Saturday and made the appointment with you before I heard anything about the stolen money. I didn't know until two hours ago that Mr. Perry had engaged you, and since we had the appointment I thought we might as well go through with it. Now you tell Mr. Perry you're acting for me, not the Seaboard, and you say I've given you a retainer for that. That's not straight. If you want to call that a retainer, it's for the business I came to see you about, not that silly rot about the money. That's nonsense."

Wolfe inquired, "What makes you think it's nonsense?"

"Because it is. I don't know what the truth of it is, but as far as I'm concerned it's nonsense."

Wolfe nodded. "I agree with you. That's what makes it dangerous."

"Dangerous? How? If you mean I'll lose my job, I don't think so. Mr. Perry is the real boss there, and he knows I'm more than competent, and he can't possibly believe I took that money. If this other business is successful, and I believe it will be, I won't want the job anyhow."

"But you will want your freedom." Wolfe sighed. "Really, Miss Fox, we are wasting time that may be valuable. Tell me, I beg you, about Mr. Perry and Mr. Muir. Mr. Muir hinted this afternoon that Mr. Perry is enjoying the usufructs of gallantry. Is that true?"

"Of course not." She frowned, and then smiled. "Calling it that, it doesn't sound bad at all, does it? But he isn't. I used to go to dinner and the theater with Mr. Perry fairly frequently, shortly after I started to work for Seaboard. That was

94

during my adventuress phase. I was going to be an adventuress."

"Did something interrupt?"

"Nothing but my disappointment. I have always been determined to get somewhere, not anywhere in particular, just somewhere. My father died when I was nine, and my mother when I was seventeen. She always said I was like my father. She paid for my schooling by sewing fat women's dresses. I loved my mother passionately, and hated the humdrum she was sunk in and couldn't get out of."

"She couldn't find George Rowley."

"She didn't try much. She thought it was fantastic. She wrote once to Harlan Scovil, but the letter was returned. After she died I tried various things, everything from hat-check girl to a stenographic course, and for three years I studied languages in my spare time because I thought I'd want to go all over the world. Finally, by a stroke of luck, I got a good job at the Seaboard three years ago. For the first time I had enough money so I could spend a little trying to find George

Rowley and the others mentioned in father's letter — I realized I'd have to find some of the others so there would be someone to recognize George Rowley. I guess mother was right when she said I'm like father; I certainly had fantastic ideas, and I'm terribly confident that I'm a very unusual person. My idea at that time was that I wanted to get money from George Rowley as soon as possible, so I could pay that old debt of my father's in California, and then go to Arabia. The reason I wanted to go to Arabia —"

She broke off abruptly, looked startled, and demanded, "What in the name of heaven started me on that?"

"I don't know." Wolfe looked patient. "You're wasting time again. Perry and Muir?"

"Well." She brushed her hair back. "Not long after I started to work for Seaboard, Mr. Perry began asking me to go to the theater with him. He said that his wife had been sick in bed for eight years and he merely wanted companionship. I knew he was a multi-millionaire, and I thought it over and decided to become an adventuress. If you think that sounds like a loony kid, don't fool yourself. For lots of women it has been a very exciting and satisfactory career. I never really expected to do anything much with Mr. Perry, because there was no stimulation in him, but I thought I could practice with him and at the same time keep my job. I even went riding with him, long after it got to be a bore. I thought I could practice with Mr. Muir, too, but I was soon sorry I had ever aroused his interest."

She drew her shoulders in a little, a shade toward the center of her, and let them out again, in delicate disgust. "It was Mr. Muir that cured me of the idea of being an adventuress, I mean in the classical sense. Of course I knew that to be a successful adventuress you have to deal with men, and they have to be rich, and seeing what Mr. Muir was like made me look around a little, and realized it would be next to impossible to find a rich man it would be any fun to be adventurous with. Mr. Muir seemed to go practically crazy after he had had dinner with me once or twice. Once he came to my apartment and almost forced his way in, and he had an enormous pearl necklace in his pocket! Of course it was disgusting in a way, but it was even more funny than it was disgusting, because I have never cared for pearls at all. But the worst thing about Mr. Muir is his stubbornness. He's a Scotsman, and apparently if he once gets an idea in his head he can't get it out again —"

Wolfe put in, "Is Mr. Muir a fool?"

"Why . . . yes, I suppose he is."

"I mean as a business man. A man of affairs. Is he a fool?"

"No. Not that way. In fact, he's very shrewd."

"Well, you are." Wolfe sighed. "You are quite an amazing fool, Miss Fox. You know that Mr. Muir, who is a shrewd man, is prepared to swear out a warrant against you for grand larceny. Do you think that he would consider himself prepared if preparations had not actually been made? Why does he insist on immediate action? So that the preparations may not be interfered with, by design, or by mischance. As soon as a warrant is in force against you, the police may search any property of yours, including that item of it where the $30,000 will be found. Couldn't Mr. Muir have taken it himself from his desk and put it anywhere he wanted to, with due circumspection?"

"Put it . . ." She stared at him. "Oh, no." She shook her head. "That would be too low. A man would have to be a dirty scoundrel to do that."

"Well? Who should know better than you, an ex-adventuress, that the race of dirty scoundrels has not yet been exterminated? By the eternal, Miss Fox, you should be tied in your cradle! Where do you live?"

"But, Mr. Wolfe . . . you could never persuade me . . ."

"I wouldn't waste time trying. Where do you live?"

"I have a little flat on East 61st Street."

"And what other items? We can disregard your desk at the office, that would not be conclusive enough. Do you have a cottage in the country? A trunk in storage? An automobile?"

"I have a little car. Nothing else whatever."

"Did you come here in it?"

"No. It's in a garage on 60th Street."

Wolfe turned to me. "Archie. What two can you get here at once?"

I glanced at the clock. "Saul Panzer in ten minutes. If Fred Durkin's not at the movies, him in twenty minutes. If he is, Orrie Cather in half an hour."

"Get them. Miss Fox will give you the key to her apartment and a note of authority, and also a note to the garage. Saul Panzer will search the apartment thoroughly. Tell him what he's looking for, and if he finds it bring it here. Fred will get the automobile and drive it to our garage, and when he gets it there go through it, and leave it there. This alone will cost us twenty dollars, twenty times the amount of Miss Fox's retainer. Everything we undertake nowadays seems to be a speculation."

I got at the telephone. Wolfe opened his eyes on Clara Fox:

"You might learn if Miss Lindquist and

Mr. Walsh will care to wash before dinner. It will be ready in five minutes."

She shook her head. "We don't need to eat. Or we can go out for a bite."

"Great hounds and Cerberus!" He was about as close to a tantrum as he ever got. "Don't need to eat! In heaven's name, are you camels, or bears in for the winter?"

She got up and went to the front room to get them.

6

My dinner was interrupted twice. Saul Panzer came before I had finished my soup, and Fred Durkin arrived while we were in the middle of the beef and vegetables. I went to the office both times and gave them their instructions and told them some hurry would do.

Wolfe made it a rule never to talk business at table, but we got a little forward at that, because he steered Hilda Lindquist and Mike Walsh into the talk and we found out things about them. She was the daughter of Victor Lindquist, now nearly 80 years old and in no shape to travel, and she lived with him on their wheat farm in Nebraska. Apparently it wasn't coffee cups she snapped in her fingers, it was threshing-machines. Clara Fox had finally found her, or rather her father, through Harlan Scovil, and she had come east for the clean-up on the chance that she might get enough to pay off a few dozen mortgages and perhaps get something extra for a new tractor, or at least a mule.

Walsh had gone through several colors before fading out to his present dim obscurity. He had made three good stakes in Nevada and California and had lost all of them. He had tried his hand as a building contractor in Colorado early in the century, made a pile, and dropped it when a sixty-foot dam had gone down the canyon three days after he had finished it. He had come back east and made a pass at this and that, but apparently had used up all his luck. At present he was night watchman on a construction job up at 55th and Madison, and he was inclined to be sore on account of the three dollars he was losing by paying a substitute in order to keep this appointment with Clara Fox. She had found him a year ago through an ad in the paper.

Wolfe was the gracious host. He saw

that Mike Walsh got two rye highballs and the women a bottle of claret, and like a gentleman he gave Walsh two extra slices of the beef, smothered with sauce, which he would have sold his soul for. But he wouldn't let Walsh light his pipe when the coffee came. He said he had asthma, which was a lie. Pipe smoke didn't bother him much, either. He was just sore at Walsh because he had had to give up the beef, and he took it out on him that way.

We hadn't any more than got back to the office, a little after nine o'clock, and settled into our chairs — the whole company present this time — when the doorbell rang. I went out to the front door and whirled the lock and slid the bolt, and opened it. Fred Durkin stepped in. He looked worried, and I snapped at him:

"Didn't you get it?"

"Sure I got it."

"What's the matter?"

"Well, it was funny. Is Wolfe here? Maybe he'd like to hear it too."

I glared at him, fixed the door, and

led him to the office. He went across and stood in front of Wolfe's desk.

"I got the car, Mr. Wolfe. It's in the garage. But Archie didn't say anything about bringing a dick along with it, so I pushed him off. He grabbed a taxi and followed me. When I left the car in the garage just now and walked here, he walked too. He's out on the sidewalk across the street."

"Indeed." Wolfe's voice was thin; he disliked after-dinner irritations. "Suppose you introduce us to the dick first. Where did you meet him?"

Fred shifted his hat to his other hand. He never could talk to Wolfe without getting fussed up, but I must admit there was often enough reason for it. Fred Durkin was as honest as sunshine, and as good a tailer as I ever saw, but he wasn't as brilliant as sunshine. Warm and cloudy today and tomorrow. He said:

"Well, I went to the garage and showed the note to the guy, and he said all right, wait there and he'd bring it down. He went off and in a couple of minutes a man with a wide mouth came up and asked me if I was going for a ride. I'd never saw him before, but I'd have known he was a city feller if I'd had my eyes shut and just touched him with my finger. I supposed he was working on something and was just looking under stones, so I just answered something friendly. He said if I was going for a ride I'd better get a horse, because the car I came for was going to remain there for the present."

Wolfe murmured, "So you apologized and went to a drug store to telephone here for instructions."

Fred looked startled. "No, sir, I didn't. My instructions was to get that car, and I got it. That dick had no documents or nothing, in fact he didn't have nothing but a wide mouth. I went upstairs with him after me. When the garage guy saw the kind of an argument it might be he just disappeared. I ran the car down on the elevator myself and got into the street and headed east. The dick jumped on the running-board, and when I reached around to brush a speck off the windshield I accidentally pushed the dick off. By that time we was at Third Avenue and he hopped a taxi and followed me. When I got to Tenth Avenue, inside your garage, I turned the car inside out, but there was nothing there but tools and an old lead pencil and a busted dog leash and a half a package of Omar cigarettes and —"

Wolfe put up a palm at him. "And the dick is now across the street?"

"Yes, sir. He was when I come in."

"Excellent. I hope he doesn't escape in the dark. Go to the kitchen and tell Fritz to give you a cyanide sandwich."

Fred shifted his hat. "I'm sorry, sir, if I —"

"Go! Any kind of a sandwich. Wait in the kitchen. If we find ourselves getting into difficulties here, we shall need you."

Fred went. Wolfe leaned back in his chair and got his fingers laced on his belly; his lips were moving, out and in, and out and in. At length he opened his eyes enough for Clara Fox to see that he was looking at her.

"Well. We were too late. I told you you were wasting time."

She lifted her brows. "Too late for what?"

"To keep you out of jail. Isn't it obvious? What reason could there be for watching your car except to catch you trying to go somewhere in it? And is it likely they would be laying for you if they had not already found the money?"

"Found it where?"

"I couldn't say. Perhaps, in the car itself. I am not a necromancer, Miss Fox. Now, before we —"

The phone rang, and I took it. It was Saul Panzer. I listened and got his story, and then told him to hold the wire and turned to Wolfe:

"Saul. From a pay station at 62nd and Madison. There was a dick playing tag with himself in front of Miss Fox's address. Saul went through the apartment and drew a blank. Now he thinks the dick is sticking there, but he's not sure. It's possible he's being followed, and if so should he shake the dick and then come here, or what?"

"Tell him to come here. By no means shake the dick. He may know the one

Fred brought, and in that case they might like to have a talk."

I told Saul, and hung up.

Wolfe was still leaning back, with his eyes half closed. Mike Walsh sat with his closed entirely, his head swaying on one side, and his breathing deep and even in the silence. Hilda Lindquist's shoulders sagged, but her face was flushed and her eyes bright. Clara Fox had her lips tight enough to make her look determined.

Wolfe said, "Wake Mr. Walsh. Having attended to urgencies — in vain — we may now at our leisure fill in some gaps. Regarding the fantastic business of the Rubber Band. —Mr. Walsh, a sharp blow with your hand at the back of your neck will help. A drink of water? Very well. —Did I understand you to say, Miss Fox, that you have found George Rowley?"

She nodded. "Two weeks ago."

"Tell me about it."

"But Mr. Wolfe . . . those detectives . . ."

"To be sure. You remember I told you you should be tied in your cradle? For the present, this house is your cradle. You

109

are safe here. We shall return to that little problem. Tell me about George Rowley."

She drew a breath. "Well . . . we found him. I began a long while ago to do what I could, which wasn't much. Of course I couldn't afford to go to England, or send someone, or anything like that. But I gathered some information. For instance, I learned the names of all the generals who had commanded brigades in the British army during the war, and as well as I could from this distance I began to eliminate them. There were hundreds and hundreds of them still alive, and of course I didn't know whether the one I wanted was alive or not. I did lots of things, and some of them were pretty bright if I am a fool. I had found Mike Walsh through an advertisement, and I got photographs of scores of them and showed them to him. Of course, the fact that George Rowley had lost the lobe of his right ear was a help. On several occasions, when I learned in the newspapers that a British general or ex-general was in New York, I managed to get a look at him, and sometimes Mike Walsh did too. Two weeks ago another one came, and in a photograph in the paper it looked as if the bottom of his right ear was off. Mike Walsh stood in front of his hotel all one afternoon when he should have been asleep, and saw him, and it was George Rowley."

Wolfe nodded. "That would be the Marquis of Clivers."

"How do you know that?"

"Not by divination. It doesn't matter. Congratulations, Miss Fox."

"Thank you. The Marquis of Clivers was going to Washington the next day, but he was coming back. I tried to see him that very evening, but couldn't get to him. I called a connection I had made in London, and learned that the marquis owned big estates and factories and mines and a yacht. I had been communicating with Hilda Lindquist and Harlan Scovil for some time, and I wired them to come on and sent them money for the trip. Mr. Scovil wouldn't take the money. He wrote me that he had never taken any woman-money and wasn't going to start." She smiled at Wolfe and me too. "I guess he was afraid of adventuresses. He said he would sell some calves. Saturday morning I got a telegram that he would get here Monday, so I telephoned your office for an appointment. When I saw him this noon I showed him two pictures of the Marquis of Clivers, and he said it was George Rowley. I had a hard time to keep him from going to the hotel after the marquis right then."

Wolfe wiggled a finger at her. "But what made you think you needed me? I detect no lack of confidence in your operations to date."

"Oh, I always thought we'd have to have a lawyer at the windup. I had read about you and admired you."

"I'm not a lawyer."

"I shouldn't think that would matter. I only know three lawyers, and if you saw them you would know why I chose you."

"You sound like a fool again." Wolfe sighed. "Do you wish me to believe that I was selected for my looks?"

"No, indeed. That would be . . . anyhow, I selected you. When I told you what your fee might be, I wasn't exaggerating. Let's say his estates and mines and so on are worth fifty million —"

"Pounds?"

"Dollars. That's conservative. He agreed to pay half of it. Twenty-five million. But there are two of the men I can't find. I haven't found a trace of Rubber Coleman, the leader, or the man called Turtle-back. I have tried hard to find Rubber Coleman, because he had the papers, but I couldn't. On the twenty-five million take off their share, one-third, and that leaves roughly sixteen million. Make allowances for all kinds of things, anything you could think of — take off, say, just for good measure, fifteen million. That leaves a million dollars. That's what I asked him for a week ago."

"You asked who for? Lord Clivers?"

"Yes."

"You said you were unable to see him him."

"That was before he went to Washington. When he came back I tried again. I had made an acquaintance . . .

he has some assistants with him on his mission — diplomats and so on — and I had got acquainted with one two weeks ago, and through him I got to the marquis, thinking I might manage it without any help. He was very unpleasant. When he found out what I was getting at, he ordered me out. He claimed he didn't know what I was talking about, and when I wanted to show him the letter my father had written in 1918, he wouldn't look at it. He told the young man whom he called to take me away that I was an adventuress."

She wasn't through. But the doorbell rang, and I went to answer it. I thought it just possible that a pair might rush me, and there was no advantage in a roughhouse, so I left the bolt and chain on until I saw it was Saul Panzer. Then I opened up and let him in, and shut the door and slid the bolt again.

Saul is about the smallest practicing dick, public or private, that I've ever seen, and he has the biggest scope. He can't push over buildings because he simply hasn't got the size, but there's no other kind of a job he wouldn't earn his money on. It's hard to tell what he looks like, because you can't see his face for his nose. He had a big long cardboard box under his arm.

I took him to the office. As he sidled past a chair to get to Wolfe's desk he passed one sharp glance around, and I knew that gave him a print of those three sitting there which would fade out only when he did.

Wolfe greeted him. "Good evening, Saul."

"Good evening, Mr. Wolfe. Of course Archie told you my phone call. There's not much to add. When I arrived the detective was there on the sidewalk. His name is Bill Purvil. I saw him once about four years ago in Brooklyn, when we had that Moschenden case. He didn't recognize me on the sidewalk, But when I went in at that entrance he followed me. I figured it was better to go ahead. There was a phone in the apartment. If I found the package I could phone Archie to come and get into the court from 60th Street, and throw it to him from a back window. When the detective saw I was going into that apartment with a key, he stopped me to ask questions, and I answered what occurred to me. He stayed out in the hall and I locked the door on the inside. I went through the place. The package isn't there. I came out and the detective followed me downstairs to the sidewalk. I phoned from a drug store. I don't think he tried to follow me, but I made sure it didn't work if he did."

Wolfe nodded. "Satisfactory. And your bundle?"

Saul got the box from under his arm and put it on the desk. "I guess it's flowers. It has a name on it, Drummond, the Park Avenue florist. It was on the floor of the hall right at the door of the apartment, apparently been delivered, addressed Miss Clara Fox. My instructions were to search only the apartment, so I hesitated to open this box, because it wasn't in the apartment. But I didn't want to leave it there, because it was barely possible that what you want was in it. So I brought it along."

"Good. Satisfactory again. May we

open it, Miss Fox?''

"Certainly."

I got up to help. Saul and I pulled off the fancy gray tape and took the lid off. Standing, we were the only ones who could see in. I said:

"It's a thousand roses."

Clara Fox jumped up to look. I reached in the box had picked up an envelope and took a card from the envelope. I squinted at it — it was scrawly writing — and read it out:

"Francis Horrocks?"

She nodded. "That's my acquaintance. The man that ejected me from the Marquis of Clivers. He's a young diplomat with a special knowledge of the Far East. Aren't they beautiful? Look, Hilda. Smell. They are *very* nice." She carried them to Wolfe. "Aren't they a beautiful color, Mr. Wolfe? Smell." She looked at Mike Walsh, but he was asleep again, so she put the box back on the desk and sat down.

Wolfe was rubbing his nose which she had tickled with the roses. "Saul. Take those to the kitchen and have Fritz put them in water. Remain there. You must see my orchids, Miss Fox, but that can wait. Mr. Walsh! Archie, wake him, please."

I reached out and gave Walsh a dig, and he jerked up and glared at me. He protested, "Hey! It's too warm in here. I'm never as warm as this after supper."

Wolfe wiggled a finger at him. "If you please, Mr. Walsh. Miss Fox has been giving us some details, such as your recognition of the Marquis of Clivers. Do you understand what I'm saying?"

"Sure." Walsh pulled the tips of his fingers across his eyes, and stretched his eyes open. "What about it?"

"Did you recognize the Marquis of Clivers as George Rowley?"

"Sure I did. Who says I didn't?"

"As yet, no one. Are you positive it was the same man?"

"Yes. I told you at the table, I'm always positive."

"So you did. Among other things. You told me that through ancient habit, and on your post as a night watchman, you carry a gun. You also told me that you suspected Harlan Scovil of being an Englishman, and that all English blood was bad blood. Do you happen to have your gun with you? Could I see it?"

"I've got a license."

"Of course. Could I see it? Just as a favor?"

Walsh growled something to himself, but after a moment's hesitation he leaned forward and reached to his hip and pulled out a gat. He looked at it, and rubbed his left palm caressingly over the barrel, and then got up and poked the butt at Wolfe. Wolfe took it, glanced at it, and held it out to me. I gave it a mild inspection. It was an old Folwell .44. It was loaded, the cylinder full, and there was no smell of any recent activity around the muzzle. I glanced at Wolfe and caught his little nod, and returned the cannon to Mike Walsh, who caressed it again before he put it back in his pocket.

Clara Fox said, "Who's wasting time now, Mr. Wolfe? You haven't told us yet —"

Wolfe stopped her. "Don't begin again, Miss Fox. Please. Give me a chance to

119

earn my share of that million. Though I must confess that my opinion is that you might all of you sell out for a ten dollar bill and call it a good bargain. What have you to go on? Really nothing. The paper which George Rowley signed was entrusted to Rubber Coleman, whom you have been unable to find. The only other basis for a legal claim would be a suit by the man called Turtle-back to recover the value of his horse, and since Mr. Walsh has told us that Turtle-back was over 50 years old in 1895, he is in all likelihood dead. There are only two methods by which you can get anything out of the Marquis of Clivers; one is to attempt to establish a legal claim by virtue of contract, for which you would need a lawyer, not a detective. You have yourself already done the detective work, quite thoroughly. The other method is to attempt to scare the marquis into paying you, through threat of public exposure of his past. That is an ancient and often effective method, Technically known as blackmail. It is not —"

She interrupted him, cool but positive.

"It isn't blackmail to try to collect something from a man that he promised to pay."

Wolfe nodded. "It's a nice point. Morally he owes it. But where's the paper he signed? Anyway, let me finish. I, myself, am in a quandary. When you first told me the nature of the commission you were offering me, I was prepared to decline it without much discussion. Then another element entered in, of which you are still ignorant, which lent the affair fresh interest. Of course, interest is not enough; before that comes the question, who is going to pay me? I shall expect —"

Mike Walsh squawked, "Ten per cent!"

Clara Fox said, "I told you, Mr. Wolfe —"

"Permit me. I shall expect nothing exorbitant. It happens that my bank account is at present in excellent condition, and therefore my cupidity is comparatively dormant. Still, I have a deep aversion to working without getting paid for it. I have accepted you, Miss Fox, as my client. I may depend on you?"

She nodded impatiently. "Of course you may. What is the other element that entered in of which I am still ignorant?"

"Oh. That." Wolfe's half-closed eyes took in all three faces. "At twenty-five minutes to six this evening, less than five hours ago, on Thirty-first Street near Tenth Avenue, Harlan Scovil was shot and killed."

Mike Walsh jerked up straight in his chair. They all gaped at Wolfe. Wolfe said:

"He was walking along the sidewalk, and someone going by in an automobile shot him five times. He was dead when a passerby reached him. The automobile has been found, empty of course, on Ninth Avenue."

Clara Fox gasped incredulously, "Harlan Scovil!" Hilda Lindquist sat with her fists suddenly clenched and her lower lip pushing her upper lip toward her nose. Mike Walsh was glaring at Wolfe. He exploded suddenly:

"Ye're a howling idiot!"

Wolfe's being called an idiot twice in one evening was certainly a record. I made a note to grin when I got time. Clara Fox was saying: "But Mr. Wolfe . . . it can't . . . how can . . ."

Walsh went on exploding, "So you hear of some shooting, and you want to smell my gun? Ye're an idiot! Of all the dirty —" He stopped himself suddenly and leaned on his hands on his knees, and his eyes narrowed. He looked pretty alert and competent for a guy seventy years old. "To hell with that. Where's Harlan? I want to see him."

Wolfe wiggled a finger at him. "Compose yourself, Mr. Walsh. All in time. As you see, Miss Fox, this is quite a complication."

"It's terrible. Why . . . it's awful. He's really *killed?*"

Hilda Lindquist spoke suddenly. "I didn't want to come here. I told you that. I thought it was a wild goose chase. My father made me. I mean, he's old and sick and he wanted me to come because he thought maybe we could get enough to save the farm."

Wolfe nodded. "And now, of course . . ."

Her square chin stuck out. "Now I'm glad I came. I've often heard my father talk about Harlan Scovil. He would have been killed anyway, whether I came or not, and now I'm glad I'm here to help. You folks will have to tell me what to do, because I don't know. But if that marquis thinks he can refuse to talk to us and then shoot us down on the street . . . we'll see."

"I haven't said the marquis shot him, Miss Lindquist."

"Who else did?"

I thought from her tone she was going to tell him not to be an idiot, but she let it go at that and looked at him. Wolfe said:

"I can't tell you. But I have other details for you. This afternoon Harlan Scovil came to this office. He told Mr. Goodwin that he came in advance of the time for the interview to see what kind of a man I was. At twenty-six minutes after five, while he was waiting to see me, he received a telephone call from a man. He left at once. You remember that shortly after you arrived this evening a caller came and you were asked to go to the front room. The caller was a city detective. He informed us of the murder, described the corpse, and said that in his pocket had been found a paper bearing my name and address, and also the names of Clara Fox, Hilda Lindquist, Michael Walsh and the Marquis of Clivers. Scovil had been shot just nine minutes after he received that phone call here and left the house."

Clara Fox said, "I saw him write those names on the paper. He did it while he was eating lunch with me."

"Just so. —Mr. Walsh. Did you telephone Scovil here at 5:26?"

"Of course not. How could I? That's a damn fool question. I didn't know he was here."

"I suppose not. But I thought possibly Scovil had arranged to meet you here. When Scovil arrived it happened that there was another man in the office, one of my clients, and Scovil approached him and told him he wasn't Mike Walsh."

"Well, was he? I'm Mike Walsh, look at me. The only arrangement I had to meet him was at six o'clock, through Miss

Fox. Shut up about it. I asked you where Harlan is. I want to see him."

"In time, sir. —Miss Fox. Did you telephone Scovil here?"

She shook her head. "No. Oh, no. I thought you said it was a man."

"So it seemed. Fritz might possibly have been mistaken. Was it you who phoned, Miss Lindquist?"

"No. I haven't telephoned anyone in New York except Clara."

"Well." Wolfe sighed. "You see the little difficulty, of course. Whoever telephoned knew that Scovil was in New York and knew he was at this office. Who knew that except you three?"

Hilda Lindquist said, "The Marquis of Clivers knew it."

"How do you know that?"

"I don't know it. I see it. Clara had been to see him and he had threatened to have her arrested for annoying him. He had detectives follow her, and they saw her this noon with Harlan Scovil, and they followed Harlan Scovil here and then notified the Marquis of Clivers. Then he telephoned —"

"Possible, Miss Lindquist. I admit it's possible. If you substitute for the detective a member of the marquis's entourage, even more possible. But granted that we rather like that idea, do you think the police will? A British peer, in this country on a government mission of the highest importance, murdering Harlan Scovil on Thirty-first Street? I have known quite a few policemen, and I am almost certain that idea wouldn't appeal to them."

Mike Walsh said, "To hell with the dumb Irish cops."

Clara Fox asked, "The detective that was here . . . the one that told you about . . . about the shooting. Our names were on that paper. Why didn't he want to see us?"

"He did. Badly. But I observed that there were no addresses on the paper except my own, so he is probably having difficulty. I decided not to mention that all of you happened to be here at the moment, because I wanted to talk with you and I knew he would monopolize your evening."

"The detective at my apartment . . .

he may have been there . . . about this . . ."

"No. There had hardly been time enough. Besides, there was one at the garage too."

Clara Fox looked at him, and took a deep breath. "I seem to be in a fix."

"Two fixes, Miss Fox." Wolfe rang for beer. "But it is possible that before we are through we may be able to effect a merger."

7

I only half heard that funny remark of Wolfe's. Parts of my brain were skipping around from this to that and finding no place to settle down. As a matter of fact I had been getting more uncomfortable all evening, ever since Slim Foltz had told us the names on that paper and Wolfe had let him go without telling him that the three people he was looking for were sitting in our front room. He was working on a murder, and the fact that the name of a bird like that marquis was on that paper meant that they weren't going to let anything slide. They would find those three people sooner or later, and when they learned where they had been at the time Slim Foltz called on us, they would be vexed. There were already two or three devoted public servants who thought

Wolfe was a little tricky, and it looked as if this was apt to give them entirely too much encouragement. I knew pretty well how Wolfe worked, and when he let Foltz go I had supposed he was going to have a little talk with our trio of visitors and then phone someone like Cramer at Headquarters or Dick Morley of the District Attorney's office, and arrange for some interviews. But here it was past ten o'clock, and he was just going on with an interesting conversation. I didn't like it.

I heard his funny remark though, about two fixes and effecting a merger. I got his idea, and that was one of the points my brain skipped to. I saw how there might possibly be a connection between the Rubber Band business and Clara Fox being framed for lifting the thirty grand. She had gone to this British gent and spilled her hand to him, and he had given her the chilly how now and had her put out. But he had been badly annoyed what. You might even say scared if he hadn't been a nobleman. And a few days later the frame-up reared its ugly head. It would be interesting to find out if the

Marquis of Clivers was acquainted with Mr. Muir, and if so to what extent. Clara Fox had said Muir was a Scotsman, so you couldn't depend on him any more than you could an Englishman, maybe not as much. As usual, Wolfe was ahead of me, but he hadn't lost me, I was panting along behind.

Meanwhile I had to listen too, for the conversation hadn't stopped. At the end of Wolfe's remark about the merger, Mike Walsh suddenly stood up and announced: "I'll be going."

Wolfe looked at him. "Not just yet, Mr. Walsh. Be seated."

But he stayed on his feet. "I've got to go. I want to see Harlan."

"Mr. Scovil is dead. I beg you, sir. There are one or two points I must still explain."

Walsh muttered, "I don't like this. You see I don't like it?" He glared at Wolfe, handed me the last half of it, and sat down on the edge of his chair.

Wolfe said, "It's getting late. We are confronted by three distinct problems, and each one presents difficulties. First, the

131

matter of the money missing from the office of the Seaboard Products Corporation. So far that appears to be the personal problem of Miss Fox, and I shall discuss it with her later. Second, there is your joint project of collecting a sum of money from the Marquis of Clivers. Third, there is your joint peril resulting from the murder of Harlan Scovil."

"Joint hell." Walsh's eyes were narrowed again. "Say we divide the peril up, mister. Along with the money."

"If you prefer. But let us take the second problem first. I see no reason for abandoning the attack on the Marquis of Clivers because Mr. Scovil has met a violent death. In fact, that should persuade us to prosecute it. My advice would be this — Archie, your notebook. Take a letter to the Marquis of Clivers, to be signed by me. Salute him democratically, 'Dear Sir:'

"I have been engaged by Mr. Victor Lindquist and his daughter, Miss Hilda Lindquist, as their agent to collect an amount which you have

132

owed them since 1895. In that year, in Silver City, Nevada, with your knowledge and consent, Mr. Lindquist purchased a horse from a man known as Turtle-back, and furnished the horse to you for your use in an urgent private emergency. You signed a paper before your departure acknowledging the obligation, but of course your debt would remain a legal obligation without that.

"At that time and place good horses were scarce and valuable; furthermore, for reasons peculiar to your situation, that horse was of extraordinary value to you at that moment. Miss Lindquist, representing her father, states that that extraordinary value can be specified as $100,000. That amount is therefore due from you, with accrued interest at 6% to date.

"I trust that you will pay the amount due without delay and without forcing us to the necessity of legal action. I am not an attorney. If you prefer to make the payment through attorneys representing both sides, we shall be glad to make that arrangement."

Wolfe leaned back. "All right, Miss Lindquist?"

She was frowning at him. "He can't pay with money for murdering Harlan Scovil."

"Certainly not. But one thing at a time. I should explain that this claim has no legal standing, since it has expired by time, but the marquis might not care to proceed to that defense in open legal proceedings. We are on the fringe of blackmail, but our hearts are pure. I should also explain that at 6% compound interest money doubles itself in something like twelve years, and that the present value of that claim as I have stated it in the letter is something over a million dollars. A high price for a horse, but we are only using it to carry us to a point of vantage. This has your approval, Miss Fox?"

Clara Fox was looking bad. Sitting there with the fingers of one hand curled tight around the fingers of the other, she wasn't nearly as cool and sweet as she had been that afternoon when Muir had declared right in front of her that she was a sneak thief.

"No," she said. "I don't think we want . . . no, Mr. Wolfe. I'm just realizing . . . it's my fault Mr. Scovil was killed, I started all this. Just for that money . . . no! Don't send that letter. Don't do anything."

"Indeed." Wolfe drank some beer, and put the glass down with his usual deliberation. "It would seem that murder is sometimes profitable, after all."

Her fingers tightened. "Profitable?"

"Obviously. If, as seems likely, Harlan Scovil was killed by someone involved in this Rubber Band business, the murderer probably had two ends in view: to remove Scovil, and to frighten the rest of you. To scare you off. He appears to have accomplished both purposes. Good for him."

"We're not scared off."

"You're ready to quit."

Hilda Lindquist put in, with her chin

135

up, "Not me. Send that letter."

"Miss Fox?"

She pulled her shoulders in, and out again. "All right. Send it."

"Mr. Walsh?"

"Deal me out. You said you wanted to explain something."

"So I did." Wolfe emptied his glass. "We'll send the letter, then. The third problem remains. I must call your attention to these facts: First, the police are at this moment searching for all three of you — in your case, Miss Fox, two separate assignments of police. Second, the police are capable of concluding that the murderer of Harlan Scovil is someone who knew him or knew of him, and was in this neighborhood this evening. Third, it is probable that there is no one in New York who ever heard of Harlan Scovil except you three and Clivers; or, if there is such a one, it is not likely that the police will discover him — in fact, the idea will not occur to them until they have exhausted all possibilities in connection with you three. Fourth, when they find you and question you, they will suspect you not only of knowledge of Scovil's murder, but also of some preposterous plot against Lord Clivers, since his name was on that paper.

"Fifth. When they question you, there will be three courses open to you. You may tell the truth, in which case your wild and extravagant tale will reinforce their suspicions and will be enough to convict you of almost anything, even murder. Or you may try to tone your tale down, tell only a little and improvise to fill in the gaps, whereupon they will catch you in lies and go after you harder than ever. Or you may assert your constitutional rights and refuse to talk at all; if you do that they will incarcerate you as material witnesses and hold you without bail. As you see, it is a dilemma with three horns and none of them attractive. As Miss Fox put it, you're in a fix. And any of the three courses will render you *hors de combat* for any further molestation of the Marquis of Clivers."

Hilda Lindquist's chin was way up in the air. Mike Walsh was leaning forward with his eyes on Wolfe narrower than ever. Clara Fox had stopped squeezing her hand and had her lips pressed tight. She opened them to say:

"All right. We're game. Which do we do?"

"None." Wolfe sighed. "None of those. Confound it, I was born romantic and I shall never recover from it. But, as I have said, I expect to be paid. I hope I have made it clear that it will not do for the police to find you until we are ready for them to. Have I demonstrated that?"

The two women asked simultaneously, "Well?"

"Well . . . Archie, bring Saul."

I jumped from habit and not from enthusiasm. I was half sore. I didn't like it. I found Saul in the kitchen drinking port wine and telling Fred and Fritz stories, and led him to the office. He stood in front of Wolfe's desk.

"Yes, sir."

Wolfe spoke, not to him. "Miss Lindquist, this is Mr. Saul Panzer. I would trust him further than might be thought credible. He is himself a bachelor, but has acquaintances who are married and possibly even friends, with the usual living quarters — an apartment or a house. Have you anything to say to him?"

But the Lindquist mind was slow. She didn't get it. Clara Fox asked Wolfe:

"May I?"

"Please do."

She turned to Saul. "Miss Lindquist would like to be in seclusion for a while — a few days — she doesn't know how long. She thought you might know of a place . . . one of your friends . . ."

Saul nodded. "Certainly, Miss Lindquist." He turned to Wolfe:

"Is there a warrant out?"

"No. Not yet."

"Shall I give the address to Archie?"

"By no means. If I need to communicate with Miss Lindquist I can do so through General Delivery. She can notify me on the telephone what branch."

"Shall we go out the back way onto Thirty-fourth Street?"

"I was about to suggest it. When you are free again, return here. Tonight." Wolfe moved his eyes. "Is there anything of value in your luggage at the hotel, Miss Lindquist?''

She was standing up. She shook her head. ''Not much. No.''

''Have you any money?''

''I have thirty-eight dollars and my ticket home.''

''Good. Opulence. Goodnight, Miss Lindquist. Sleep well.''

Clara Fox was up too. She went to the other woman and put her hands on her shoulders and kissed her on the mouth. ''Goodnight, Hilda. It's rotten, but . . . keep your chin up.''

Hilda Lindquist said in a loud voice, ''Goodnight, everybody,'' and turned and followed Saul Panzer out of the room. In a few seconds I could hear their footsteps on the stairs leading down to the basement, where a door opened onto the court in the rear. We were all looking at Wolfe, who was opening a bottle of beer. I was thinking, the old lummox certainly fancies he's putting on a hot number, I suppose he'll send Miss Fox to board with his mother in Buda Pesth. It looked to me like he was stepping off over his head.

He looked at Mike Walsh. "Now, sir, your turn. I note your symptoms of disapproval, but we are doing the best we can. In the kitchen is a man named Fred Durkin, whom you have seen. Within his capacity, he is worthy of your trust and mine. I would suggest —"

"I don't want any Durkin." Walsh was on his feet again. "I don't want anything from you at all. I'll just be going."

"But Mr. Walsh." Wolfe wiggled a finger at him. "Believe me, it will not pay to be headstrong. I am not by nature an alarmist, but there are certain features of this affair —"

"So I notice." Walsh stepped up to the desk. "The features is what I don't like about it." He looked at Clara Fox, then at me, then at Wolfe, letting us know what the features were. "I may be past me prime, but I'm not in a box yet. What kind of a shenanigan would ye like to try on an old man, huh? I'm to go out and hide, am I? Do I get to ask a question or two?"

"That's three." Wolfe sighed. "Go ahead."

Walsh whirled on me. "You, Goodwin's your name? Was it you that answered the phone yesterday, the call that came for Harlan Scovil?"

"No." I grinned at him. "I wasn't here."

"Where was you?"

"At the office of the Seaboard Products Corporation, where Miss Fox works."

"Ha! Was you indeed. You wasn't here. I suppose it couldn't have been you that phoned here to Harlan."

"Sure it could have, but it wasn't. Listen, Mr. Walsh —"

"I've listened enough. I've been listening to this Clara Fox for a year and looking at her pretty face, and I had no reason to doubt her maybe, and this is what's come out of it, I've helped lead my old friend Harlan Scovil into an ambush to his death. My old friend Harlan." He stopped abruptly, and shut his lips tight, and looked around at us while a big fat tear suddenly popped out of each of his eyes and rolled on down, leaving a mark across his wrinkles. He went on, "I ate a meal with you. A meal and three drinks.

Maybe I'd like to puke it up some day. Or maybe you're all square shooters, I don't know, but I know somebody ain't, and I'm going to find out who it is. What's this about them being after Miss Fox for stealing money? I can find out about that too. And if I want anything collected from this English Marquis nobleman, I can collect it myself. Goodnight to ye all." He turned and headed for the door.

Wolfe snapped, "Get him, Archie."

Remembering the gun on his hip, I went and folded myself around him and locked him. He let out a snarl and tried some twisting and unloosed a couple of kicks at my shins, but in four seconds he had sense enough to see it was no go. He quivered a little and then stood quiet, but I kept him tight. He said:

"It's me now, is it?"

Wolfe spoke across the room at him. "You called me an idiot, Mr. Walsh. I return the compliment. What is worse, you are hotheaded. But you are an old man, so there is humanity's debt to you. You may go where you please, but I must warn you that every step you take may be a dangerous step. Furthermore, when you talk, every word may be dangerous not only to you but to Miss Fox and Miss Lindquist. I strongly advise you to adopt the precautions —"

"I'll do me own precautions."

"Mike!" Clara Fox came, her hand out. "Mike, you can't be thinking . . . what Mr. Wolfe says is right. Don't desert us now. Turn him loose, Mr. Goodwin. Shake hands, Mike."

He shook his head. "Did you see him grab me, and all I was doing was walking out on me own feet? I hate the damn detectives and always have, and what was he doing at your office? And if you're my enemy, Clara Fox, God help you, and if not then you can be my friend. Not now. When he turns me loose I'll be going."

Wolfe said, "Release him, Archie. Goodnight, Mr. Walsh."

I let my muscles go and stepped back. Mike Walsh put a hand up to feel his ribs, turned to look at me, and then to Wolfe. He said:

"But I'm no idiot. Show me that back way."

Clara Fox begged him, "Don't go, Mike."

He didn't answer her. I started for the kitchen, and he followed me after stopping in the hall for his hat and coat. I told Fred to see him through the court and the fence and the passage leading to 34th Street, and switched on the basement light for them. I stood and watched them go down. I hadn't cared much for Wolfe's hot number anyhow, and now it looked like worse than a flop, with that wild Irishman in his old age going out to do his own precautions. But I hadn't argued about letting him go, because I knew that kind as well as Wolfe did and maybe better.

When I went back to the office Clara Fox was still standing up. She asked, "Did he really go?"

I nodded. "With bells on."

"Do you think he meant what he said?" She turned to Wolfe. "I don't think he meant it at all. He was just angry and frightened and sorry. I know how he felt. He felt that Harlan Scovil was killed because we started this business, and

145

now he doesn't want to go away and hide. I don't either. I don't want to run away."

"Then it is lucky you won't have to." Wolfe emptied his glass, returned it to the tray, and slid the tray around to the other side of the pen block. That meant that he had decided he had had enough beer for the day, and therefore that he would probably open only one more bottle before going upstairs, provided he went fairly soon. He sighed. "You understand, Miss Fox, this is something unprecedented. It has been many years since any woman has slept under this roof. Not that I disapprove of them, except when they attempt to function as domestic animals. When they stick to the vocations for which they are best adapted, such as chicanery, sophistry, self-adornment, cajolery, mystification and incubation, they are sometimes splendid creatures. Anyhow . . . you will find our south room, directly above mine, quite comfortable. I may add that I am foolishly fond of good form, good color, and fine texture, and I have good taste in those matters. It is a pleasure to look at you. You have unusual beauty. I say that to inform you that while the idea of a woman sleeping in my house is theoretically insupportable, in this case I am willing to put up with it."

"Thank you. Then I'm to hide here?"

"You are. You must keep to your room, with the curtains drawn. Elaborate circumspection will be necessary and will be explained to you. Mr. Goodwin will attend to that. Should your stay be prolonged, it may be that you can join us in the dining-room for meals; eating from a tray is an atrocious insult both to the food and the feeder; and in that case, luncheon is punctually at one and dinner at eight. But before we adjourn for the night there are one or two things I need still to know; for instance, where were you and Miss Lindquist and Mr. Walsh from five to six o'clock this evening?"

Clara Fox nodded. "I know. That's why you asked me if I had killed anybody, and I thought you were being eccentric. But of course you don't believe that. I've told you we were looking for

Harlan Scovil."

"Let's get a schedule. Put it down, Archie. Mr. Goodwin informed me that you left the Seaboard office at a quarter past five."

She glanced at me. "Yes, about that. That was the time I was supposed to get Harlan Scovil at his hotel on Forty-fifth Street, and I didn't get there until nearly half-past five. He wasn't there. I looked around on the street and went a block to another hotel, thinking possibly he had misunderstood me, and then went back again and he still wasn't there. They said he had been out all afternoon as far as they knew. Hilda was at a hotel on Thirtieth Street, and I had told Mike Walsh to be there in the lobby at a quarter to six, and I was to call there for them. Of course I was late, it was six o'clock when I got there, and we decided to try Harlan Scovil's hotel once more, but he wasn't there. We waited a few minutes and then came on without him, and got here at six-thirty." She stopped, and chewed on her lip. "He was dead . . . then. While we were there waiting for him. And I was planning . . . I thought . . ."

"Easy, Miss Fox. We can't resurrect. So you know nothing of Miss Lindquist's and Mr. Walsh's whereabouts between five and six. —Easy, I beg you. Don't tell me again I'm an idiot or you'll have me believing it. I am merely filling in a picture. Or rather, a rough sketch. I think perhaps you should leave us here with it and go to bed. Remember, you are to keep to your room, both for your own safety and to preserve me from serious annoyance. Mr. Goodwin —"

"I know." She frowned at him and then at me. "I thought of that when you said I was to stay here. You mean what they call accessory after the fact —"

"Bosh." Wolfe straightened in his chair and his hand went forward by automatism, but there was no beer there. He sent a sharp glance at me to see if I noticed it, and sat back again. "I can't be an accessory after a fact that never existed. I am acting on the assumption that you are not criminally involved either in larceny or in murder. If you are, say so and get out. If you are not, go to bed.

Fritz will show you your room." He pushed the button. "Well?"

"I'll go to bed." She brushed her hair back. "I don't think I'll sleep."

"I hope you will, even without appetite for it. At any rate, you won't walk the floor, for I shall be directly under you." The door opened, and Wolfe turned to it. "Fritz. Please show Miss Fox to the south room, and arrange towels and so on. In the morning, take her roses to her with breakfast, but have Theodore slice the stems first. — And by the way, Miss Fox, you have nothing with you. The niceties of your toilet you will have to forego, but I believe we can furnish a sleeping-garment. Mr. Goodwin owns some handsome silk pajamas which his sister sent him on his birthday, from Ohio. They are hideous, but handsome. I'm sure he won't mind. I presume, Fritz, you'll find them in the chest of drawers near the window. Unless . . . would you prefer to get them for Miss Fox yourself, Archie?"

I could have thrown my desk at him. He knew damn well what I thought of those pajamas. I was so sore I suppose it showed in my cheeks, because I saw Fritz pull in his lower lip with his teeth. I was slower on the come-back than usual, and I never did get to make one, for at that instant the doorbell rang, which was a piece of luck for Nero Wolfe. I got up and strode past them to the hall.

I was careless for two reasons. I was taking it for granted it was Saul Panzer, back from planting Hilda Lindquist in seclusion; and the cause of my taking something for granted when I shouldn't, since that's always a bad thing to do in our business, was that my mind was still engaged with Wolfe's vulgar attempt to be funny. Anyhow, the fact remains that I was careless. I whirled the lock and took off the bolt and pulled the door open.

They darned near toppled me off my pins with the edge of the door catching my shoulder. I saved myself from falling and the rest was reflex. There were two of them, and they were going right on past in a hurry. I sprang back and got in front and gave one of them a knee in the belly and used a stiff-arm on the other. He started to swing, but I didn't bother about it; I picked up the one that had stopped my knee and just used him for a whisk-broom and depended on speed and my 180 pounds. The combination swept the hall out. We went through the door so fast that the first guy stumbled and fell down the stoop, and I dropped the one I had in my arms and turned and pulled the door shut and heard the lock click. Then I pushed the bell-button three times. The guy that had fallen down the stoop, the one who had tried to plug me, was on his feet again and coming up, with words.

"We're officers —"

"Shut up." I heard footsteps inside, and I called through the closed door. "Fritz? Tell Mr. Wolfe a couple of gentlemen have called and we're staying out on the porch for a talk. And hey! Those things are in the bottom drawer."

8

I said, "What do you mean, officers? Army or navy?"

He looked down at me. He was an inch taller than me to begin with, and he was stretching it. He made his voice hard enough to scare a schoolgirl right out of her socks. "Listen, bud. I've heard about you. How'd you liked to take a good nap on some concrete?"

The other officer was back on his ankles too, but he was a short guy. He was built something like a whisk-broom, at that. I undertook to throw oil on the troubled waters. Ordinarily I might have enjoyed a nice rough cussing-match, but I wanted to find out something and get back inside. I summoned a friendly grin.

"What the hell, how did I know you had badges? Okay, thanks, sergeant. All

I knew was the door bumping me and a cyclone going by. Is that a way to inspire confidence?"

"All right, you know we've got badges now." The sergeant humped up a shoulder and let it drop, and then the other one. "Let us in. We want to see Nero Wolfe."

"I'm sorry, he's got a headache."

"We'll cure it for him. Listen. A friend of mine warned me about you once. He said the time would come when you would have to be taken down. Maybe that's the very thing I came here for. But so far it's a matter of law. Open that door or I'll open it myself. I want to see Mr. Wolfe on police business."

"There's no law about that. Unless you've got a warrant."

"You couldn't read it anyhow. Let us in."

I got impatient. "What's the use wasting time? You can't go in. The floor's just been scrubbed. Wolfe wouldn't see you anyhow, at this time of night. Tell me what you want like gentleman and a cop, and I'll see if I can help you."

He glared at me. Then he put his hand

inside to his breast pocket and pulled out a document, and I had a feeling in my knees like a steering-wheel with a shimmy. If it was a search warrant the jig was up right there. He unfolded it and held it for me to look, and even in the dim light from the street lamp one glance was enough to start my heart off again. It was only a warrant to take into custody. I peered at it and saw among other things the name Ramsey Muir, and nodded.

The sergeant grunted, "Can you see the name? Clara Fox."

"Yeah, it's a nice name."

"We're going in after her. Open up."

I lifted the brows. "In here? You're crazy."

"All right, we're crazy. Open the door."

I shook my head, and got out a cigarette, and lit up. I said, "Listen, sergeant. There's no use wasting the night in repartee. You know damn well you've got no more right to go through that door than a cockroach unless you've got a search warrant. Ordinarily Mr. Wolfe is more than willing to cooperate with you guys; if you don't know that, ask Inspector Cramer. So am I. Hell, some of my best friends are cops. I'm not even sore because you tried to rush me and I got excited and thought you were mugs and pushed you. But it just happens that we don't want company of any kind at present."

He grunted and glared. "Is Clara Fox in there?"

"Now that's a swell question." I grinned at him. "Either she isn't, in which case I would say no, or she is and I don't want you to know it, in which case would I say yes? I might at that, if she was somewhere else and I didn't want you to go there to look for her."

"Is she in there?"

I just shook my head at him.

"You're harboring a fugitive from justice."

"I wouldn't dream of such a thing."

The short dick, the one I had swept the hall with, piped up in a tenor, "Take him down for resisting an officer."

I reproved him: "The sergeant knows better than that. He knows they wouldn't book me, or if they did I read about a man once that collected enough to retire on for false arrest."

The big one stood and stared into my frank eyes for half a minute, then turned and descended the stoop and looked up and down the street. I didn't know whether he expected to see the Russian army or a place to buy a drink. He called up to his brother in arms:

"Stay here, Steve. Cover that door. I'll go and phone a report and probably send someone to cover the rear. When that bird turns his back to go in the house give him a kick in the ass."

I waved at him. "Goodnight, sergeant," pushed the button three shorts, took my key from my pocket, unlocked the door and went in. If that tenor had tickled me I'd have pulled his nose. I slid the bolt in place. Fritz was standing in the middle of the hall with my automatic in his hand. I said:

"Watch out, that thing's loaded."

He was serious. "I know it is, Archie. I thought possibly you might need it."

"No, thanks. I bit their jugulars. It's a trick."

Fritz giggled and handed me the gun, and went to the kitchen. I strolled into the office. Clara Fox was gone, and I was reflecting that she might be looking at herself in the mirror with my silk pajamas on. I had tried them on once, but had never worn them. I had no more than got inside the office when the doorbell rang. As I returned to the entrance and opened the door, leaving the bolt and chain on, I wondered if it was the tenor calling me back to get my kick. But this time it was Saul Panzer. He stood there and let me see him. I asked him through the crack:

"Did you find her?"

"No. I lost her. Lost the trail."

"You're a swell bird dog."

I opened up and let him in, and took him to the office. Wolfe was leaning back in his chair with his eyes closed. The tray had been moved back to its usual position, and there was a glass on it with fresh foam sticking to the sides, and two bottles. He was celebrating the hot number he was putting on.

I said, "Here's Saul."

"Good." The eyes stayed shut. "All right, Saul?"

"Yes, sir."

"Of course. Satisfactory. Can you sleep here?"

"Yes, sir. I stopped by and got a toothbrush."

"Indeed. Satisfactory. The north room, Archie, above yours. Tell Fred he is expected at eight in the morning, and send him home. If you are hungry, Saul, go to the kitchen; if not, take a book to the front room. There will be instructions shortly."

I went to the kitchen and pried Fred Durkin out of his chair and escorted him to the hall and let him out, having warned him not to stumble over any foreign objects that might be found on the stoop. But the dick had left the stoop and was propped against a fire plug down at the curb. He jerked himself up to take a stare at Fred, and I was hoping he'd be dumb enough to suspect it was Clara Fox with pants on, but that was really too much to expect. I barricaded again and returned

159

to the office.

Saul had gone to the front room to curl up with a book. Wolfe stayed put behind his desk. I went to the kitchen and negotiated for a glass of milk, and then went back and got into my own swivel and started sipping. When a couple of minutes passed without any sign from Wolfe, I said indifferently:

"That commotion in the hall a while ago was the Mayor and the Police Commissioner calling to give you the freedom of the city prison. I cut their throats and put them in the garbage can."

"One moment, Archie. Be quiet."

"Okay. I'll gargle my milk. It'll probably be my last chance for that innocent amusement before they toss us in the hoosegow. I remember you told me once that there is no moment in any man's life too empty to be dramatized. You seem to think that's an excuse for filling life up with —"

"Confound you." Wolfe sighed, and I saw his eyelids flicker. "Very well. Who was it in the hall?"

"Two city detectives, one a sergeant no less, with a warrant for the arrest of Clara Fox sworn to by Ramsey Muir. They tried to take us by storm, and I repulsed them single-handed and single-footed. Satisfactory?"

Wolfe shuddered. "I grant there are times when there is no leisure for finesse. Are they camping?"

"One's out there on a fire plug. The sergeant went to telephone. They're going to cover the back. It's a good thing Walsh and Hilda Lindquist got away. I don't suppose —"

The phone rang. I circled on the swivel and put down my milk and took it. "Hello, this is the office of Nero Wolfe." Someone asked me to wait. Then someone else:

"Hello, Wolfe? Inspector Cramer."

I asked him to hold it and turned to Wolfe. "Cramer. Up at all hours of the night."

As Wolfe reached for the phone on his desk he tipped me a nod, and I kept my receiver and reached for a pencil and notebook.

Cramer was snappy and crisp, also he was surprised and his feelings were hurt. He had a sad tale. It seemed that Sergeant Heath, one of the best men in his division, in pursuance of his duty to make a lawful arrest, had attempted to call at the office of Nero Wolfe for a consultation and had been denied admittance. In fact, he had been forcibly ejected. What kind of cooperation was that?

Wolfe was surprised too, at this protest. At the time that his assistant, Mr. Goodwin, had hurled the intruders into the street single-handed, he had not known they were city employees; and when that fact was disclosed, their actions had already rendered their friendly intentions open to doubt. Wolfe was sorry if there had been a misunderstanding.

Cramer grunted. "Okay. There's no use trying to be slick about it. What's it going to get you, playing for time? I want that girl, and the sooner the better."

"Indeed." Wolfe was doing slow motion. "You want a girl?"

"You know I do. Goodwin saw the warrant."

"Yes, he told me he saw a warrant. Larceny, he said it was. But isn't this unusual, Mr. Cramer? Here it is nearly midnight, and you, an inspector, in a vindictive frenzy over a larceny —"

"I'm not in a frenzy. But I want that girl, and I know you've got her there. It's no use, Wolfe. Less than half-an-hour ago I got a phone call that Clara Fox was at that moment in your office."

"It costs only a nickel to make a phone call. Who was it?"

"That's my business. Anyhow, she's there. Let's talk turkey. If Heath goes back there now, can he get her? Yes or no."

"Mr. Cramer." Wolfe cleared his throat. "I shall talk turkey. First, Heath or anyone else coming here now will not be permitted to enter the house without a search warrant."

"How the hell can I get a search warrant at midnight?"

"I couldn't say. Second, Miss Clara Fox is my client, and, however ardently I may defend her interests, I do not expect to violate the law. Third, I will not for the present answer any question, no matter what its source, regarding her whereabouts.''

"You won't. Do you call that cooperation?''

"By no means. I call it common sense. And there is no point in discussing it.''

There was a long pause, then Cramer again: "Listen, Wolfe. This is more important than you think it is. Can you come down to my office right away?''

"Mr. Cramer!'' Wolfe was aghast. "You know I cannot.''

"You mean you won't. Forget it for once. I shouldn't leave here. I tell you this is important.''

"I'm sorry, sir. As you know, I leave my house rarely, and only when impelled by exigent personal considerations. The last time I left it was in the taxicab driven by Dora Chapin, for the purpose of saving the life of my assistant, Mr. Goodwin.''

Cramer cussed a while. "You won't come?''

"No.''

"Can I come there?''

"I should think not, under the

circumstances. As I said, you cannot enter without a search warrant."

"To hell with a search warrant. I've got to see you. I mean, come and talk with you."

"Just to talk? You are making no reservations?"

"No. This is straight. I'll be there in ten minutes."

"Very well." I saw the creases in Wolfe's cheeks unfolding. "I'll try to restrain Mr. Goodwin."

We hung up. Wolfe pushed the button for Fritz. I shut my notebook and tossed it to the back of the desk, and picked up the glass and took a sip of milk. Then, glancing at the clock and seeing it was midnight, I decided I had better reinforce my endurance and went to the cabinet and poured myself a modicum of bourbon. It felt favorable going down, so I took another modicum. Fritz had brought Wolfe some beer, and it was already flowing to its destiny.

I said, "Tell me where Mike Walsh is and I'll go and wring his neck. He must have gone to the first drug store and phoned headquarters. We should have had Fred tail him."

Wolfe shook his head. "You always dive into the nearest pool, Archie. Some day you'll hit a rock and break your neck."

"Yeah? What now? Wasn't it Walsh that phoned him?"

"I have no idea. I'm not ready to dive. Possibly Mr. Cramer will furnish us a sounding. Tell Saul to go to bed and come to my room for instructions at eight o'clock."

I went to the front room and gave Saul the program, and bade him goodnight, and went back to my desk again. There was a little white card lying there, fallen out of my notebook, where I had slipped it some hours before and forgotten about it. I picked it up and looked at it. *Francis Horrocks.*

I said, "I wonder how chummy Clara Fox got with that acquaintance she made. The young diplomat that sent her the roses. It was him that got her in to see his boss. Where to you suppose he fits in?"

"Fits in to what?"

So that was the way he felt. I waved a hand comprehensively. "Oh, life. You know, the mystery of the universe. The scheme of things."

"I'm sure I don't know. Ask him."

"Egad, I shall. I just thought I'd ask you first. Don't be so damn snooty. The fact is, I feel rotten. That Harlan Scovil that got killed was a good guy. You'd have liked him; he said no one could ever get to know a woman well enough to leave her around loose. Though I suppose you've changed your mind, now that there's a woman sleeping in your bed —"

"Nonsense. My bed —"

"You own all the beds in this house except mine, don't you? Certainly it's your bed. Is her door locked?"

"It is. I instructed her to open it only to Fritz's voice or yours."

"Okay. I'm apt to wander in there any time. Is there anything you want to tell me before Cramer gets here? Such as who shot Harlan Scovil and where that thirty grand is and what will happen when they pick Mike Walsh up and he tells them

167

all about our convention this evening? Do you realize that Walsh was here when Saul took Hilda Lindquist away? Do you realize that Walsh may be in Cramer's office right now? Do you realize —"

"That will do, Archie. Definitely." Wolfe sat up and poured beer. "I realize up to my capacity. As I told Mr. Walsh, I am not an alarmist, but I certainly realize that Miss Fox is in more imminent danger than any previous client I can call to mind; if not danger of losing her life, then of having it irretrievably ruined. That is why I am accepting the hazard of concealing her here. As for the murder of Harlan Scovil, a finger of my mind points straight in one direction, but that is scarcely enough for my own satisfaction and totally insufficient for the safety of Miss Fox or the demands of legal retribution. We may learn something from Mr. Cramer, though I doubt it. There are certain steps to be taken without delay. Can Orrie Cather and Johnny Keems be here at eight in the morning?"

"I'll get them. I may have to pull Johnny off —"

"Do so. Have them here by eight if possible, and send them to my room." He sighed. "A riot for a levee, but there's no help for it. You will have to keep to the house. Before we retire certain arrangements regarding Miss Fox will need discussion. And by the way, the letter I dictated on behalf of our other client, Miss Lindquist, should be written and posted with a special delivery stamp before the early morning collection. Send Fritz out with it."

"Then I'd better type it now, before Cramer gets here."

"As you please."

I turned and got the typewriter up and opened my notebook, and rattled it off. I grinned as I wrote the "dear sir," but the grin was bunk, because if Wolfe hadn't told me to be democratic I would have been up a stump and probably would have had to try something like "dearest marquis." From the article I had read the day before I knew where he was, Hotel Portland. Wolfe signed it, and I got Fritz and let him out the front door and waited there till he came back. The short dick

169

was still out there.

I was back in the office but not yet on my sitter again, when the doorbell rang. I wasn't taking any chances, since Fred had gone home and Saul was upstairs asleep. I pulled the curtain away from the glass panel to get a view of the stoop, including corners, and when I saw Cramer was there alone I opened up. He stepped in and I shut the door and bolted it and then extended a paw for his hat and coat. And it wasn't so silly that I kept a good eye on him either, since I knew he had been enforcing the law for thirty years.

He mumbled, "Hello, son. Wolfe in the office?"

"Yeah. Walk in."

9

Wolfe and the inspector exchanged greetings. Cramer sat down and got out a cigar and bit off the end, and held a match to it. Wolfe got a hand up and pinched his nostrils between a thumb and a forefinger to warn the membranes of the assault that was coming. I was in my chair with my notebook on my knee, not bothering to camouflage.

Cramer said, "You know, you're a slick son-of-a-gun. Do you know what I was trying to decide on my way over here?"

Wolfe shook his head. "I couldn't guess."

"I bet you couldn't. I decided it was a toss-up. Whether you've got that Fox woman here and you're playing for time or waiting for daylight to spring something, or whether you've sent her

171

away for her health and you're kidding us to make us think she's here so we won't start nosing for her trail. For instance, I don't suppose it could have been this Goodwin here that phoned my office at half-past eleven?"

"I shouldn't think so. Did you, Archie?"

"No, sir. On my honor I didn't."

"Okay." Cramer got smoke in his windpipe and coughed it out. "I know there's no use trying to play poker with you, Wolfe. I quit that years ago. I've come to lay some cards on the table and ask you to do the same. In fact, the Commissioner says we're not asking, we're demanding. We're taking no chances —"

"The Police Commissioner? Mr. Hombert?" Wolfe's brows were up.

"Right. He was in my office when I phoned you. I told you, this is more important than you think it is. You've stepped into something."

"You don't say so." Wolfe sighed. "I was sure to, sooner or later."

"Oh, I'm not trying to impress you. I've quit that too. I'm just telling you.

As I told the Commissioner, you're tricky and you're hard to get ahead of, but I've never known you to slip in the mud. By and large, and of course making allowances, you've always been a good citizen."

"Thank you. Let us go on from there."

"Right." Cramer took a puff and knocked off ashes. "I said I'd show you some cards. First, there's the background, I'd better mention that. You know how it is nowadays, everybody's got it in for somebody else, and half of them have gone cuckoo. When a German ship lands here a bunch of Jews go and tear the flag off it and raise general hell. If a Wop professor that's been kicked out of Italy tries to give a lecture a gang of Fascists haul him down and beat him up. When you try your best to feed people that haven't got a job they turn Communist on you and start a riot. It's even got so that when a couple of bank presidents have lunch at the White House, the servants have to search the floor for banana peels that they may have put there for the President to slip on. Everyone has gone nuts."

Wolfe nodded. "Doubtless you are correct. I don't get around much. It sounds bewildering."

"It is. To get down to particulars, when any prominent foreigners come here, we have to watch our step. We don't want anything happening. For instance, you'd be surprised at the precautions we have to take when the German Ambassador comes up from Washington for a banquet. You might think there was a war on. As a matter of fact, there is! No one's ready for a scrap but everyone wants to hit first. Whoever lands at this port nowadays, you can be sure there's someone around that's got it in for him."

"It might be better if everybody stayed at home."

"Huh? Oh. That's their business. Anyway, that's the background. A couple of weeks ago a man called the Marquis of Clivers came here from England."

"I know. I've read about him."

"Then you know what he came for."

Wolfe nodded. "In a general way. A high diplomatic mission. To pass out

174

slices of the Orient.''

''Maybe. I'm not a politician, I'm a cop. I was when I pounded the pavement thirty years ago, and I still am. But the Marquis of Clivers seems to be as important as almost anybody. I understand we get the dope on that from the Department of State. When he landed here a couple of weeks ago we gave him protection, and saw him off to Washington. When he came back, eight days ago, we did the same.''

''The same? Do you mean you have men with him constantly?''

Cramer shook his head. ''Not constantly. All public appearances, and a sort of general eye out. We have special men. If we notice anything or hear of anything that makes us suspicious, we're on the job. That's what I'm coming to. At 5:28 this afternoon, just four blocks from here, a man was shot and killed. In his pocket he had a paper —''

Wolfe showed a palm. ''I know all about that, Mr. Cramer. I know the man's name, I know he had left my office only a few minutes before he was killed, and

I know that the name of the Marquis of Clivers was on the paper. The detective that was here, Mr. Foltz I believe his name was, showed it to me."

"Oh. He did. Well?"

"Well . . . I saw the names on the paper. My own was among them. But, as I explained to Mr. Foltz, I had not seen the man. He had arrived at our office, unexpected and unannounced, and Mr. Goodwin had —"

"Yeah." Cramer took his cigar from his mouth and hitched forward. "Look here, Wolfe. I don't want to get into a chinning match with you, you're better at it then I am, I admit it. I've talked with Foltz, I know what you told him. Here's my position: there's a man in this town representing a foreign government on important business, and I'm responsible both for his safety and his freedom from annoyance. A man is shot down on the street, and on a paper in his pocket we find the name of the Marquis of Clivers, and other names. Naturally I wouldn't mind knowing who killed Harlan Scovil, but finding that name there makes it a good deal more than just another homicide. What's the connection and what does it mean? The Commissioner says we've got to find out damned quick or it's possible we'll have a first-rate mess on our hands. It's already been bungled a little. Like a dumb flatfoot rookie, Captain Devore went to see the Marquis of Clivers this evening without first consulting headquarters."

"Indeed. Will you have some beer, Mr. Cramer?"

"No. The marquis just stared at Devore as if he was one of the lower animals, which he was, and said that possibly the dead man was an insurance salesman and the paper was a list of prospects. Later on the Commissioner himself telephoned the marquis, and by that time the marquis had remembered that a week ago today a woman by the name of Clara Fox had called on him with some kind of a wild tale, trying to get money, and he had had her put out. So there's a tie-up. It's some kind of a plot, no doubt about it, and since it's interesting enough so that someone took the trouble to bump off this Harlan Scovil, you couldn't call it tiddly-winks. Your name was on that paper. I know what you told Foltz. Okay. What I've got to do is find those other three, and I should have been in bed two hours ago. First let me ask you a plain straight question: what do you know about the connection between Clara Fox, Hilda Lindquist, Michael Walsh, and the Marquis of Clivers?"

Wolfe shook his head, slowly. "That won't do, Mr. Cramer."

"It'll do me. Will you answer it?" Cramer stuck his cigar in his mouth and tilted it up.

Wolfe shook his head again. "Certainly not. —Permit me, please. Let us frame the question differently, like this: What have I been told regarding the relations between those four people which would either solve the problem of the murder of Harlan Scovil, or would threaten the personal safety of the Marquis of Clivers or subject him to undeserved or illegal annoyance? Will you accept that as your question?"

Cramer scowled at him. "Say it again."

Wolfe repeated it. Cramer said:

"Well . . . answer it."

"The answer is, nothing."

"Huh? Bellywash. I'm asking you, Wolfe —"

Wolfe's palm stopped him, and Wolfe's tone was snappy. "No more. I've finished with that. I admit your right to call on me, as a citizen enjoying the opportunities and privileges of the City of New York, not to hinder — even to some extent assist — your efforts to defend a distinguished foreign guest against jeopardy and improper molestation. Also your efforts to solve a murder. But here are two facts for you. First, it is possible that your two worthy enterprises will prove to be incompatible. Second, as far as I am concerned, for the present at least, that question and answer are final. You may have other questions that I may be disposed to reply to. Shall we try?"

Cramer, chewing his cigar, looked at him. "You know something, Wolfe? Some day you're going to fall off and get hurt."

"You said those very words to me, in this room, eight years ago."

"I wouldn't be surprised if I did." Cramer put his dead half-chewed cigar in the ashtray, took out a fresh one, and sat back. "Here's a question. What do you mean about incompatible? I suppose it was the Marquis of Clivers that pumped the lead in Harlan Scovil. There's a thought."

"I've already had it. It might very well have been. Has he an alibi?"

"I don't know. I guess the Commissioner forgot to ask him. You got any evidence?"

"No. No fragment." Wolfe wiggled a finger. "But I'll tell you this. It is important to me, also, that the murder of Harlan Scovil be solved. In the interest of a client. In fact, two."

"Oh. You've got clients."

"I have. I have told you that there are various questions I might answer if you cared to ask them. For instance, do you know who was sitting in your chair three hours ago? Clara Fox. And in that one? Hilda Lindquist. And in that? Michael Walsh. That, I believe, covers the list on that famous paper, except for the Marquis

180

of Clivers. I am sorry to say he was absent.''

Cramer had jerked himself forward. He leaned back again and observed, "You wouldn't kid me."

"I am perfectly serious."

Cramer stared at him. He scraped his teeth around on his upper lip, took a piece of tobacco from his tongue with his fingers, and kept on staring. Finally he said, "All right. What do I ask next?"

"Well . . . nothing about the subject of our conference, for that was private business. You might ask where Michael Walsh is now. I would have to reply, I have no idea. No idea whatever. Nor do I know where Miss Lindquist is. She left here about two hours ago. The commission I have undertaken for her is a purely civil affair, with no impingements on the criminal law. My other client is Clara Fox. In her case the criminal law is indeed concerned, but not the crime of murder. As I told you on the telephone, I will not for the present answer any question regarding her whereabouts."

"All right. Next?"

"Next you might perhaps permit me a question. You say that you want to see these people on account of the murder of Harlan Scovil, and in connection with your desire to protect the Marquis of Clivers. But the detectives you sent, whom Mr. Goodwin welcomed so oddly, had a warrant for her arrest on a charge of larceny. Do you wonder that I was, and am, a little skeptical of your good faith?"

"Well," Cramer looked at this cigar. "If you collected all the good faith in this room right now you might fill a teaspoon."

"Much more, sir, if you included mine." Wolfe opened his eyes at him. "Miss Fox is accused of stealing. How do you know, justly or unjustly? You thought she was in my house. Had you any reason to suppose that I would aid a person suspected of theft to escape a trial by law? No. If you thought she was here, could you not have telephoned me and arranged to take her into custody tomorrow morning, when I could have got her release on bail? Did you need to assault my privacy and insult my dignity by having your bullies burst in my door in order to carry off a sensitive and lovely young woman to a night in jail? For shame, sir! Pfui!" Wolfe poured himself a glass of beer.

Cramer shook his head, slowly back and forth. "By God, you're a world-beater. I hand it to you. You know very well, Wolfe, I wasn't interested in any larceny. I wanted to talk with her about murder and about this damned marquis."

"Bah. After your talk, would she or would she not have been incarcerated?"

"I suppose she would. Hell, millions of innocent people have spent a night in jail, and sometimes much longer."

"The people I engage to keep out of it don't. If what you wanted was a talk, why the warrant? Why the violent and hostile onslaught?"

Cramer nodded. "That was a mistake. I admit it. I'll tell you the truth, the Commissioner was there demanding action. And the phone call came. I don't know who it was. He not only told me that Clara Fox was in your house, he also told me that the same Clara Fox was wanted for stealing money from the Seaboard Products Corporation. I got in touch with another department and learned that a warrant for her arrest had been executed late this afternoon. It was the Commissioner's idea to get the warrant and use it to send here and get her in a hurry."

I went on and got the signs for that down in my notebook, but my mind wasn't on that, it was on Mike Walsh. It was fairly plain that Wolfe had let one get by when he had permitted Walsh to walk out with no supervision, considering that New York is full not only of telephones, but also of subways and railroad trains and places to hide. And for the first time I put it down as a serious speculation whether Walsh could have had a reason to croak his dear old friend Harlan Scovil. Seeing Wolfe's lips moving slowly out and in, I suspected that the taste in his mouth was about the same as mine. Cramer was saying:

"Come on, Wolfe, forget it. You know what most Police Commissioners are like. They're not cops. They think all you have to do is flash a badge and strong men burst into tears. Be a sport and help me out once. I want to see this Fox woman. I'll take your word for Walsh and Lindquist and keep after them, but help me out on Clara Fox. If you've got her here, trot her out. If you haven't, tell me where to find her. If you've turned her loose too, which isn't a bad trick, show me her trail. She may be your client, but I'm not kidding when I say that the best thing you can do for her right now, and damn quick, is to let me see her. I don't care anything about any larceny —"

Wolfe interrupted. "She does. I do." He shook his head. "The larceny charge is of course in charge of the District Attorney's office; you haven't the power to affect it one way or another. I know that. As for the Marquis of Clivers, he is in no danger from Clara Fox that you need to protect him from. And as regards the murder of Harlan Scovil, she knows as little about that as I do. In fact, even less, since it is barely possible that I know who killed him."

Cramer looked at him. He puffed his

cigar and kept on looking. At length he said, "Well. It's a case of murder. I'm in charge of the Homicide squad. I'm listening."

"That's all. I volunteered that."

Cramer looked disgusted. "It can't be all. It's either too much or not enough. You've said enough to make you a material witness. You know what we can do with material witnesses if we want to."

"Yes, I know." Wolfe sighed. "But you can't very well lock me up, for then I wouldn't be free to unravel this tangle for my client — and for you. I said, barely possible." He sat up straight, abruptly. "Barely possible, sir! Confound all of you! You marquises that need protection, you hyenas of finance, you upholders of the power to persecute and defame! And don't mistake this outburst as a display of moral indignation; it is merely the practical protest of a man of business who finds his business interfered with by ignorance and stupidity. I expect to collect a fee from my client, Miss Fox. To do that I need to prosecute a claim for her, for a legal debt, I need to clear her from the false accusation of larceny, and I fear I need to discover who murdered Harlan Scovil. Those are legitimate needs, and I shall pursue them. If you want to protect your precious marquis, for God's sake do so! Surround him with a ring of iron and steel, or immerse him in antiseptic jelly! But don't annoy me when I'm trying to work! It is past one o'clock, and I must be up shortly after six, and Mr. Goodwin and I have things to do. I have every right to advise Miss Fox to avoid unfriendly molestation. If you want her, search for her. I have said that I will answer no question regarding her whereabouts, but I will tell you this much: if you undertake to invade these premises with a search warrant, you won't find her here."

Wolfe's half a glass of beer was flat, but he didn't mind that. He reached for it and swallowed it. Then he took the handkerchief from his breast pocket and wiped his lips. "Well, sir?"

Cramer put his cigar stub in the tray, rubbed the palms of his hands together for a while, pulled at the lobe of his ear, and stood up. He looked down at Wolfe.

"I like you, you know. You know damn well I do. But this thing is to some extent out of my hands. The Commissioner was talking on the telephone this evening with the Department of Justice. That's the kind of a lay-out it is. They might really send and get you. That's a friendly warning."

"Thank you, sir. You're going? Mr. Goodwin will let you out."

I did. I went to the hall and held his coat for him, and when I pulled the curtain aside to survey the stoop before opening the door he chuckled and slapped me on the back. That didn't make me want to kiss him. Naturally he knew when an apple was too high to reach without a ladder, and naturally there's no use letting a guy know you're going to sock him until you're ready to haul off. I saw his big car with a driver there at the curb, and there was a stranger on the sidewalk. Apparently the tenor had been relieved.

I went back to the office and sat down and yawned. Wolfe was leaning back with his eyes wide open, which meant he was sleepy. We looked at each other. I said:

"So if he comes with a search warrant he won't find her here. That's encouraging. It's also encouraging that Mike Walsh is being such a big help. Also that you know who killed Harlan Scovil, like I know who put the salt in the ocean. Also that we're tied hand and foot with the Commissioner himself sore at us." I yawned. "I guess I'll prop myself up in bed tomorrow and read and knit."

"Not tomorrow, Archie. The day after, possibly. Your notebook."

I got it, and a pencil, Wolfe began:

"Miss Fox to breakfast with me in my room at seven o'clock. Delay would be dangerous. Do not forget the gong. You are not to leave the house. Saul, Fred, Orrie and Keems are to be sent to my room immediately upon arrival, but singly. Arrange tonight for a long distance connection with London at eight-thirty, Hitchcock's office. From Miss Fox, where does Walsh live and where is he employed as night watchman. As early as possible, call Morley of the District Attorney's office and I'll talk to him. Have Fritz bring me a copy of this when he wakes me at six-thirty. From Saul, complete information from Miss Lindquist regarding her father, his state of health, could he travel in an airplane, his address and telephone number in Nebraska. Phone Murger's — they open at eight-thirty — for copies of *Metropolitan Biographies,* all years available. Explain to Fritz and Theodore procedure regarding Miss Fox, as follows: . . ."

He went on, in the drawling murmur that he habitually used when giving me a set-up. I was yawning, but I got it down. Some of it sounded like he was having hallucinations or else trying to make me think he knew things I didn't know. I quit yawning for grinning while he was explaining the procedure regarding Miss Fox.

He went to bed. After I finished the typing and giving a copy to Fritz and a few other chores, I went to the basement to take a look at the back door, and I looked out the front to direct a Bronx cheer at the gumshoe on guard. Up the stairs, I continued to the third floor to take a look at the door of the south room, but I didn't try to see if it was locked, thinking it might disturb her. Down again, in my room, I looked in the bottom drawer to see if Fritz had messed it up getting out the pajamas. It was all right. I hit the hay.

10

When I leave my waking up in the morning to the vagaries of nature, it's a good deal like other acts of God — you can't tell much about it ahead of time. So Tuesday at six-thirty I staggered out of bed and fought my way across the room to turn off the electric alarm clock on the table. Then I proceeded to cleanse the form and the phiz and get the figure draped for the day. By that time the bright October sun had a band across the top fronts of the houses across the street, and I thought to myself it would be a pity to have to go to jail on such a fine day.

At seven-thirty I was in my corner in the kitchen, with Canadian bacon, pancakes, and wild thyme honey which Wolfe got from Syria. And plenty of coffee. The wheels had already started to turn. Clara

Fox, who had told Fritz she had slept like a log, was having breakfast with Wolfe in his room. Johnny Keems had arrived early, and he and Saul Panzer were in the dining-room punishing pancakes. With the telephone I had pulled Dick Morley, of the District Attorney's office, out of bed at his home, and Wolfe had talked with him. It was Morley who would have lost his job, and maybe something more, but for Wolfe pulling him out of a hole in the Banister-Schurman business about three years before.

With my pancakes I went over the stories of Scovil's murder in the morning papers. They didn't play it up much, but the accounts were fairly complete. The tip-off was that he was a Chicago gangster, which gave me a grin, since he looked about as much like a gangster as a prima donna. The essentials were there, provided they were straight: no gun had been found. The car had been stolen from where some innocent perfume salesman had parked it on 29th Street. The closest eyewitness had been a man who had been walking along about thirty feet behind

Harlan Scovil, and it was he who had got the license number before he dived for cover when the bullets started flying. In the dim light he hadn't got a good view of the man in the car, but he was sure it was a man, with his hat pulled down and a dark overcoat collar turned up, and he was sure he had been alone in the car. The car had speeded off across 31st Street and turned at the corner. No one had been found who had noticed it stopping on Ninth Avenue, where it had later been found. No fingerprints . . . and so forth and so forth.

I finished my second cup of coffee and got up and stretched and from then on I was as busy as a pickpocket on New Year's Eve. When Fred and Orrie came I let them in, and after they had got their instructions from Wolfe I distributed expense money to all four of them and let them out again. The siege was still on. There were two dicks out there now, one of them about the size of Charles Laughton before he heard beauty calling, and every time anyone passed in or out he got the kind of scrutiny you read about. I got the long distance call through to London, and Wolfe talked from his room to Ethelbert Hitchcock, which I consider the all-time low for a name for a snoop, even in England. I phoned Murger's for the copies of *Metropolitan Biographies,* and they delivered them within a quarter of an hour and I took them up to the plant rooms, as Wolfe had said he would glance at them after nine o'clock . As I was going out I stopped where Theodore Horstmann was turning out some old *Cattleyas trianae* and growled at him:

"You're going to get shot in the gizzard."

I swear to God he looked pale.

I phoned Henry H. Barber, the lawyer that we could count on for almost anything except fee-splitting, to make sure he would be available on a minute's notice all day, and to tell him that he was to consider himself retained, through us, by Miss Clara Fox, in two actions: a suit to collect a debt from the Marquis of Clivers, and a suit of damages through false arrest against Ramsey Muir. Likewise, in the first case, Miss

Hilda Lindquist.

It looked as if I had a minute loose, so I mounted the two flights to the south room and knocked on the door, and called out my name. She said come in, and I entered.

She was in the armchair, with books and magazines on the table, but none of them was opened. Maybe she had slept like a log, but her eyes looked tired. She frowned at me. I said:

"You shouldn't sit so close to the window. If they wanted to bad enough they could see in here from that 34th Street roof."

She glanced around. "I shouldn't think so, with those curtains."

"They're pretty thin. Let me move you back a little, anyhow." She got up, and I shoved the chair and table toward the bed. "I'm not usually nervous, but this is a stunt we're pulling."

She sat down again and looked up at me. "You don't like it, do you, Mr. Goodwin? I could see last night you didn't approve of it. Neither do I."

I grinned at her. "Bless your dear little

heart, what difference does that make? Nero Wolfe is putting on a show and we're in the cast. Stick to the script, don't forget that."

"I don't call it a show." She was frowning again. "A man has been murdered and it was my fault. I don't like to hide, and I don't want to. I'd rather —"

I showed her both palms. "Forget it. You came to get Wolfe to help you, didn't you? All right, let him. He may be a nut, but you're lucky that he spotted the gleam of honesty in your eye or you'd be in one sweet mess this minute. You behave yourself. For instance, if that phone there on the stand is in any way a temptation . . ."

She shook her head. "If it is, I'll resist it."

"Well, there's no use leaving it here anyhow." I went and pulled the connection out of the plug and gathered the cord and instrument under my arm. "I learned about feminine impulses in school. —There goes the office phone. Don't open the door and don't go close to the windows."

I beat it and went down two steps at a time. It was Dick Morley on the phone, with a tale. I offered to connect him with Wolfe in the plant rooms, but he said not to disturb him, he could give it to me. He had had a little trouble. The Clara Fox larceny charge was being handled by an Assistant District Attorney named Frisbie whom Morley knew only fairly well, and Frisbie hadn't seemed especially inclined to open up, but Morley had got some facts. A warrant for Clara Fox's arrest, and a search warrant for her apartment, had been issued late Monday afternoon. The apartment had not been searched because detectives under Frisbie's direction had gone first to the garage where she kept her car, and had found in it, wrapped in a newspaper under the back seat, a package of hundred dollar bills amounting to $30,000. The case was considered airtight. Frisbie's men no longer had the warrant for arrest because it had been turned over to Inspector Cramer at the request of the Police Commissioner.

I thanked Morley and hung up and went upstairs to the plant rooms and told Wolfe the sad story. He was in the tropical room trimming wilts. When I finished he said:

"We were wrong, Archie. Not hyenas. Hyenas wait for a carcass. Get Mr. Perry on the phone, connect it here, and take it down.

I went back to the office. It wasn't so easy to get Perry. His secretary was reluctant, or he was, or they both were, but I finally managed to get him on and put him through to Wolfe. Then I began a fresh page of the notebook.

Perry said he was quite busy, he hoped Wolfe could make it brief. Wolfe said he hoped so too, that first he wished to learn if he had misunderstood Perry Monday afternoon. He had gathered that Perry had believed Miss Fox to be innocent, had been opposed to any precipitate action, and had desired a careful and complete investigation. Perry said that was correct.

Wolfe's tone got sharp. "But you did not know until after seven o'clock last evening that I was not going to investigate for you, and the warrant for Miss Fox's arrest was issued an hour earlier than that. You would not call that precipitate?''

Perry sounded flustered. ''Well . . . precipitate . . . yes, it was. It was, yes. You see . . . you asked me yesterday if I am not the fount of justice in this organization. To a certain extent, yes. But there is always . . . well . . . the human element. I am not a czar, neither in fact nor by temperament. When you phoned me last evening you may have thought me irritable — as a matter of fact, I thought of calling you back to apologize. The truth is I was chagrined and deeply annoyed. I knew then that a warrant had been issued for the arrest at the instance of Mr. Muir. Surely you can appreciate my position. Mr. Muir is a high official of my corporation. When I learned later in the evening that the money had been found in Miss Fox's car, I was astounded . . . I couldn't believe it . . . but what could I do? I was amazed . . .''

''Indeed.'' Wolfe still snapped. ''You've

got your money back. Do you intend to proceed with the prosecution?"

"You don't need to take that tone, Wolfe." Perry sharpened a little. "I told you there is the human element. I'm not a czar. Muir makes an issue of it. I'm being frank with you. I can't talk him off. Granted that I could kick the first vice-president out of the company if I wanted to, which is a good deal to grant, do you think I should? After all, he has the law —"

"Then you're with him on it?"

A pause. "No. No, I'm not. I . . . I have the strongest . . . sympathy for Clara — Miss Fox. I would like to see her get something . . . much more human than justice. For instance, if there is any difficulty about bail for her I would be glad to furnish it."

"Thank you. We'll manage bail. You asked me to be brief, Mr. Perry. First, I suggest that you arrange to have the charge against Miss Fox quashed immediately. Second, I wish to inform you of our intentions if that is not done. At ten o'clock tomorrow morning I shall have Miss Fox submit herself to arrest and shall have her at once released on bail. She will then start an action against Ramsey Muir and the Seaboard Products Corporation to recover one million dollars in damages for false arrest. We deal in millions here now. I think there is no question but that we shall have sufficient evidence to uphold our action. If they try her first, so much the better. She'll be acquitted."

"But how can . . . that's absurd . . . if you have evidence . . ."

"That's all, Mr. Perry. That's my brevity. Goodbye."

I heard the click of Wolfe hanging up. Perry was sputtering, but I hung up too. I tossed the notebook away and got up and stuck my hands in my pockets and walked around. Perhaps I was muttering. I was thinking to myself, if Wolfe takes that pot with nothing but a dirty deuce he's a better man than he thinks he is, if that was possible. On the face of it, it certainly looked as if his crazy conceit had invaded the higher centers of his brain and stopped his mental processes completely; but there was one thing that made such a supposition unlikely, namely, that he was spending money. He had four expensive men riding around in taxis and he had got London on the phone as if it had been a delicatessen shop. It was a thousand to one he was going to get it back.

Still another expenditure was imminent, as I learned when the phone rang again. I sat down to get it, half hoping it was Perry calling back to offer a truce. But what I heard was Fred Durkin's low growl, and he sounded peeved.

"That you, Archie?"

"Right. What have you got?"

"Nothing. Less than that. Look here. I'm talking from the Forty-seventh Street Station."

"The . . . what? What for?"

"What the hell do you suppose for? I got arrested a little."

I made a face and took a breath. "Good for you," I said grimly. "That's a big help. Men like you are the backbone of the country. Go on."

His growl went plaintive. "Could I help it? They hopped me at the garage when

I went there to ask questions. They say I committed something when I took that car last night. I think they're getting ready to send me somewhere, I suppose Centre Street. What the hell could I do, run and let him tag me? I wouldn't be phoning now if it hadn't happened that a friend of mine is on the desk here."

"Okay. If they take you to the D. A.'s office keep your ears open and stick to the little you know. We'll get after it."

"You better. If I — hey! Will you phone the missis?"

I assured him he would see the missis as soon as she was expecting him, and hung up. I sat and scratched my nose a minute and then made for the stairs. It was looking as if being confined to the house wasn't going to deprive me of my exercise.

Wolfe was still in the tropical room. He kept on snipping stems and listened without looking around. I reported the development. He said, "These interruptions are abominable."

I said, "All right, let him rot in a dungeon."

Wolfe sighed. "Phone Mr. Barber. Can

you pick Keems up? No, you can't. When you hear from him let me talk to him."

I went back down and got Barber's office and asked him to send someone out to make arrangements for Fred to sleep with his missis that night, and gave him the dope.

I had no idea when I might hear from Johnny Keems. They had all got their instructions direct from Wolfe, and as usual he was keeping my head clear of unnecessary obstructions. As I had let Orrie Cather out he had made some kind of a crack about being the only electrician in New York who understood directors' rooms, and of course I knew Saul Panzer had a contact on with Hilda Lindquist, but beyond that their programs were outside my circle. I guessed Fred had gone back to the garage to see if he could get a line on a plant, which made it appear that Wolfe didn't even have a dirty deuce, but of course he had talked with Clara Fox nearly an hour that morning, so that was all vague. But it did seem that Frisbie or someone around the District Attorney's office was busting with ardor over an ordinary larceny on which they already had the evidence, leaving a dick at the garage; but that was probably part of the net they were holding for Clara Fox. It might even have been one of Cramer's men.

I went on being a switchboard girl. A little before ten Saul Panzer called, and from upstairs Wolfe listened to him while I put down the details he had collected from Hilda Lindquist regarding her father in Nebraska. She thought that if riding in an airplane didn't kill him it would scare him to death. Apparently Saul had further instructions, for Wolfe told him to proceed. A little later Orrie phoned in, and what he reported to Wolfe gave me my first view of a new slant that hadn't occurred to me at all. Introducing himself to Sourface Vawter as an electrician, he had been admitted to the directors' room of the Seaboard Products Corporation, and had learned that besides the double door at the end of the corridor it had another door leading into the public hall. It had been locked but could be opened from the inside, and Orrie had himself gone out that way and around the hall to the elevators. Wolfe told Orrie to wait and talked to me:

"Don't type a note on that, Archie. Any that you do type, put them in the safe at once. Leave Orrie on with me and be sure the other line is open. A call I am expecting hasn't come. When Keems calls I'll talk to him, but I'll give Orrie Fred's assignment."

Taking the hint that he didn't want to burden my ears with Orrie's schedule, I hung up. I filed some notes in the safe and loaded Wolfe's pen and tested it, a chore that I hadn't been able to get around to before — absentmindedly, because I was off on a new track. I had no idea what had started Wolfe in that direction. It had beautiful possibilities, no doubt of that, but a 100 to 1 shot in a big handicap is a beautiful possibility too, and how often would you collect on it? After taxing the brain a few minutes, this looked more like a million to one. I would probably have gone on to add more ciphers to that if I hadn't been interrupted by the doorbell. Of course I was still on that job too. I went to the hall and pulled the curtain to see through the glass panel, and got a surprise. It was the first time Wolfe's house had ever been taken for a church, but there wasn't any other explanation, for either that specimen on the stoop was scheduled for best man at a wedding or Emily Post had been fooling me for years.

The two dicks were down on the sidewalk, looking up at the best man as if it was too much of a problem for them. They had nothing on me. I opened the door and let it come three inches, leaving the chain on, and said in a well bred tone:

"Good morning."

He peered through at me. "I say, that crack is scarcely adequate. Really." He had a well trained voice but a little squawky.

"I'm sorry. This is a bad neighborhood and we have to be careful. What can I do for you?"

He went on peering. "Is this the house of Mr. Nero Wolfe?"

"It is."

He hesitated, and turned to look down at the snoops on the sidewalk, who were staring up at him in the worst possible taste. Then he came closer and pushed his face up against the crack and said in a tone nearly down to a whisper:

"From Lord Clivers. I wish to see Mr. Wolfe."

I took a second for consideration and then slid the bolt off and opened up. He walked in and I shut the door and shot the bolt again. When I turned he was standing there with his stick hung over his elbow, pulling his gloves off. He was six feet, spare but not skinny, about my age, fair-skinned with chilly blue eyes, and there was no question about his being dressed for it. I waved him ahead and followed him into the office, and he took his time getting his paraphernalia deposited on Wolfe's desk before he lowered himself into a chair. Meantime I let him know that Mr. Wolfe was engaged and would be until eleven o'clock, and that I was the confidential assistant and was at his service. He got seated and looked at me as if he would have to get around to admitting my right to exist before we could hope to make any headway.

But he spoke. "Mr. Goodwin? I see. Perhaps I got a bit ahead at the door. That is . . . I really should see Mr. Wolfe without delay."

I grinned at him. "You mean because you mentioned the Marquis of Clivers? That's okay. I wrote that letter. I know all about it. You can't see Mr. Wolfe before eleven. I can let him know you're here . . ."

"If you will be so good. Do that. My name is Horrocks — Francis Horrocks."

I looked at him. So this was the geezer that bought roses with three-foot stems. I turned on the swivel and plugged in the plant rooms and pressed the button. In a minute Wolfe was on and I told him:

"A man here to see you, Mr. Francis Horrocks. From the Marquis of Clivers. . . . Yeah, in the office. . . . Haven't asked him. . . . I told him, sure. . . . Okay."

I jerked the plugs and swivelled again. "Mr. Wolfe says he can see you at eleven o'clock, unless you'd care to try me. He suggests the latter.''

''I should have liked to see Mr. Wolfe.'' The blue eyes were going over me. ''Though I merely bring a message. First, though, I should . . . er . . . perhaps explain . . . I am here in a dual capacity. It's a bit confusing, but really quite all right. I am here, as it were, personally . . . and also semi-officially. Possibly I should first deliver my message from Lord Clivers.''

''Okay. Shoot.''

''I beg your pardon? Oh, quite. Lord Clivers would like to know if Mr. Wolfe could call at his hotel. An hour can be arranged —''

''I can save you breath on that. Mr. Wolfe never calls on anybody.''

''No?'' His brows went up. ''He is not . . . that is, bedridden?''

''Nope, only house-ridden. He doesn't like it outdoors. He never has called on anybody and never will.''

''You don't say.'' His forehead showed wrinkles. ''Well. Lord Clivers wishes very much to see him. You say you wrote that letter?''

I nodded. ''Yeah, I know all about it. I suppose Mr. Wolfe would be glad to talk with the Marquis on the telephone —''

''He prefers not to discuss it on the telephone.''

''Okay. I was going to add, or the marquis can come here. Of course the legal part of it is being handled by our attorney.''

The young diplomat sat straight with his arms folded and looked at me. ''You have engaged a solicitor?''

''Certainly. If it comes to a lawsuit, which we hope it won't, we don't want to waste any time. We understand the marquis will be in New York another week, so we'd have to be ready to serve him at once.''

He nodded. ''Just so. That's a bit candid.'' He bit his lip and cocked his head a little. ''We appear to have reached a dead end. Your position seems quite clear. I shall report it, that's all I can do.'' He hitched his feet back and cleared his throat. ''Now, if you don't mind, I assume my private capacity. I remarked that I am here personally. My name is Francis Horrocks.''

"Yeah. Your personal name.''

"Just so. And I would like to speak with Miss Fox. Miss Clara Fox.''

I felt myself straightening out my face and hoped he didn't see me. I said, "I can't say I blame you. I've met Miss Fox. Go to it.''

He frowned. "If you would be so good as to tell her I am here. It's quite all right. I know she's having a spot of seclusion, but it's quite all right. Really. You see, when she telephoned me this morning I insisted on knowing the address of her retreat. In fact, I pressed her on it. I confess she laid it on me not to come here to see her, but I made no commitment. Also, I didn't come to see her; I came semi-officially. What? Being here, I ask to see her, which is quite all right. What?''

My face was under control after the first shock. I said, "Sure it's quite all right. I mean, to ask. Seeing her is something else. You must have got the address wrong or maybe you were phoning in your sleep.''

"Oh, no. Really." He folded his arms again. "See here, Mr. Goodwin, let's cut across. It's a fact, I actually must see Miss Fox. As a friend, you understand. For purely personal reasons. I'm quite determined about this."

"Okay. Find her. She left no address here."

He shook his head patiently. "It won't do, I assure you it won't. She telephoned me. Is she in distress? I don't know. I shall have to see her. If you will tell her —"

I stood up. "Sorry, Mr. Horrocks. Do you really have to go? I hope you find Miss Fox. Tell the Marquis of Clivers —"

He sat tight, shook his head again, and frowned. "Damn it all. I dislike this, really. I've never set eyes on you before. What? I've never seen this Mr. Wolfe. Could Miss Fox have been under duress when she was telephoning? You see the possibility, of course. Setting my mind at rest and all that. If you put me out, it will really be necessary for me to tell those policemen outside that Miss Fox telephoned me from this address at nine o'clock this morning. Also I should have to take the precaution of finding a telephone at once to repeat the information to your police headquarters. What?"

I stared down at him, and I admit he was too much for me. Whether he was deep and desperate or dumb and determined I didn't know. I said:

"Wait here. Mr. Wolfe will have to know about you. Kindly stay in this room."

I left him there and went to the kitchen and told Fritz to stand in the hall, and if an Englishman emerged from the office, yodel. Then I bounced up two flights to the south room, called not too loud, and when I heard the key turn, opened the door and entered. Clara Fox stood and brushed her hair back and looked at me half alarmed and half hopeful.

I said, "What time this morning did you phone that guy Francis Horrocks?"

She stared. It got her. She swallowed. "But I . . . he . . . he promised . . ."

"So you did phone him. Swell. You forgot to mention it when I asked you about it a while ago."

"But you didn't ask me if I *had* phoned?"

"Oh, didn't I? Now that was careless." I threw up my hands. "To hell with it. Suppose you tell me what you phoned him about. I hope it wasn't a secret."

"No, It wasn't." She came a step to me. "Must you be so sarcastic? There was nothing . . . it was just personal."

"As for instance?"

"Why, it was really nothing. Of course, he sent those roses. Then . . . I had had an engagement to dine with him Monday evening, and when I made the appointment with Mr. Wolfe I had to cancel the one with Mr. Horrocks, and when he insisted I thought that three hours would be enough with Mr. Wolfe, so I told Mr. Horrocks I would go with him at ten o'clock to dance somewhere, and probably he went to the apartment and waited around there I don't know how long, and this morning I supposed he would keep phoning there and of course there would be no answer, and he couldn't get me at the office either, and besides, I hadn't thanked him for the roses . . ."

I put up a palm. "Take a breath. I see, romance. It'd be still more romantic if he came to visit you in jail. You're quite an adventuress, being as you are over 90% nincompoop. I don't suppose you know that according to an article in yesterday's *Times* this Horrocks is the nephew of the Marquis of Clivers and next in line for the title."

"Oh yes. He explained to me . . . that is . . . that's all right. I knew that. And Mr. Goodwin, I don't like —"

"We'll discuss your likes later. Here's something you don't know. Horrocks is downstairs in the office saying that he's got to see you or he'll run and get the police."

"What! He isn't."

"Yep. Somebody is, and from his looks I'm willing to admit it's Horrocks."

"But he shouldn't . . . he promised . . . send him away!"

"He won't go away. If I throw him out he'll yell for a cop. He thinks you're here under duress and need to be rescued — that's his story. You're a swell client, you are. With the chances Nero Wolfe's taking for you — all right. Anyhow, whether he's straight or not, there's no way out of it now. I'm going to bring him up here, and for God's sake make it snappy and let him go back to his uncle."

"But I . . . good heavens!" She brushed her hair back. "I don't want to see him. Not now. Tell him . . . of course I could . . . yes, that's it . . . I'll go down and just tell him —"

"You will not. Next you'll be wanting to go and walk around the block with him. You stay here."

Outside in the hall I hesitated, uncertain whether to go up and tell Wolfe of the party we were having, but decided there was no point in riling him. I went back down, tossing Fritz a nod as I passed by, and found the young diplomat sitting in the office with his arms still folded. He put his brows up at me. I told him to come on, and let him go first. Behind him on the stairs I noticed he had good springs in his legs, and at the top his air-pump hadn't speeded up any. Keeping fit for dear old England and the bloody empire.

I opened the door and bowed him in and followed him.

Clara Fox came across to him. He looked at her with a kind of sickening grin and put out his hand. She shook her head:

"No, I won't shake hands with you. Aren't you ashamed of yourself? You promised me you wouldn't. Causing Mr. Goodwin all this trouble . . ."

"Now, really. I say." His voice was different from what it had been downstairs, sort of sweet and concentrated. Silly as hell. "After all, you know, it was fairly alarming . . . with you gone and all that . . . couldn't find a trace of you . . . and you look frightful, very bad in the eyes . . ."

"Thank you very much." All of a sudden she began to laugh. I hadn't heard her laugh before. It showed her teeth and put color in her cheeks. She laughed at him until if I had been him I'd have thought up some kind of a remark. Then she stuck out her hand. "All right, shake. Mr. Goodwin says you were going to rescue me. I warned you to let American girls alone — you see the sort of thing it leads to?"

With his big paw he was hanging onto her hand as if he had a lease on it. He was staring at her. "You know, they do, though. I mean the eyes. You're really quite all right? You couldn't expect me —"

I butted in because I had to. I had left the door open and the sound of the front doorbell came up plain. I glanced at Francis Horrocks and decided that if he really was a come-on I would at least have the pleasure of seeing how long he looked lying down, before he got out of that house, and I got brusque to Clara Fox:

"Hold it. The doorbell. I'm going to shut this door and go down to answer it, and it would be a good idea to make no sounds until I get back." The bell started ringing again. "Okay?"

Clara Fox nodded.

"Okay, Mr. Horrocks?"

"Certainly. Whatever Miss Fox says."

I beat it, closing the door behind me. Some smart guy was leaning on the button, for the bell kept on ringing as

I went down the two flights. Fritz was standing in the hall, looking belligerent; he hated people that got impatient with the bell. I went to the door and pulled the curtain and looked out, and felt mercury running up my backbone. It was a quartet. Only four, and I recognized Lieutenant Rowcliff in front. It was him on the button. I hadn't had such a treat for a long while. I turned the lock and let the door come as far as the chain.

Rowcliff called through: "Well! We're not ants. Come on, open up."

I said: "Take it easy. I'm just the messenger boy."

"Yeah? Here's the message." He unfolded a paper he had in his hand. Having seen a search warrant before, I didn't need a magnifying glass. I looked through the crack at it. Rowcliff said:

"What are you waiting for? Do you want me to count ten?"

11

I said, "Hold your horses, lieutenant. If what you want is in here it can't get out, since I suppose you've got the rear and the roof covered. This isn't my house, it belongs to Nero Wolfe and he's upstairs. Wait a minute, I'll be right back."

I went up three steps at a time, paying no attention to Rowcliff yelling outside. I went in the south room; they were standing there. I said to Clara Fox, "They're here. Make it snappy. Take Horrocks with you, and if he's in on this I'll kill him."

Horrocks started, "Really —"

"Shut up! Go with Miss Fox. For God's sake —"

She might have made an adventuress at that; she was okay when it came to action. She darted to the table and grabbed her handbag and handkerchief, dashed back and got Horrocks by the hand, and pulled him through the door with her. I took a quick look around to make sure there were no lipsticks or powder puffs left behind, shoved the table towards the window where it looked more natural, and beat it. In the hall I stopped one second to shake myself. Noises of Rowcliff bellowing on the stoop floated up. Horrocks and Clara Fox had disappeared. I went down to the front door and slid the bolt and flung it open.

"Welcome," I grinned. "Mr. Wolfe says he wants the warrant for a souvenir."

They trooped in behind Rowcliff. He grunted. "Where's Wolfe?"

"Up with the plants. Until eleven o'clock. He told me to tell you this, that of course you have the legal right to search the entire premises, but that the city will pay for every nickel's worth of damage that's done if he has to go to City Hall himself to collect it."

"No! Don't scare me to death. Come on, boys. Where does that go to?"

"Front room." I pointed. "Office.

Kitchen. Basement stairs. The rear door is down there, onto the court."

He turned, and then whirled to me again. "Look here, Goodwin. You've had your bluff called. Why not save time? Why don't you bring this Fox woman down here, or up here, and call it a trick? It'd save a lot of messing around."

I said, coldly, "Pish-tush. Which isn't for you, lieutenant; I know you've got orders. It's for Inspector Cramer, and you can take it to him. The horse-laugh he'll get over this will be heard at Bath Beach. Does he think Nero Wolfe is simple enough to try to hide a woman under his bed? Go on and finish your button-button-who's-got-the-button and get the hell out of here."

He grunted and started off with his army toward the door of the basement stairs. I followed. I wanted to keep an eye on them anyway, on general principles, but besides that, I had decided to ride him. Wolfe had told me to use my judgment, and I knew that was the best way to put a bird like Rowcliff in the frame of mind we wanted him in. So I was right behind them going down, and while they poked around all over the basement, pulling the curtains back from the shelves, opening trunks and looking into empty packing cartons, I exercised the tongue. Rowcliff tried to pass it back once or twice and then pretended not to hear me. I opened the door to the insulated bottle department, and kept jerking my head around at them as if I expected to catch them in a snatch at a quart of rye. They finished up down there by taking a look at the court out of the back door, and after I got the door locked again I followed them back up to the first floor.

Rowcliff stationed a man at the door to the basement stairs and then began at the kitchen and worked forward. I hung on his tail. I said, "Up here, now, you've got to take soundings. The place is lousy with trap-doors," and when he involuntarily looked down at his feet I turned loose a haw-haw. In the office I asked him, "Want me to open the safe? There's a piece of her in there. That's the way he worked it, cut her up and scattered her around." By the time we started for the second floor he was boiling and trying not to show it, and about 97% convinced. He left a man at the head of the stairs and tackled Wolfe's room. Fritz had come along to see that nothing got hurt, thinking maybe that my mind was on something else, for there was a lot of stuff in there. I'll admit they didn't get rough, though they were thorough. Wolfe's double mattress looked pretty thick under its black silk coverlet, and one of them wiggled under it to have a look. Rowcliff went around the rows of bookshelves taking measurements with his eyes for a concealed closet, and where the poker-dart board was hanging on a screen he pulled the screen around to look behind it. All the time I was making remarks as they occurred to me.

In my room, as Rowcliff was looking back of the clothes in the closet, I said, "Listen, I've got a suggestion. I'll put on an old mother hubbard I won once at a raffle and you take me to Cramer and tell him I'm Clara Fox. After this performance there's no question but what he's too damn dumb to know the difference."

He backed out of the closet, straightened up, and glared at me. He bellowed, "You shut your trap, see? Or I will take you somewhere, and it won't be to Cramer!"

I grinned at him. "That's childish, lieutenant. Make saps out of yourselves and then try to take it out on citizens. Oh, wait! Baby, wait till this gets out!"

He tramped to the hall and started up the next flight with his army behind. I'll admit I was a little squeamish as they entered the south room; it's hard for anyone to stay in a room ten hours and not leave a trace; but they weren't looking for traces, they were looking for a live woman. Anyway, she had followed Wolfe's instructions to the letter and it looked all right. That only took a couple of minutes, and the same for the north room, where Saul Panzer had slept. When they came out to the hall again I opened the door to the narrow stairs going up, and held it for them.

"Plant rooms fourth and last stop. And take it from me, if you knock over a bench of orchid pots you'll find more trouble here than you brought with you."

Rowcliff was licked. He wasn't saying so, and he was trying not to look it, but he was. He growled:

"Wolfe up there?"

"He is."

"All right. Come along, Jack. You two wait here."

The three of us got to the top in single file and I called to him to push in. We entered and he saw the elevator standing there with the door gaping. He opened the door to the stairs and called down, "Hey, Al! Come up and give this elevator a go and look over the shaft!" Then he rejoined us.

Those plant rooms had been considered impressive by better men than Lieutenant Rowcliff — for example among many others, by Pierre Fracard, President of the Horticultural Society of France. I was in and out of them ten times a day and they impressed me, though I pretended to Theodore Horstmann that they didn't. Of course they were more startling in February than they were in October, but Wolfe and Horstmann had developed a technique of forcing that made them worth looking at no matter when it was. Inside the door of the first room, which had Odontoglossums, Oncidiums and Miltonia hybrids, Rowcliff and the dick stopped short. The angle-iron staging gleamed in its silver paint, and on the concrete benches and shelves three thousand pots of orchids showed greens and blues and yellows and reds. It looked spotty to me, since I had seen it at the top of its glory, but it was nothing to sniff at. I said:

"Well, do you think you're at the flower show? You didn't pay to get in. Get a move on, huh?"

Rowcliff led the way. He didn't leave the center aisle. Once he stopped to stoop for a peek under a bench, and I let a laugh bust out and then choked it and said, "Excuse me, lieutenant, I know you have your duty to perform." He went on with his shoulders up, but I knew the eager spirit of the chase had oozed down into his shoes.

In the next room, Cattleyas, Laelias,

hybrids and miscellaneous, Theodore Horstmann was over at one side pouring fertilizer on a row of Cymbidiums, which are terrestrials, and Rowcliff took a look at him but didn't say anything. The dick in between us stopped to bend down and stick his nose against a big lilac hybrid, and I told him, "Nope. If you smell anything sweet, it's me."

We went on through the tropical room, where it was hot with the sun shining and the lath screens already off, and continued to the potting room. It had enough free space to move around in, and it also had inhabitants. Francis Horrocks, still unsoiled, stood leaning with his back against an angle-iron, talking to Nero Wolfe, who was using the pressure spray. A couple of boards had been laid along the top of a long low wooden box which was filled with osmundine, and on the boards had been placed 35 or 40 pots of Laeliocattleya Lustre. Wolfe was spraying them with high pressure, and it was pretty wet around there. Horrocks was saying:

"It really seems a devilish lot of

trouble. What? Of course, you know, it's perfectly proper for every chap . . ."

Rowcliff looked around. There were sphagnum, sand, charcoal, crock for drainage, stacks of hundreds of pots. Rowcliff moved forward, and Wolfe shut off the spray and turned to him.

I closed in. "Mr. Nero Wolfe, Lieutenant Rowcliff."

Wolfe inclined his head one inch. "How do you do." He looked toward the door, where the dick stood. "And your companion?"

He was using his aloof tone, and it was good. Rowcliff said, "One of my men. We're here on business."

"So I understand. If you don't mind, introduce him. I like to know the names of people who enter my house."

"Yeah? His name's Loedenkrantz."

"Indeed." Wolfe looked at him and inclined his head on inch again. "How do you do, sir."

The dick said without moving, "Pleased to meetcha."

Wolfe returned to Rowcliff. "And you are a lieutenant. Reward of merit?

Incredible." His voice deepened and accelerated. "Will you take a message for me to Mr. Cramer? Tell him that Nero Wolfe pronounces him to be a prince of witlings and an unspeakable ass! Pfui!" He turned on the spray, directed it on the orchids, and addressed Francis Horrocks. "But my dear sir, since all life is trouble, the only thing is to achieve a position where we may select varieties . . ."

I said to Rowcliff. "There's a room there at the side, the gardener's. You don't want to miss that."

He went with me and looked in, and I hand it to him that he had enough face left to enter and look under the bed and open the closet door. He came out again, and he was done. But as he moved for the door he asked me, "How do you get out to the roof?"

"You don't. This covers all of it. Anyhow you've got it spotted. Haven't you? Don't tell me you overlooked that."

We were returning the way we had come, and I was behind them again. He didn't answer. Mr. Loedenkrantz didn't stop to smell an orchid. There was a grin inside of me trying to burst into flower, but I was warning it, not yet, sweetheart, they're not out yet. We left the plant rooms and descended to the third floor, and Rowcliff said to the pair he had left there:

"Fall in."

One began, "I thought I heard a noise —"

"Shut up."

I followed them down, on down. After all the diversion I had been furnishing I didn't think it advisable to go suddenly dumb, so I manufactured a couple of nifties during the descent. In the lower hall, before I unlocked the door, I squared off to Rowcliff and told him:

"Listen. I've been free with the lip, but it was my day. We all have to take it sometimes, and hey-nonny-nonny. I'm aware it wasn't you that pulled this boner."

But being a lieutenant, he was stern and unbending. "Much obliged for nothing. Open the door."

I did that, and they went. On the sidewalk they were joined by their brothers who had been left there. I shut the door, heard the lock snap, and put on the bolt. I turned and went to the office. I seldom took a drink before dark, but the idea of a shot of bourbon seemed pleasing, so I went to the cabinet and helped myself. It felt encouraging going down. In my opinion, there was very little chance that Rowcliff had enough eagerness left in him to try a turn-around, but I returned to the entrance and pulled the curtain and stood looking out for a minute. There was no one in sight that had the faintest resemblance to a city employee. So I mounted the stairs, clear to the plant rooms, and went through to the potting room. Wolfe and Horrocks were standing there, and Wolfe looked at me inquiringly.

I waved a hand. "Gone. Done."

Wolfe hung the spray tube on its hook and called, "Theodore!"

Horstmann came trotting. He and I together lifted the pots of Laeliocattleyas, which Wolfe had been spraying, from the boards, and put them on a bench. Then we removed the boards from the long box of osmundine; Horrocks took one. Wolfe said:

"All right, Miss Fox."

The mossy fibre, dripping with water, raised itself out of the box, fell all around us, and spattered our pants. We began picking off patches of it that were clinging to Clara Fox's soaked dress, and she brushed back her hair and blurted:

"Thank God I wasn't born a mermaid!"

Horrocks put his fingers on the sleeve of her dress. "Absolutely saturated. Really, you know —"

He may have been straight, but he had no right to be in on it. I cut him off: "I know you'll have to be going. Fritz can attend to Miss Fox. If you don't mind?"

12

At twelve o'clock noon Wolfe and I sat in the office. Fred Durkin was out in the kitchen eating pork chops and pumpkin pie. He had made his appearance some twenty minutes before, with the pork chops in his pocket, for Fritz to cook, and a tale of injured innocence. One of Barber's staff had found him in a detention room down at headquarters, put there to weigh his sins after an hour of displaying his ignorance to Inspector Cramer. The lawyer had pried him loose without much trouble and sent him on his way, which of course was West 35th Street. Wolfe hadn't bothered to see him.

Up in the tropical room was the unusual sight of Clara Fox's dress and other items of apparel hanging on a string to dry out, and she was up in the south room sporting the dressing gown Wolfe had given me for Christmas four years before. I hadn't seen her, but Fritz had taken her the gown. It looked as if we'd have to get her out of the house pretty soon or I wouldn't have a thing to put on.

Francis Horrocks had departed, having accepted my hint without any whats. Nothing had been explained to him. Wolfe, of course, wasn't openly handing Clara Fox anything, but it was easy to see that she was one of the few women he would have been able to think up a reason for, from the way he talked about her. He told me that when she and Horrocks had come running into the potting room she had immediately stepped into the osmundine box, which had been all ready for her, and standing there she had fixed her eyes on Horrocks and said to him, "No questions, no remarks, and you do what Mr. Wolfe says. Understand." And Horrocks had stood and stared with his mouth open as she stretched herself out in the box and Horstmann had piled osmundine on her three inches deep while Wolfe got the spray ready. Then he had come to and helped with the boards and the pots.

In the office at noon, Wolfe was drinking beer and making random remarks as they occurred to him. He observed that since Inspector Cramer was sufficiently aroused to be willing to insult Nero Wolfe by having his house invaded with a search warrant, it was quite possible that he had also seen fit to proceed to other indefensible measures, such as tapping telephone wires, and that therefore we should take precautions. He stated that it had been a piece of outrageous stupidity on his part to let Mike Walsh go Monday evening before asking him a certain question, since he had then already formed a surmise which, if proven correct, would solve the problem completely. He said he was sorry that there was no telephone at the Lindquist prairie home in Nebraska, since it meant that the old gentleman would have to endure the rigors of a nine-mile trip to a village in order to talk over long distance; and he hoped that the connection with him would be made at one o'clock as arranged. He also hoped that Johnny Keems would be able to find Mike Walsh and escort him to the office without interference, fairly soon, since a few words with Walsh and a talk with Victor Lindquist should put him in a position where he could proceed with arrangements to clean up the whole affair. More beer. And so forth.

I let him rave on, thinking he might fill in a couple of gaps by accident, but he didn't.

The phone rang. I took it, and heard Keems' voice. I stopped him before he got started:

"I can't hear you, Johnny. Don't talk so close."

"What?"

"I said, don't talk so close."

"Oh. Is this better?"

"Yeah."

"Well . . . I'm reporting progress backwards. I found the old lady in good health and took care of her for a couple of hours, and then she got hit by a brown taxi and they took her to the hospital."

"That's too bad. Hold the wire a minute." I covered the transmitter and turned to Wolfe: "Johnny found Mike Walsh and tailed him for two hours, and a dick picked him up and took him to headquarters."

"Picked up Johnny?"

"No. Walsh."

Wolfe frowned, and his lips went out and in, and again. He sighed. "The confounded meddlers. Call him in."

I told the phone, "Come on in, and hurry," and hung up.

Wolfe leaned back with his eyes shut, and I didn't bother him. It was a swell situation for a tantrum, and I didn't feel like a dressing-down. If his observations had been anything at all more than shooting off, this was a bad break, and it might lead to almost anything, since if Mike Walsh emptied the bag for Cramer there was no telling what might be thought necessary for protecting the Marquis of Clivers from a sinister plot. I didn't talk, but got out the plant records and pretended to go over them.

At a quarter to one the doorbell rang,

and I went and admitted Johnny Keems. I was still acting as hallboy, because you never could tell about Cramer. Johnny, looking like a Princeton boy with his face washed, which was about the only thing I had against him, followed me to the office and dropped into a chair without an invitation. He demanded:

"How did I come through on the code? Not so bad, huh?"

I grunted. "Perfectly marvelous. You're a wonder. Where did you find Walsh?"

He threw one leg over the other. "No trouble at all. Over on East 64th Street, where he boards. Your instructions were not to approach him until I had a line or in case of emergency, so I found out by judicious inquiry that he was in there and then I stuck around. He came out at a quarter to ten and walked to Second Avenue and turned south. West on 58th to Park. South on Park —"

Wolfe put in, "Skip the itinerary."

Johnny nodded. "We were about there anyhow. At 56th Street he went into the Hotel Portland."

"Indeed."

"Yep. And he stayed there over an hour. He used the phone and then took an elevator, but I stayed in the lobby because the house dick knows me and he saw me and I knew he wouldn't stand for it. I knew Walsh might have got loose because there are two sets of elevators, but all I could do was stick, and at a quarter past eleven he came down and went out. He headed south and turned west on 55th, and across Madison he went in at a door where it's boarded up for construction. That's the place you told me to try if I drew a blank at 64th Street, the place where he works as a night watchman. I waited outside, thinking I might get stopped if I went in, and hoping he wouldn't use another exit. But he didn't. In less than ten minutes he came out again, but he wasn't alone any more. A snoop had him and was hanging onto him. They walked to Park and took a taxi, and I hopped one of my own and followed to Centre Street. They went in at the big doors, and I found a phone."

Wolfe, leaning back, shut his eyes. Johnny Keems straightened his necktie and looked satisfied with himself. I tossed my notebook to the back of the desk, with his report in it, and tried to think of some brief remark that would describe how I felt. The telephone rang.

I took it. A voice informed me that Inspector Cramer wished to speak to Mr. Goodwin, and I said to put him on and signalled to Wolfe to take his line.

The sturdy inspector spoke: "Goodwin? Inspector Cramer. How about doing me a favor?"

"Surest thing you know." I made it hearty. "I'm flattered."

"Yeah? It's an easy one. Jump in your wagon and come down to my office."

I shot a glance at Wolfe, who had his receiver to his ear, but he made no sign. I said, "Maybe I could, except for one thing. I'm needed here to inspect cards of admission at the door. Like search warrants, for instance. You have no idea how they pile in on us."

Cramer laughed. "All right, you can have that one. There'll be no search warrants while you're gone. I need you down here for something. Tell Wolfe you'll be back in an hour."

"Okay. Coming."

I hung up and turned to Wolfe. "Why not? It's better than sitting here crossing my fingers. Fred and Johnny are here, and together they're a fifth as good as me. Maybe he wants me to help him embroider Mike Walsh. I'd be glad to."

Wolfe nodded. "I like this. There's something about it I like. I may be wrong. Go, by all means."

I shook my pants legs down, put the notebook and plant record away in the drawers, and got going. Johnny came to bolt the door behind me.

I hadn't been on the sidewalk for nearly twenty hours, and it smelled good. I filled the chest, waved at Tony with a cart of coal across the street, and opened up my knees on the way to the garage. The roadster whinnied as I went up to it, and I circled down the ramp, scared the daylights out of a truck as I emerged, and headed downtown with my good humor coming in again at every pore. I doubt if anything could ever get me so low that it wouldn't perk me up to get out and enjoy

244

nature, anywhere between the two rivers from the Battery to 110th Street, but preferably below 59th.

I parked at the triangle and went in and took an elevator. They sent me right in to Cramer's little inside room, but it was empty except for a clerk in uniform, and I sat down to wait. In a minute Cramer entered. I was thinking he might have the decency to act a little embarrassed, but he didn't; he was chewing a cigar and he appeared hearty. He didn't go to his desk, but stood there. I thought it wouldn't hurt to rub it in, so I asked him:

"Have you found Clara Fox yet?"

He shook his head. "Nope. No Clara Fox. But we will. We've got Mike Walsh."

I lifted the brows. "You don't say. Congratulations. Where'd you find him?"

He frowned down at me. "I'm not going to try to bluff you, Goodwin. It's a waste of time. That's what I asked you to come down here for, this Mike Walsh. You and Wolfe have been cutting it pretty thin up there, but if you help me out on this we'll call it square. I want you to pick this Mike Walsh out for me. You won't have to appear, you can look through the panel."

"I don't get you. I thought you said you had him."

"Him hell." Cramer bit his cigar. "I've got eight of 'em."

"Oh," I grinned at him sympathetically. "Think of that, eight Mike Walshes! It's a good thing it wasn't Bill Smith or Abe Cohen."

"Will you pick him out?"

"I don't like to." I pulled a hesitation. "Why can't the boys grind it out themselves?"

"Well, they can't. We've got nothing at all to go on except that Harlan Scovil had his name on a piece of paper and he was at your place last night. We couldn't use a hose on all eight of them even if we were inclined that way. The last one was brought in less than an hour ago, and he's worse than any of the others. He's a night watchman and he's seventy if he's a day, and he says who he knows or doesn't know is none of our damn business, and I'm inclined to believe him. Look here,

Goodwin. This Walsh isn't a client of Wolfe's. You don't owe him anything, and anyway we're not going to hurt him unless he needs it. Come on and take a look and tell me if we've got him."

I shook my head. "I'm sorry. It wouldn't go with the program. I'd like to, but I can't."

Cramer took his cigar from his mouth and pointed it at me. "Once more I'm asking you. Will you do it?"

I just shook my head.

He walked around the desk to his chair and sat down. He looked at me if he regretted something. Finally he said, "It's too much, Goodwin. This time it's too much. I'm going to have to put it on to you and Wolfe both for obstructing justice. It's all set for a charge. Even if I hated to worse than I do, I've got upstairs to answer to."

He pushed a button on his desk. I said, "Go ahead. Then, pretty soon, go ahead and regret it for a year or two and maybe longer."

The door opened and a gumshoe came in. Cramer turned to him. "You'll have to turn 'em loose, Nick. Put shadows on all of them except the kid that goes to N. Y. U. and the radio singer. They're out. Take good men. If one of them gets lost you've got addresses to pick him up again. Any more they pick up, I'll see them after you've got a record down."

"Yes, sir. The one from Brooklyn, the McGrue Club guy, is raising hell."

"All right. Let him out. I'll phone McGrue later."

The gumshoe departed. Cramer tried to get his cigar lit. I said: "And as far as upstairs is concerned, to hell with the Commissioner. How does he know whether or not it's justice that Wolfe's obstructing? How about that cripple Paul Chapin and that bird Bowen? Did he obstruct justice that time? If you ask me, I think you had a nerve to ask me to come down here. Are we interfering with your legal right to look for these babies? You even looked for one of them under Wolfe's bed and under my bed. Do Wolfe and I wear badges, and do we line up on the first and fifteenth for a city check? We do not."

Cramer puffed. "I ought to charge you."

I lifted the shoulders and let them drop. "Sure. You're just sore. That's one way cops and newspaper reporters are all alike, they can't bear to have anyone know anything they won't tell." I looked at my wrist watch and saw it was nearly two o'clock. "I'm hungry. Where do I eat, inside or out?"

Cramer said, "I don't give a damn if you never eat. Beat it."

I floated up and out, down the hall, down in the elevator, and back to the roadster. I looked around comprehensively, reflecting that within a radius of a few blocks eight Mike Walshes were scattering in all directions, six of them with tails, and that I would give at least two bits to know where one of them was headed for. But even if he had gone by my elbow that second I wouldn't have dared to take it up, since that would have spotted him for them, so I hopped in the roadster and swung north.

When I got back to the house Wolfe and Clara Fox were in the dining-room, sitting with their coffee. They were so busy they only had time to toss me a nod, and I sat down at my end of the table and Fritz brought me a plate. She had on my dressing-gown, with the sleeves rolled up, and a pair of Fritz's slippers with her ankles bare. Wolfe was reciting Hungarian poetry to her, a line at a time, and she was repeating it after him; and he was trying not to look pleased as she leaned forward with an ear cocked at him and her eyes on his lips, asking as if she was really interested, "Say it again, slower, please do."

The yellow dressing-gown wasn't bad on her, at that, but I was hungry. I waded through a plate of minced lamb kidneys with green peppers, and a dish of endive, and as Fritz took the plate away and presented me with a hunk of pie I observed to the room:

"If you've finished with your coffee and have any time to spare, you might like to hear a report."

Wolfe sighed. "I suppose so. But not here." He arose. "If Fritz could serve your coffee in the office? And you, Miss

Fox . . . upstairs.''

"Oh, my lord. Must I dig in again?"

"Of course. Until dinnertime." He bowed, meaning that he inclined his head two inches, and went off.

Clara Fox got up and walked to my end. "I'll pour your coffee."

"All right, Black and two lumps."

She screwed up her face. "With all this grand cream here? Very well. You know, Mr. Goodwin, this house represents the most insolent denial of female rights the mind of man has ever conceived. No woman in it from top to bottom, but the routine is faultless, the food is perfect, and the sweeping and dusting are impeccable. I have never been a housewife, but I can't overlook this challenge. I'm going to marry Mr. Wolfe, and I know a girl that will be just the thing for you, and of course our friends will be in and out a good deal. This place needs some upsetting."

I looked at her. The hem of the yellow gown was trailing the floor. The throat of it was spreading open, and it was interesting to see where her shoulders came to and how the yellow made her hair look. I said:

"You've already upset enough. Go upstairs and behave yourself. Wolfe has three wives and nineteen children in Turkey."

"I don't believe it. He has always hated women until he saw how nicely they pack in osmundine."

I grinned at her and got up. "Thanks for the coffee. I may be able to persuade Wolfe to let you come down for dinner."

I balanced my cup and saucer in one hand while I opened the door for her with the other, and then went to the office and got seated at my desk and started to sip. Wolfe had his middle drawer open and was counting bottle caps to see how much beer he had drunk since Sunday morning. Finally he closed it and grunted.

"I don't believe it for a moment. Bah. Statistics are notoriously unreliable. I had a very satisfactory talk with Mr. Lindquist over long distance, and I am more than ever anxious for a few words with Mr. Walsh. Did you see him?"

"No. I declined the invitation." I

reported my session with Cramer in detail, mostly verbatim, which was the way he liked it. Wolfe listened, and considered.

"I see. Then Mr. Walsh is loose again."

"Yeah. Not only is he loose, but I don't see how we can approach him, since there's a tail on him. The minute we do they'll know it's him and grab him away from us."

"I suppose so." Wolfe sighed. "Of course it would not do to abolish the police. For nine-tenths of the prey that the law would devour they are the ideal hunters, which is as it should be. As for Walsh, it is essential that I see him . . . or that you do. Bring Keems."

I went to the front room, where Johnny was taking ten cents a game from Fred Durkin with a checkerboard, and shook him loose. He sat down next to the desk and Wolfe wiggled a finger at him.

"Johnny, this is important. I don't send Archie because he is needed here, and Saul is not available."

"Yes, sir. Shoot."

"The Michael Walsh whom you followed this morning has been released by the police because they don't know if he is the one they want. They have put a shadow on him, so it would be dangerous for you to pick him up even if you knew where to look. It is very important for Archie to get in touch with him. Since he is pretending to the police that he is not the man they seek, there is a strong probability that he will stick to the ordinary routine of his life; that is, that he will go to work this evening. But if he does that he will certainly be followed there and a detective will be covering the entrance all evening; therefore Archie could not enter that way to see him. I am covering all details so that you will know exactly what we want. Is it true that when a building project is boarded up, there is boarding where the construction adjoins the sidewalk but not on the other sides, where there are buildings? I would think so; at least it may be so sometimes. Very well, I wish to know by what means Archie can enter that building project at, say, seven o'clock this evening. Explore them all. I understand from Miss Fox, who was there last Thursday evening to talk with Mr. Walsh, that they have just started the steel framework.

"Miss Fox also tells me that Mr. Walsh goes to work at six o'clock. I want to know if he does so today. You can watch the entrance at that time, or you may perhaps have found another vantage point for observing him from inside. Use your judgment and your wit. Should you phone here, use code as far as possible. Be here by six-thirty with your report."

"Yes, sir." Johnny stood up. "If I have to sugar anybody around the other buildings in order to get through, I'll need some cash."

Wolfe nodded with some reserve. I got four fives from the safe and passed them over and Johnny tucked them in his vest. Then I took him to the hall and let him out.

I went back to my desk and fooled around with some things, made out a couple of checks and ran over some invoices from Richardt. Wolfe was drinking beer and I was watching him out of the corner of my eye. I was keyed up, and I knew why I was, it was something about him. A hundred times I tried to decide just what it was that made it so plain to me when he had the feeling that he was closing in and was about ready for the blow-up. Once I would think that it was only that he sat differently in his chair, a little further forward, and another time I would guess that it was the way he made movements, not quicker exactly but closer together, and still another time I would light on something else. I doubt if it was any of those. Maybe it was electric. There was more of a current turned on inside of him, and somehow I felt it. I felt it that day, as he filled his glass, and drained it and filled it again. And it made me uncomfortable, because I wasn't doing anything, and because there was always the danger that Wolfe would go off half cocked when he was keeping things to himself. So at length I offered an observation:

"And I just sit here? What's the idea, do you think those gorillas are coming back? I don't. They're not even watching the front. What was the matter with leaving Fred and Johnny here and letting me go to 55th Street to do my own scouting? That might have been sensible, if you want me to see Mike Walsh by seven o'clock. All I'm suggesting is a little friendly chat. I've heard you admit you've got lots of bad habits, but the worst one is the way you dig up odd facts out of phone calls and other sources when my back is turned and then expect me . . ." I waved a hand.

Wolfe said, "Nonsense. When have my expectations of you ventured beyond your capacity?"

"Never. How could they? But for instance, if it's so important for me to see Mike Walsh it might be a good idea for me to know why, unless you want him wrapped up and brought here."

Wolfe shook his head. "Not that, I think. I'll inform you, Archie. In good time." He reached out and touched the button, then sighed and pushed the tray away. "As for my sending Johnny and letting you sit here, you may be needed. While you were out Mr. Muir telephoned to ask if he might call here at half-past-two. It is that now —"

"The devil he did. Muir?"

"Yes. Mr. Ramsey Muir. And as for my keeping you in ignorance of facts, you already interfere so persistently with my mental processes that I am disinclined to furnish you further grounds for speculation. In the present case you know the general situation as well as I do. Chiefly you lack patience, and my exercise of it infuriates you. If I know who killed Harlan Scovil — and since talking with Mr. Lindquist over long distance I think I do — why do I not act at once? Firstly because I require confirmation, and secondly because our primary interest in this case is not the solution of a murder but the collection of a debt. If I expect to get the confirmation I require from Mr. Walsh, why do I not get him at once, secure my confirmation, and let the police have him? Because the course they would probably take, after beating his story out of him, would make it difficult to collect from Lord Clivers, and would greatly complicate the matter of clearing Miss Fox of the larceny charge. We have three separate goals to reach, and since it will be necessary to arrive at all of them simultaneously — but there is the doorbell. Mr. Muir is three minutes late."

I went to the hall and took a look through the panel. Sure enough, it was Muir. I opened up and let him in. From the way he stepped over the doorsill and snapped out that he wanted to see Wolfe, it was fairly plain that he was mad as hell. He had on a brown plaid topcoat cut by a tailor that was out of my class, but 25 years too young for him, and apparently he wasn't taking it off. I motioned him ahead of me into the office and introduced him, and allowed myself a polite grin when I saw that he wasn't shaking hands any more than Wolfe was. I pushed a chair around and he sat with his hat on his knees.

Wolfe said, "Your secretary, on the telephone, seemed not to know what you wished to see me about. My surmise was, your charge against Miss Clara Fox. You understand of course that I am representing Miss Fox."

"Yes. I understand that."

"Well, sir?"

The bones of Muir's face seemed to show, and his ears seemed to point forward, more than they had the day before. He kept his lips pressed together and his jaw was working from side to side as if all this emotion in his old age was nearly too much for him. I remembered how he had looked at Clara Fox the day before and thought it was remarkable that he could keep his digestion going with all the stew there must have been inside of him. He said:

"I have come here at the insistence of Mr. Perry." His voice trembled a little, and when he stopped his jaw slid around. "I want you to understand that I know she took that money. She is the only one who could have taken it. It was found in her car." He stopped a little to control his jaw. "Mr. Perry told me of your threat to sue for damages. The insinuation in it is contemptible. What kind of a blackguard are you, to protect a thief by hinting calumnies against men who . . . men above suspicion?"

He paused and compressed his lips. Wolfe murmured, "Well, go on. I don't answer questions containing two or more unsupported assumptions.''

I don't think Muir heard him; he was only hearing himself and trying not to blow up. He said, "I'm here only for one reason, for the sake of the Seaboard Products Corporation. And not on account of your dirty threat either. That's not where the dirt is in the Seaboard Products Corporation that has got to be concealed.'' His voice trembled again. "It's the fact that the president of the corporation has to satisfy his personal sensual appetite by saving a common thief from what she deserves! That's why she can laugh at me! That's why she can stand behind your dirty threats! Because she knows what Perry wants, and she knows how —''

"Mr. Muir!'' Wolfe snapped at him. "I wouldn't talk like that if I were you. It's so futile. Surely you didn't come here to persuade me that Mr. Perry has a sensual appetite.''

Muir made a movement and his hat rolled from his knees to the floor, but he paid no attention to it. His movement was for the purpose of getting his hand into his inside breast pocket, from which he withdrew a square manila envelope. He looked in it and fingered around and took out a small photograph, glanced at it, and handed it to Wolfe. "There," he said, "look at that."

Wolfe did so, and passed it to me. It was a snapshot of Clara Fox and Anthony D. Perry seated in a convertible coupe with the top down. I laid it on the edge of the desk and Muir picked it up and returned it to the envelope. His jaw was moving. He said, "I have more than thirty of them. A detective took them for me. Perry doesn't know I have them. I want to make it clear to you that she deserves . . . that she has a hold on him . . ."

Wolfe put up a hand. "I'm afraid I must interrupt you again, Mr. Muir. I don't like photographs of automobiles. You say that Mr. Perry insisted on your coming here. I'll have to insist on your telling me what for."

"But you understand —"

"No. I won't listen. I understand enough. Perhaps I had better put a question or two. Is it true that you have recovered all the missing money?"

Muir glared at him. "You know we have. It was found under the back seat of her car."

"But if that was her car in the photograph, it has no back seat."

"She bought a new one in August. The photograph was taken in July. I suppose Perry bought it. Her salary is higher than any other woman in our organization."

"Splendid. But about the money. If you have it back, why are you determined to prosecute?"

"Why shouldn't we prosecute? Because she's guilty! She took it from my desk, knowing that Perry would protect her! With her body, with her flesh, with her surrender —"

"No, Mr. Muir." Wolfe's hand was up again. "Please. I put the question wrong, I shouldn't have asked why. I want to know, are you determined to prosecute?"

Muir clamped his lips. He opened them, and clamped them again. At last he spoke, "We were. I was."

"Was? Are you still?"

No reply. "Are you still, Mr. Muir?"

"I . . . no."

"Indeed." Wolfe's eyes narrowed. "You are prepared to withdraw the charge?"

"Yes . . . under certain circumstances."

"What circumstances?"

"I want to see her." Muir stopped because his voice was trembling again. "I have promised Perry that I will withdraw the charge provided I can see her, alone, and tell her myself." He sat up and his jaw tightened. "That . . . those are the circumstances."

Wolfe looked at him a moment and then leaned back. He sighed. "I think possibly that can be arranged. But you must first sign a statement exonerating her."

"Before I see her?"

"Yes."

"No. I see her first." Muir's lips worked. "I must see her and tell her myself. If I had already signed a statement, she wouldn't . . . no. I won't do that."

"But you can't see her first." Wolfe

sounded patient. "There is a warrant in force against her, sworn to by you. I do not suspect you of treachery, I merely protect my client. You say that you have promised Mr. Perry that you will withdraw the charge. Do so. Mr. Goodwin will type the statement, you will sign it, and I will arrange a meeting with Miss Fox later in the day."

Muir was shaking his head. He muttered, "No. No . . . I won't." All at once he broke loose worse than he had in Perry's office the day before. He jumped up and banged his hand on the desk and leaned over at Wolfe. "I tell you I must see her! You damn blackguard, you've got her here! What for? What do you get out of it? What do you and Perry . . ."

I had a good notion to slap him one, but of course he was too old and too little. Wolfe, leaning back, opened his eyes to look at him and then closed them. Muir went on raving. I got out of my chair and told him to sit down, and he began yelling at me, something about how I had looked at her in Perry's office yesterday. That sounded as if he might really be going to have a fit, so I took a step and got hold of his shoulders with a fairly good grip and persuaded him into his chair, and he shut up as suddenly as he had started and pulled a handkerchief from his pocket and began wiping his face with his hand trembling.

As he did that and I stepped back, the doorbell rang. I wasn't sure about leaving Wolfe there alone with a maniac, but when I didn't move he lifted his brows at me, so I went to see who the customer was.

I looked through the panel. It was a rugged-looking guy well past middle age in a loose-hanging tweed suit, with a red face, straight eyebrows over tired gray eyes, and no lobe on his right ear. Even without the ear I would have recognized him from the *Times* picture. I opened the door and asked him what he wanted and he said in a wounded tone:

"I'd like to see Mr. Nero Wolfe. Lord Clivers."

13

I nodded. "Right. Hop the sill."

I proceeded to tax the brain. Before I go on to describe that, I'll make a confession. I had not till that moment seriously entertained the idea that the Marquis of Clivers had killed Harlan Scovil. And why not? Because like most other people, and maybe especially Americans, there was a sneaky feeling in me that men with noble titles didn't do things like that. Besides, this bird had just been to Washington and had lunch at the White House, which cinched it that he wasn't a murderer. As a matter of fact, I suspect that noblemen and people who eat lunch at the White House commit more than their share of murders compared to their numerical strength in the total population. Anyhow, looking at this one in the flesh, and reflecting that he carried a pistol and knew how to use one, and considering how well he was fixed in the way of motive, and realizing that since Harlan Scovil had been suspicious enough to make an advance call on Nero Wolfe he might easily have done the same on the Marquis of Clivers, I revised some of the opinions I had been forming. It looked wide open to me.

That flashed through my mind. Also, as I disposed of his hat and stick and gloves for him, I wondered if it might be well to arrange a little confrontation between Muir and the marquis, but I didn't like to decide that myself. So I escorted him to a seat in the front room, telling him Wolfe was engaged, and then returned to the hall and wrote on a piece of paper, "Old man Clivers," and went to the office and handed the paper to Wolfe.

Wolfe glanced at it, looked at me, and winked his right eye. I sat down. Muir was talking, much calmer but just as stubborn. They passed it back and forth for a couple of minutes without getting anywhere, until Wolfe said:

"Futile, Mr. Muir. I won't do it. Tell Mr. Perry that I shall proceed with the program I announced to him this morning. That's final. I'll accept nothing less than complete and unconditional exoneration of my client. Good day, sir; I have a caller waiting."

Muir stood up. He wasn't trembling, and his jaw seemed to be back in place, but he looked about as friendly as Mussolini talking to the world. He didn't say anything. He shot me a mean glance and looked at Wolfe for half a minute without blinking, and then stooped to pick up his hat and straightened up and steered for the door. I followed and let him out, and stood on the stoop a second watching him start off down the sidewalk as if he had half a jag on. He was like the mule in the story that kept running into trees; he wasn't blind, he was just so mad he didn't give a damn.

I stood shaking my head more in anger than in pity, and then went back to the office and said to Wolfe:

"I would say you hit bottom that time. He's staggering. If you called that foxy, what would you say if you saw a rat?''

Wolfe nodded faintly. I resumed, "I showed you that paper because I thought you might deem it advisable to let Clivers and Muir see each other. Unexpected like that, it might have been interesting. It's my social instinct."

"No doubt. But this is a detective bureau, not a fashionable salon. Nor a menagerie — since Mr. Muir is plainly a lecherous hyena. Bring Lord Clivers."

I went through the connecting door to the front room, and Clivers looked around surprised at my entering from a new direction. He was jumpy. I pointed him ahead and he stopped on the threshold and glanced around before venturing in. Then he moved spry enough and walked over to the desk. Wolfe took him in with his eyes half shut, and nodded.

"How do you do, sir." Wolfe indicated the chair Muir had just vacated. "Be seated."

Clivers did a slow motion circle. He turned all the way around, encompassing with his eyes the book shelves, the wall maps, the Holbein reproductions, more book shelves, the three-foot globe on its stand, the engraving of Brillat-Savarin, more book shelves, the picture of Sherlock Holmes above my desk. Then he sat down and looked at me with a frown and pointed a thumb at me.

"This young man," he said.

Wolfe said, "My confidential assistant, Mr. Goodwin. There would be no point in sending him out, for he would merely find a point of vantage we have prepared, and set down what he heard."

"The devil he would." Clivers laughed three short blasts, haw-haw-haw, and gave me up. He transferred the frown to Wolfe. "I received your letter about that horse. It's preposterous."

Wolfe nodded. "I agree with you. All debts are preposterous. They are the envious past clutching with its cold dead fingers the throat of the living present."

"Eh?" Clivers stared at him. "What kind of talk is that? Rot. What I mean to say is, two hundred thousand pounds for a horse. And uncollectible."

"Surely not." Wolfe sighed. He leaned forward to press the button for Fritz, and back again. "The best argument against you is your presence here. If it is uncollectible, why did you come? Will you have some beer?"

"What kind of beer?"

"American. Potable."

"I'll try it. I came because my nephew gave me to understand that if I wanted to see you I would have to come. I wanted to see you because I had to learn if you are a swindler or a dupe."

"My dear sir." Wolfe lifted his brows. "No other alternatives? —Another glass and bottle, Fritz." He opened his, and poured. "But you seem to be a direct man. Let's not get mired in irrelevancies. Frankly, I am relieved. I feared that you might even dispute the question of identity and create a lot of unnecessary trouble."

"Dispute identity?" Clivers glared. "Why the devil should I?"

"You shouldn't, but I thought you might. You were, forty years ago in Silver City, Nevada, known as George Rowley?"

"Certainly I was. Thanks, I'll pour it myself."

"Good." Wolfe drank, and wiped his

lips. "I think we should get along. I am aware that Mr. Lindquist's claim against you has no legal standing on account of the expiration of time. The same is true of the claim of various others; besides, the paper you signed which originally validated it is not available. But it is a sound and demonstrable moral obligation, and I calculated that rather than have that fact shown in open court you would prefer to pay. It would be an unusual case and would arouse much public interest. Not only are you a peer of England, you are in this country on an important and delicate diplomatic mission, and therefore such publicity would be especially undesirable. Would you not rather pay what you owe, or at least a fraction of it, than permit the publicity? I calculated that you would. Do you find the beer tolerable?"

Clivers put down his glass and licked his lips. "It'll do." He screwed up his mouth and looked at Wolfe. "By God, you know, you might mean that."

"Verily, sir."

"Yes, by God, you might. I'll tell you what I thought. I thought you were basing the claim on that horse with the pretense that it was additional to the obligation I assumed when I signed that paper. The horse wasn't mentioned in the paper. Not a bad idea, an excellent go at blackmail. It all sounds fantastic now, but it wasn't then. If I hadn't signed that paper and if it hadn't been for that horse I would have had a noose around my neck. Not so damn pleasant, eh? And of course that's what you're doing, claiming extra for the horse. But it's preposterous. Two hundred thousand pounds for a horse? I'll pay a thousand."

Wolfe shook his head. "I dislike haggling. Equally I dislike quibbling. The total claim is in question, and you know it. I represent not only Mr. and Miss Lindquist but also the daughter of Gilbert Fox, and indirectly Mr. Walsh; and I was to have represented Mr. Scovil, who was murdered last evening." He shook his head again. "No, Lord Clivers. In my letter I based the claim on the horse only because the paper you signed is not available. It is the total claim we are discussing, and, strictly speaking, that would mean half of your entire wealth. As I said, my clients are willing to accept a fraction.''

Clivers had a new expression on his face. He no longer glared, but looked at Wolfe quietly intent. He said, ''I see. So it's a serious game, is it? I would have paid a thousand for the horse, possibly even another thousand for the glass of beer. But you're on for a real haul by threatening to make all this public and compromise my position here. Go to hell.'' He got up.

Wolfe said patiently, ''Permit me. It isn't a matter of a thousand or two for a horse. Precisely and morally, you owe these people half of your wealth. If they are willing —''

''Bah! I owe them nothing! You know damn well I've paid them.''

Wolfe's eyes went nearly shut. ''What's that? You've paid them.''

''Of course I have, and you know it. And I've got their receipt, and I've got the paper I signed.'' Clivers abruptly sat down again. ''Look here. Your man is here, and I'm alone, so why not talk straight? I don't resent your being a crook, I've dealt with crooks before, and more pretentious ones than you. But cut out the pretense and get down to business. You have a good lever for blackmail, I admit it. But you might as well give up the idea of a big haul, because I won't submit to it. I'll pay three thousand pounds for a receipt from the Lindquists for that horse."

Wolfe's forefinger was tapping gently on the arm of his chair, which meant he was dodging meteors and comets. His eyes were mere slits. After a moment he said, "This is bad. It raises questions of credibility." He wiggled the finger. "Really bad, sir. How am I to know whether you really have paid? And if you have, how are you to know whether I was really ignorant of the fact and acting in good faith? Have you any suggestions?" He pushed the button. "I need some beer. Will you join me?"

"Yes. It's pretty good. Do you mean to say you didn't know I had paid?"

"I do. I do indeed. Though the possibility should certainly have occurred to me. I was too intent on the path under my feet." He stopped to open bottles, pushed one across to Clivers, and filled his glass. "You say you paid them. What *them?* When? How much? What with? They signed a receipt? Tell me about it."

Clivers, taking his time, emptied his glass and set it down. He licked his lips, screwed up his mouth, and looked at Wolfe, considering. Finally he shook his head. "I don't know about you. You're clever. Do you mean that if I show evidence of having paid, and their receipt, you will abandon this preposterous claim for the horse on payment of a thousand pounds?"

"Satisfactory evidence?" Wolfe nodded. "I'll abandon it for nothing."

"Oh, I'll pay a thousand. I understand the Lindquists are hard up. The evidence will be satisfactory, and you can see it tomorrow morning."

"I'd rather see it today."

"You can't. I haven't got it. It will arrive this evening on the *Berengaria*. My dispatch bag will reach me tonight, but I shall be engaged. Come to my hotel any time after nine in the morning."

"I don't go out. I am busy from nine to

eleven. You can bring your evidence here any time after eleven.''

''The devil I can.'' Clivers stared at him, and suddenly laughed his three blasts again. Haw-haw-haw. He turned it off. ''You can come to my hotel. You don't look infirm.''

Wolfe said patiently, ''If you don't bring it here, or send it, I won't get to see it and I'll have to press the claim for the horse. And by the way, how does it happen to be coming on the *Berengaria?*''

''Because I sent for it. Monday of last week, eight days ago, a woman saw me. She got in to me through my nephew — it seems they had met socially. She represented herself as the daughter of Gil Fox and made demands. I wouldn't discuss it with her. I thought it was straight blackmail and I would freeze her out. She was too damned good-looking to be honest. But I thought it worth while to cable to London for these items from my private papers, in case of developments. They'll be here tonight.''

''And this payment — when was it made?''

"Nineteen-six or seven. I don't know. I haven't looked at those papers for twenty years."

"To whom was the payment made?"

"I have the receipt signed by all of them."

"So you said. And you have the paper which you had signed. The man called Rubber Coleman had that paper. Did he get the money?"

Clivers opened his mouth and shut it again. Then he said, "I've answered enough questions. You'll see the check in the morning, signed by me, endorsed by the payee, and cancelled paid." He looked at his empty glass. "I hadn't tried American lager before. It's pretty good."

Wolfe pressed the button. "Then why not anticipate it by a few hours? I'm not attempting a cross-examination, Lord Clivers. I merely want information. Was it Coleman?"

"Yes."

"How much did he get?"

"Two hundred and some odd thousand pounds. A million dollars. He came to me

279

— July I think it was — about a year after I succeeded to the title. It must have been nineteen-six. He made exorbitant demands. Much of my property was entail. He was unreasonable. We finally agreed on a million dollars. Of course I needed time to get that much cash together. He returned to the States and came back in a couple of months with a receipt signed by all of them. Besides, he was deputized in the original paper, which he surrendered. My solicitor wanted me to send over here and have the signatures verified, but Coleman said he had had difficulty in persuading them to agree to the amount and I was afraid to reopen the question. I paid him."

"Where is Coleman now?"

"I don't know. I've never seen him since, nor heard of him. I wasn't interested; it was a closed chapter. I'm not greatly interested now. If he swindled them and kept the money, they shouldn't have trusted him with their signatures." Clivers hesitated, then resumed, "It's a fact that when the Fox woman saw me a week ago I took it for blackmail, but when Harlan Scovil called to see me yesterday afternoon I had my doubts. Scovil was a square man, he was born square, and I didn't think even forty years could turn him into a blackmailer. When I learned from the police last evening that he had been killed, there was no longer any doubt about a stink in the wind, but I couldn't tell them what I didn't know, and what I did know was my own business."

"So Harlan Scovil saw you yesterday?" Wolfe rubbed his nose. "That's int —"

"He didn't see me. I was out. When I returned in the late afternoon I was told he had been there." Clivers drank his beer. "Then this morning your letter came and it looked like blackmail again. With a murder involved in it also, it appeared that publicity was inevitable if I consulted the official police. The only thing left was to deal with you. All you wanted was money, and I have a little of it left in spite of taxes and revolutions. I don't for a minute believe that you're prepared to drop it merely because I show evidence that I've paid. You want money. You present a front that shows you're not a damned piker." He pointed. "Look at that globe, the finest I ever saw, couldn't have cost less than a hundred pounds. Twice as big as the one in my library. I'll pay three thousand for Lindquist's receipt for that horse."

"Indeed." Wolfe sighed. "Back to three thousand again. I'm sorry, sir, that you persist in taking me for a horse trader. And I do want money. That globe was made by Gouchard and there aren't many like it." He suddenly straightened up. "By the way, was it Mr. Walsh who told you that the Lindquists are hard up?"

Clivers stared. "How the devil do you know that?" He looked around. "Is Walsh here?"

"No, he isn't here. I didn't know it, I asked. I was aware that Mr. Walsh had called at the Hotel Portland this morning, so you had a talk with him. You haven't been entirely frank, Lord Clivers. You knew when you came here that Mr. Walsh never got any of that money, possibly that he never signed the receipt."

"I knew he said he hadn't."

"Don't you believe him?"

"I don't believe anybody. I know damn well I'm a liar. I'm a diplomat." He did his three blasts again, haw-haw-haw. "Look here. You can forget about Walsh, I'll deal with him myself. I have to keep this thing clear, at least as long as I'm in this country. I'll deal with Walsh. Scovil is dead, God rest his soul. Let the police do what they can with that. As for the Lindquists, I'll pay them two thousand for the horse, and you would get a share of that. The Fox woman can look after herself; anyone as young and handsome as she is doesn't need any of my money. As far as I'm concerned, that clears it up. If you can find Coleman and put a twist on him, go ahead, but that would take doing. He was hard and tricky, and it's a safe bet he still is. You may see the documents tomorrow morning, but I won't bring them here and I won't send them. If you can't come, send your man to look at them. I'll see him, and we can arrange for the payment to the Lindquists and their receipt. Actually, a thousand pounds should be enough for a horse. Eh?"

Wolfe shook his head. He was leaning

back again, with his fingers twined on his belly, and if you didn't know him you might have thought he was asleep. Clivers sat and frowned at him. I turned a new page of my notebook and wondered if we would have to garnishee Clara Fox's wages to collect our fee. Finally Wolfe's eyelids raised enough to permit the conjecture that he was conscious.

"It would have saved a lot of trouble," he murmured, "if they had hanged you in 1895. Isn't that so? As it stands, Lord Clivers, I wish to assure you again of my complete good faith in this matter, and I suggest that we postpone commitments until your evidence of payment has been examined. Tomorrow, then." He looked at me. "Confound you, Archie. I have you to thank for this acarpous entanglement."

It was a new one, but I got the idea. He meant that he had drawn his sword in defense of Clara Fox because I had told him that she was the ideal of my dreams. I suppose it was me that sat and recited Hungarian poetry to her.

14

When Wolfe came down to the office from the plant rooms at six o'clock, Saul Panzer and Orrie Cather were there waiting for him. Fred Durkin, who had spent most of the afternoon in the kitchen with the cookie jar, had been sent home at five, after I had warned him to cross the street if he saw a cop.

Nothing much had happened, except that Anthony D. Perry had telephoned a little after Fred had left, to say that he would like to call at the office and see Wolfe at seven o'clock. Since I would be leaving about that time to sneak up on Mike Walsh, I asked him if he couldn't make it at six, but he said other engagements prevented. I tried a couple of leading questions on him, but he got brusque and said his business was with

Nero Wolfe. I knew Saul would be around, or Johnny Keems, so I said okay for seven.

There had been no word from Johnny. The outstanding event of the afternoon had been the arrival of another enormous box of roses from the Horrocks person, and he had had the brass to have the delivery label addressed to me, with a card on the inside scribbled "Thanks Goodwin for forwarding," so now in addition to acting as hallboy and as a secondhand ladies' outfitter, apparently I was also expected to be a common carrier.

I had lost sixty cents. At a quarter to four, a few minutes after Clivers had gone, Wolfe had suggested that since I hadn't been out much a little exercise wouldn't hurt me any. He had made no comments on the news from Clivers, and I thought he might if I went along with him, but I told him I couldn't see it at two bits. He said, all right, a dime. So I mounted the stairs while he took the elevator and we met in his room. He took his coat and vest off, exhibiting about eighteen square feet of canary yellow shirt, and chose the darts with yellow feathers, which were his favorites. The first hand he got an ace and two bull's eyes, making three aces. By four o'clock, time for him to go to the plant rooms, it had cost me sixty cents and I had got nothing out of it because he had been too concentrated on the game to talk.

I went on up to the south room and was in there nearly an hour. There were three reasons for it: first, Wolfe had instructed me to tell Clara Fox about the visits from Muir and Clivers; second, she was restless and needed a little discipline; and third, I had nothing else to do anyhow. She had her clothes on again. She said Fritz had given her an iron to press with, but her dress didn't look as if she had used it much. I told her I supposed an adventuress wouldn't be so hot at ironing. When I told her about Muir she just made a face and didn't seem disposed to furnish any remarks, but she was articulate about Clivers. She thought he was lying. She said that she understood he was considered one of the ablest of British diplomats, and it was to be expected he would use his talents for private business as well as public. I said that I hadn't observed anything particularly able about him except that he could empty a glass of beer as fast as Nero Wolfe; that while he might not be quite as big a sap as his nephew Francis Horrocks he seemed fairly primitive to me, even for a guy who had spent most of his life on a little island.

She said it was just a difference in superficial mannerisms, that she too had thought Horrocks a sap at first, that I would change my mind when I knew him better, and that after all traditions weren't necessarily silly just because they weren't American. I said I wasn't talking about traditions, I was talking about saps, and as far as I was concerned saps were out, regardless of race, nationality or religion. It went on from there until she said she guessed she would go up and take advantage of Mr. Wolfe's invitation to look at the orchids, and I went down to send Fred home.

When Wolfe came down I was at my desk working on some sandwiches and milk, for I didn't know when I might get back from my trip uptown. I told him about the phone call from Perry. He went into the front room to get reports from Saul and Orrie, which made me sore as usual, but when he came back and settled into his chair and rang for beer I made no effort to stimulate him into any choice remarks about straining my powers of dissimulation, because he didn't give me a chance. Having sent Orrie home and Saul to the kitchen, he was ready for me, and he disclosed the nature of my mission with Mike Walsh. It wasn't precisely what I had expected, but I pretended it was by keeping nonchalant and casual. He drank beer and wiped his lips and told me:

"I'm sorry, Archie, if this bores you."

I said, "Oh, I expect it. Just a matter of routine."

He winked at me, and I turned and picked up my milk to keep from grinning back at him, and the telephone rang.

It was Inspector Cramer. He asked for Wolfe and I passed the signal, and of course kept my own line. Cramer said:

"What about this Clara Fox? Are you

going to bring her down here, or tell me where to send for her?''

Wolfe murmured into the transmitter, ''What is this, Mr. Cramer? A new tactic? I don't get it.''

''Now listen, Wolfe!'' Cramer sounded hurt and angry. ''First you tell me you've got her hid because we tried to snatch her on a phoney larceny charge. Now that that's out of the way, do you think you're going to pull —''

''What?'' Wolfe stopped him. ''The larceny charge out of the way?''

''Certainly. Don't pretend you didn't know it, since of course you did it, though I don't know how. You can put over the damnedest tricks.''

''No doubt. But please tell me how you learned this.''

''Frisbie over at the District Attorney's office. It seems that a fellow named Muir, a vice-president up at that Seaboard thing where she worked, is a friend of Frisbie's. He's the one that swore out the warrant. Now he's backed up, and it's all off, and I want to see this Miss Fox and hear her tell me that she never heard of Harlan

Scovil, like all the Mike Walshes we got.'' Cramer became sarcastic. "Of course this is all news to you.''

"It is indeed.'' Wolfe sent a glance at me, with a lifted brow. "Quite pleasant news. Let's see. I suspect it would be too difficult to persuade you that I know nothing of Miss Fox's whereabouts, so I shan't try. It is now six-thirty, and I shall have to make some inquiries. Where can I telephone you at eight?''

"Oh, for God's sake.'' Cramer sounded disgusted. "I wish I'd let the Commissioner pull you in, as he wanted to. I don't need to tell you why I hate to work against you, but have a heart. Send her down here, I won't bite her. I was going to a show tonight.''

"I'm sorry, Mr. Cramer.'' Wolfe affected his sweet tone, which always made me want to kick him. "I must first verify your information about the larceny charge, and then I must get in touch with Miss Fox. You'll be there until eight o'clock.''

Cramer grunted something profane, and we hung up.

"So." I tossed down my notebook. "Mr. Muir is yellow after all, and Mr. Perry is probably coming to find out how you knew he would be. Shake-up in the Seaboard Products Corporation. But where the devil is Johnny — ah, see that? All I have to do is pronounce his name and he rings the doorbell."

I went to the entrance and let him in. One look at his satisfied handsomeness was enough to show that he had been marvelous all over again. As a matter of fact, Johnny Keems unquestionably had an idea at the back of his head — and still has — that it would be a very fine thing for the detective business if he got my job. Which doesn't bother me a bit, because I know Wolfe would never be able to stand him. He puts slick stuff on his hair and he wears spats, and he would never get the knack of keeping Wolfe on the job by bawling him out properly. I know what I get paid high wages for, though I've never been able to decide whether Wolfe knows that I know.

I took Johnny to the office and he sat down and began pulling papers out of his pocket. He shuffled through them and announced:

"I thought it would be better to make diagrams. Of course I could have furnished Archie with verbal descriptions, but along with my shorthand I've learned —"

Wolfe put in, "Is Mr. Walsh there now?"

Johnny nodded. "He came a few minutes before six. I was watching from the back of a restaurant that fronts on 56th Street, because I knew he'd have a shadow and I didn't want to run a risk of being seen, a lot of those city detectives know me. By the way, there's only the one entrance to the boarding, on 55th." He handed the papers across to Wolfe. "I dug up nine other ways to get in. Some of them you couldn't use, but with two of them, a restaurant and a pet shop that's open until nine, it's a cinch."

Instead of taking the papers, Wolfe nodded at me. "Give them to Archie. Is there anyone in there besides Mr. Walsh?"

"I don't think so. It's mostly steel men on the job now, and they quit at five. Of course it was dark when I left, and it isn't lit up much. There's a wooden shed at one side with a couple of tables and a phone and so on, and a man was standing there talking to Walsh, a foreman, but he looked as if he was ready to leave. The reason I was a little late, after I got out of there I went around to 55th to see if there was a shadow on the job, and there was. I spotted him easy. He was standing there across the street, talking to a taxi-driver.''

"All right. Satisfactory. Go over the diagrams with Archie.''

Johnny explained to me how good the diagrams were, and I had to agree with him. They were swell. Five of them I discarded, because four of them were shops that wouldn't be open and the other was the Orient Club, which wouldn't be easy to get into. Of the remaining four, one was the pet shop, one a movie theater with a fire alley, and two restaurants. After Johnny's detailed description of the relative advantages and disadvantages, I picked one of the restaurants for the first stab. It seemed like a lot of complicated organization work for getting ready to stop in and ask a guy a question, but considering what the question led to in Wolfe's mental arrangements it seemed likely that it might be worth the trouble. By the time we were through with Johnny's battle maps it lacked only a few minutes till seven, and I followed my custom of chucking things in the drawers, plugging the phone for all the house connections, and taking my automatic and giving it a look and sticking it in my pocket. I got up and pushed my chair in.

I asked Johnny, "Can you hang around for a couple of hours' overtime?"

"I can if I eat."

"Okay. You'll find Saul in the kitchen. There's a caller expected at seven and he'll tend to the door. Stick around. Mr. Wolfe may want you to exercise your shorthand."

Johnny strode out. I think he practiced striding. I started to follow, but turned to ask Wolfe, "Are you going to grab time by the forelock? Will there be a party when I get back?"

"I couldn't say." Wolfe's hand was

resting on the desk; he was waiting for the door to close behind me, to ring for beer. "We'll await the confirmation."

"Shall I phone?"

"No. Bring it."

"Okay." I turned.

The telephone rang. From force of habit I wheeled again and stepped to my desk for it, though I saw that Wolfe had reached for his receiver. So we both heard it, a voice that sounded far away but thin and tense with excitement:

"Nero Wolfe! Nero —"

I snapped, "Yes. Talking."

"I've got him! Come up here . . . 55th Street . . . Mike Walsh this is . . . I've got him covered . . . come up —"

It was cut off by the sound of a shot in the receiver — a sound of an explosion so loud in my ear that it might have been a young cannon. Then there was nothing. I said "Hello, Walsh, Walsh!" a few times, but there was no answer.

I hung up and turned to Wolfe. "Well, by Godfrey. Did you hear anything?"

He nodded. "I did. And I don't understand it."

"Indeed. That's a record. What's the program, hop up there?"

Wolfe's eyes were shut, and his lips were moving out and in. He stayed that way a minute. I stood and watched him. Finally he said, "If Walsh shot someone, who was it? But if someone shot him, why now? Why not yesterday or a week ago? In any case, you might as well go and learn what happened. It may have been merely a steel girder crashing off its perch; there was enough noise."

"No. That was a gun."

"Very well. Find out. If you — ah! The doorbell. Indeed. You might attend to that first. Mr. Perry is punctual."

As I entered the hall Saul Panzer came out of the kitchen, and I sent him back. I turned on the stoop light and looked through the panel because it was getting to be a habit, and saw it was Perry. I opened the door and he stepped inside and put his hat and gloves on the stand.

I followed him into the office.

Wolfe said, "Good evening sir. —I have reflected, Archie, that the less one meddles the less one becomes involved.

You might have Saul phone the hospital that there has been an accident. —Oh no, Mr. Perry, nothing serious, thank you."

I went to the kitchen and told Saul Panzer: "Go to Allen's on 34th Street and phone headquarters that you think you heard a shot inside the building construction on 55th near Madison and they'd better investigate at once. If they want to know who you are, tell them King George. Make it snappy."

That was a nickel wasted, but I didn't know it then.

15

Perry glanced at me as I got into my chair and opened my notebook. He was saying, "I don't remember that anything ever irritated me more. I suppose I'm getting old. You mustn't think I bear any ill-will; if you preferred to represent Miss Fox, that was your right. But you must admit I played your hand for you; so far as I know there wasn't the faintest shred of evidence with which you could have enforced your threat." He smiled. "You think, of course, that my personal — er — respect for Miss Fox influenced my attitude and caused me to bring pressure on Muir. I confess that had a great deal to do with it. She is a charming young landy and also an extremely competent employee."

Wolfe nodded. "And my client.

Naturally, I was pleased to learn that the charge had been dropped."

"You say you heard it from the police? I hoped I was bringing the good news myself."

"I got it from Inspector Cramer." Wolfe had got his beer. He poured some, and resumed, "Mr. Cramer told me that he had been advised of it by a Mr. Frisbie, an Assistant District Attorney. It appears that Mr. Frisbie is a friend of Mr. Muir."

"Yes. I am acquainted with Frisbie. I know Skinner, the District Attorney, quite well." Perry coughed, watched Wolfe empty his glass, and resumed, "So I'm not the bearer of glad tidings. But," he smiled, "that wasn't the chief purpose of my call."

"Well, sir?"

"Well . . . I think you owe me something. Look at it this way. By threatening me with a procedure which would have meant most distasteful publicity for my corporation, you forced me to exert my authority and compel Muir to drop his charge. Muir isn't an employee; he is the highest officer of the

300

corporation after myself and he owns a fair proportion of the stock. It wasn't easy." Perry leaned forward and got crisper. "I surrendered to you. Now I have a right to know what I surrendered to. The only possible interpretation of your threat was that Miss Fox had been framed, and you wouldn't have dared to make such a threat unless you had some sort of evidence for it." He sat back and finished softly, "I want to know what that evidence is."

"But, Mr. Perry." Wolfe wiggled a finger. "Miss Fox is my client. You're not."

"Ah." Perry smiled. "You want to be paid for it? I'll pay a reasonable amount."

"Whatever information I have gathered in the interest of Miss Fox is not for sale to others."

"Rubbish. It has served her well. She has no further use for it." He leaned forward again. "Look here, Wolfe. I don't need to try to explain Muir to you, you've talked with him. If he has got so bad that he tries to frame a girl out of senile chagrin and vindictiveness, don't you think I ought to know it? He is our senior vice-president. Wouldn't our stockholders think so?"

"I didn't know stockholders think." Wolfe sighed. "But to answer your first question: yes, sir, I do think you ought to know it. But you won't learn it from me. Let us not go on pawing the air, Mr. Perry. This is definite: I did have evidence to support my threat, but under no circumstances will you get from me any proof that you could use against Mr. Muir. So we won't discuss that. If there is any other topic . . ."

Perry insisted. He got frank. His opinion was that Muir was such an old goat that his active services were no longer of any value to the corporation. He wanted to deal fairly with Muir, but after all his first duty was to the organization and its stockholders. And so on. He had suspected from the first that there was something odd about the disappearance of that $30,000, and he reasserted his right to know what Wolfe had found out about it. Wolfe let him ramble on quite a while, but finally he sighed and sat up and got positive. Nothing doing.

Perry seemed determined to keep his temper. He sat and bit his lower lip and looked at me and back at Wolfe again.

Wolfe asked, "Was there anything else, sir?"

Perry hesitated. Then he nodded. "There was, yes. But I don't suppose . . . however . . . I want to see Miss Fox."

"Indeed." Wolfe's shoulders went up an inch and down again. "The demand for that young woman seems to be universal. Did you know the police are still looking for her? They want to ask her about a murder."

Perry's chin jerked up. "Murder? What murder?"

"Just a murder. A man on the street with five bullets in him. I would have supposed Frisbie had told you of it."

"No. Muir said Frisbie said something . . . I forget what . . . but this sounds serious. How can she possibly be connected with it? Who was killed?"

"A man named Harlan Scovil. Murder is often serious. But I think you needn't worry about Miss Fox; she really had nothing to do with it. You see, she is still my client. At present she is rather inaccessible, so if you could just tell me what you want to see her about . . ."

I saw a spot of color on Perry's temple, and it occurred to me that he was the fourth man I had that day seen badly affected in the emotions by either the presence or the name of Clara Fox. She wasn't a woman, she was an epidemic. But obviously Perry wasn't going to repeat Muir's performance. I watched the spot of color as it faded. At length he said to Wolfe quietly:

"She is in this house. Isn't she?"

"The police searched this house today and didn't find her."

"But you know where she is?"

"Certainly." Wolfe frowned at him. "If you have a message for her, Mr. Goodwin will take it."

"Can you tell me when and where it will be possible to see her?"

"No. I'm sorry. Not at present. Tomorrow, perhaps . . ."

Perry arose from his chair. He stood

and looked down at Wolfe, and all of a sudden smiled. "All right," he said. "I can't say that my call here has been very profitable, but I'm not complaining. Every man has a right to his own methods if he can get away with them. As you suggest, I'll wait till tomorrow; you may feel differently about it." He put out his hand.

Wolfe glanced at the outstretched hand, then opened his eyes to look directly at Perry's face. He shook his head. "No, sir. You are perfectly aware that in view of this . . . event, I am no friend of yours."

Perry's temple showed color again. But he didn't say anything. He turned and steered for the door. I lifted myself and followed him. He already had his hat and gloves by the time I got to the hall stand, and when I opened the door for him I saw that he had a car outside, one of the new Wethersill convertibles. I watched him climb in, and waited until he had glided off before I re-entered and slid the bolt to.

I stopped in the kitchen long enough to learn from Saul that he had phoned the message to headquarters but hadn't been able to convince them that he was King George and so had rung off.

In the office, Wolfe sat with his eyes closed and his lips moving. After sitting down and glancing over my notebook and putting it in the drawer, I observed aloud:

"He's wise."

No reply, no acknowledgment. I added, "Which is more than you are." That met with the same lack of encouragement. I waited a courteous interval and resumed, "The poor old fellow would give anything in the world to forestall unpleasant publicity for the Seaboard Products Corporation. Just think what he has sacrificed! He has spent the best part of his life building up that business, and I'll bet his share of the profits is no more than a measly half a million a year. But what I want to know —"

"Shut up, Archie." Wolfe's eyes opened. "I can do without that now." He grimaced at his empty glass. "I am atrociously uncomfortable. It is sufficiently annoying to deal with inadequate information, which is what one usually has, but to sit thus while surmises, the mere ghosts of facts, tumble idiotically in my brain, is next to insupportable. It would have been better, perhaps, if you had gone to 55th Street. With prudence. At any rate, we can try for Mr. Cramer. I told him I would telephone him by eight, and it lacks only ten minutes of that. I particularly resent this sort of disturbance at this time of day. I presume you know we are having guinea chicken *Braziliera*. See about Mr. Cramer."

That proved to be a job. Cramer's extension seemed to be permanently busy. After five or six tries I finally got it, and was told by someone that Cramer wasn't there. He had left shortly after seven o'clock, and it wasn't known where he was, and he had left no word about any expected message from Nero Wolfe. Wolfe received the information standing up, for Fritz had appeared to announce dinner. I reported Cramer's absence and added, "Why don't I go uptown now and see if something fell and broke? Or send Saul."

Wolfe shook his head. "No. The police are there, and if there is anything to hear we shall hear it later by reaching Mr. Cramer, without exposing ourselves." He moved to the door. "There is no necessity for Johnny to sit in the kitchen at a dollar and a half an hour. Send him home. Saul may remain. Bring Miss Fox."

I performed the errands.

At the dinner table, of course, business was out. Nothing was said to Clara Fox about the call for help from Mike Walsh or Perry's visit. In spite of the fact that she had a rose pinned on her, she was distinctly down in the mouth and wasn't making any effort in the way of peddling charm, but even so, appraising her coolly, I could see that she might be a real problem for any man who was at all impressionable. She had been in the plant rooms with Wolfe for an hour before six o'clock, and during dinner he went on with a conversation which they had apparently started then, about folk dances and that sort of junk. He even hummed a couple of tunes for her, after the guinea chicken had been disposed of, which caused me to take a firm hold on myself so as not to laugh the salad out of my mouth. At that, it was better than when he tried to whistle, for he did produce some kind of a noise.

With the coffee he told her that the larceny charge had been dropped. She opened her eyes and her mouth both.

"No, really? Then I can go!" She stopped herself, and put out a hand to touch his sleeve, and color came to her cheeks. "Oh, I don't mean . . . that was terrible, wasn't it? But you know how I feel, hiding . . ."

"Perfectly." Wolfe nodded. "But I'm afraid you must ask us to tolerate you a little longer. You can't go yet."

"Why not?"

"Because, first, you might get killed. Indeed, it is quite possible, though I confess not very likely. Second, there is a development that must still be awaited. On that you must trust me. I know, since Archie told you of Lord Clivers's statement that he has paid —"

I didn't hear the finish, because the doorbell rang and I wasn't inclined to delay about answering it. I was already on pins and I would soon have been on needles if something hadn't happened to open things up. I loped down the hall.

It was only Johnny Keems whom I had sent home over an hour before. Wondering what for, I let him in. He said, "Have you seen it?"

I said, "No, I'm blind. Seen what?"

He pulled a newspaper from his pocket and stuck it at me. "I was going to a movie on Broadway and they were yelling this extra, and I was nearby so I thought it would be better to run over with it than to phone —"

I had looked at the headlines. I said, "Go to the office. No, go to the kitchen. You're on the job, my lad. Satisfactory."

I went to the dining-room and moved Wolfe's coffee cup to one side and spread the paper in front of him. "Here," I said, "here's that development you're awaiting." I stood and read it with him while Clara Fox sat and looked at us.

MARQUIS ARRESTED!
BRITAIN'S ENVOY
FOUND STANDING OVER MURDERED MAN!

Gazette Reporter
Witnesses Unprecedented Drama!

At 7:05 this evening the Marquis of Clivers, special envoy of Great Britain to this country, was found by a city detective, within the cluttered enclosure of a building under construction on 55th Street, Manhattan, standing beside the body of a dead man who had just been shot through the back of the head. The dead man was Michael Walsh, night watchman. The detective was Purley Stebbins of the Homicide Squad.

At seven o'clock a *Gazette* reporter, walking down Madison Avenue, seeing a crowd collected at 55th Street, stopped to investigate. Finding that it was only two cars with shattered windshields and other minor damages from a collision, he strolled on, turning into 55th. Not far from the corner he saw a man stepping off the curb to cross the street. He recognized the man as Purley

Stebbins, a city detective, and was struck by something purposeful in his gait. He stopped, and saw Stebbins push open the door of a board fence where a building is being constructed.

The reporter crossed the street likewise, through curiosity, and entered the enclosure after the detective. He ventured further, and saw Stebbins grasping by the arm a man elegantly attired in evening dress, while the man tried to pull away. Then the reporter saw something else: the body of a man on the ground.

Advancing close enough to see the face of the man in evening dress and recognizing him at once, the reporter was quick-witted enough to call sharply. "Lord Clivers!"

The man replied, "Who the devil are you?"

The detective, who was feeling the man for a weapon, instructed the reporter to telephone headquarters and get Inspector Cramer. The body was lying in such a position that the reporter had to step over it to get at the telephone on the wall of a wooden shed. Meanwhile Stebbins had blown his whistle and a few moments later a patrolman in uniform entered. Stebbins spoke to him, and the patrolman leaned over the body and exclaimed, "It's the night watchman, old Walsh!"

Having phoned police headquarters, the reporter approached Lord Clivers and asked him for a statement. He was brushed aside by Stebbins, who commanded him to leave. The reporter persisting, Stebbins instructed the patrolman to put him out, and the reporter was forcibly ejected.

The superintendent of the construction, reached on the telephone, said that the name of the night watchman was Michael Walsh. He knew of no possible connection between Walsh and a member of the British nobility.

No information could be obtained from the suite of Lord Clivers at the Hotel Portland.

At 7:30 Inspector Cramer and various members of the police force had arrived on the scene at 55th Street, but no one

was permitted to enter the enclosure
and no information was forthcoming.

There was a picture of Clivers, taken
the preceding week on the steps of the
White House.

I was raving. If only I had gone up
there! I glared at Wolfe: "Be prudent!
Don't expose ourselves! I could have been
there in ten minutes after that phone call!
Great God and Jehosaphat!"

I felt a yank at my sleeve and saw it was
Clara Fox. "What is it? What —"

I took it out on her. I told her savagely,
"Oh, nothing much. Just another of your
playmates bumped off. You haven't got
much of a team left. Mike Walsh shot and
killed dead, Clivers standing there —"

Wolfe had leaned back and closed his
eyes, with his lips working. I reached for
the paper and pushed it at her. "Sure,
go ahead, hope you enjoy it." As she
leaned over the paper I heard her breath
go in. I said, "Of all the goddam
wonderful management —"

Wolfe cut in sharply, "Archie!"

I muttered, "Go to hell everybody,"

and sat down and bobbed my head from side to side in severe pain. The cockeyed thing had busted wide open and instead of going where I belonged I had sat and eaten guinea chicken Brazilisomething and listened to Wolfe hum folk tunes. Not only that, it had busted at the wrong place and Nero Wolfe had made a fool of himself. If I had gone I would have been there before Cramer or anyone else. . . .

Wolfe opened his eyes and said quietly, "Take Miss Fox upstairs and come to the office." He lifted himself from his chair.

So did Clara Fox. She arose with her face whiter than before and looked from one to the other of us. She announced, "I'm not going upstairs. I . . . I can't just stay here. I'm going . . . I'm going . . ."

"Yes." Wolfe lifted his brows at her. "Where?"

She burst out, "How do I know where? Don't you see I . . . I've got to do something?" She suddenly flopped back into her chair and clasped her hands and began to tremble. "Poor old Mike Walsh . . . why in the name of God . . . why did I ever . . ."

Wolfe stepped to her and put his hand on her shoulder. "Look here," he snapped. "Do you wonder I'd rather have ten thousand orchids than a woman in my house?"

She looked up at him, and shivered. "And it was you that let Mike Walsh go, when you knew —"

"I knew very little. Now I know even less. —Archie, bring Saul."

"Johnny is here —"

"No. Saul."

I went to the kitchen and got him. Wolfe asked him: "How long will it take to get Hilda Lindquist here?"

Saul considered half an instant. "Fifty minutes if I phone. An hour and a half if I go after her."

"Good. Telephone. You had better tell her on the phone that Mike Walsh has been killed, since if she sees a *Gazette* on the way she might succumb also. Is there someone to bring her?"

"Yes, sir."

"Use the office phone. Tell her not to delay unnecessarily, but there is no great urgency. Wipe the spot of grease off of the left side of your nose."

"Yes, sir," Saul went, pulling his handkerchief from his pocket.

Clara Fox said, in a much better tone, "I haven't succumbed." She brushed back her hair, but her hand was none too steady. "I didn't mean, when I said you let Mike Walsh go —"

"Of course not." Wolfe didn't relent any. "You weren't in a condition to mean anything. You still are not. Archie and I have one or two things to do. You can't leave this house, certainly not now. Will you go upstairs and wait till Miss Lindquist gets here? And don't be conceited enough to imagine yourself responsible for the death of Michael Walsh. Your meddlings have not entitled you to usurp the fatal dignity of Atropos; don't flatter yourself. Will you go upstairs and command patience?"

"Yes." She stood up. "But I want . . . if someone should telephone for me I want to talk."

Wolfe nodded. "You shall. Though I fancy Mr. Horrocks will be too occupied with this involvement of his chief for social impulses.''

But it was Wolfe's off day; he was wrong again. A phone call from Horrocks, for Clara Fox, came within fifteen minutes. In the interim Wolfe and I had gone to the office and learned from Saul that he had talked to Hilda Lindquist and she was coming, and Wolfe had settled himself in his chair, disposed of a bottle of beer, and repudiated my advances. Horrocks didn't mention the predicament of his noble uncle; he just asked for Clara Fox, and I sent Saul up to tell her to take it in Wolfe's room, since there was no phone in hers. I should have listened in as a matter of business, but I didn't, and Wolfe didn't tell me to.

Finally Wolfe sighed and sat up. "Try for Mr. Cramer."

I did so. No result. They talked as if, for all they knew, Cramer might be up in Canada shooting moose.

Wolfe sighed again. "Archie. Have we ever encountered a greater jumble of nonsense?"

"No, sir. If only I had gone —''

"Don't say that again, or I'll send you

upstairs with Miss Fox. Could that have ordered the chaos? The thing is completely ridiculous. It forces us to measures no less ridiculous. We shall have to investigate the movements of Mr. Muir since six o'clock this evening, to trust Mr. Cramer with at least a portion of our facts, to consider afresh the motivations and activities of Lord Clivers, to discover how a man can occupy two different spots of space at the same moment, and to make another long distance call to Nebraska. I believe there is no small firearm that will shoot fifteen hundred miles, but we seem to be confronted with a determination and ingenuity capable of almost anything, and before we are through with this we may need Mr. Lindquist badly. Get that farm — the name is Donvaag?"

I nodded and got busy. At that time of night, going on ten o'clock, the lines were mostly free, and I had a connection with Plainview, Nebraska, in less than ten minutes. It was a person to person call and a good clear connection; Ed Donvaag's husky voice, from his farmhouse out on the western prairie, was in my ear as plain as Francis Horrocks' had been from the Hotel Portland. Wolfe took his line.

"Mr. Donvaag? This is Nero Wolfe . . . That's it. You remember I talked to you this afternoon and you were good enough to go after Mr. Lindquist for a conversation with me. . . . Yes, sir. I have to ask another favor of you. Can you hear me well? Good. It will be necessary for you to go again to Mr. Lindquist tonight or the first thing tomorrow morning. Tell him there is reason to suspect that someone means him injury and may attempt it. . . . Yes. We don't know how. Tell him to be circumspect — to be careful. Does he eat candy? He might receive a box of poisoned candy in the mail. Even, possibly, a bomb. Anything. He might receive a telegram saying his daughter had died — with results expected from the shock to him. . . . No, indeed. His daughter is well and there is nothing to fear for her. . . . Well, this is a peculiar situation; doubtless you will hear all about it later. Tell him to be careful and to suspect anything at all unusual. . . . You can go at once? Good. You are a good neighbor, sir. Goodnight."

Wolfe rang off and pushed the button for beer. He sighed. "That desperate fool has a good deal to answer for. Another four dollars. —Three? Oh, the night rate. —Bring another, Fritz. —Archie, give Saul the necessary facts regarding Mr. Muir and send him out. We want to know where he was from six to eight this evening."

I went to the kitchen and did that. Johnny Keems was helping Fritz with the dishes and Saul was in my breakfast corner with the remainder of the dish of ripe olives. He didn't write anything down; he never had to. He pointed his long nose at me and gathered up the last of the olives into a handful, and departed. I let him out.

Back in the office, I asked Wolfe if he wanted me to try for Cramer again. He shook his head. He was leaning back with his eyes closed, and the faint movement of his lips in and out informed me that he was in conference with himself. I sat down and put my feet on my desk. In a few minutes I got up again and went to the cabinet and poured myself a shot of bourbon, smelled it, and poured it back into the bottle. It wasn't whiskey I wanted. I went to the kitchen and asked Johnny some more questions about the layout up at 55th Street, and drank a glass of milk.

It was ten o'clock when Hilda Lindquist arrived. There was a man with her, but when I told him Saul wasn't there he didn't come in. I told him Saul would fix it with him and he beat it. Hilda's square face and brown dress didn't look any the worse for wear during the twenty-four hours since she had gone off, but her eyes were solemn and determined. She said of course the thing was all off, since they had caught the Marquis of Clivers and he would be executed for murder, and her father would be disappointed because he was old and they would lose the farm, and would she be able to get her bag which she had left at the hotel, and she would like to start for home as soon as there was a train. I told her to drive in and park a while, there was still some fireworks left in the bag, but by the way she turned her eyes on me I saw that she might develop into a real problem, so I put her in the front room and asked her to wait a minute.

I ran up to the south room and said to Clara Fox: "Hilda Lindquist is downstairs and I'm going to send her up. She thinks the show is over and she has to go back home to her poor old dad with her sock empty, and by the look in her eye it will take more than British diplomacy to keep her off of the next train. Nero Wolfe is going to work this out. I don't know how and maybe he don't either this minute, but he'll do it. Nero Wolfe is probably even better than I think he is, and that's a mouthful. You wrote the music for this piece, and half your band has been killed, and it's up to you to keep the other half intact. Well?"

I had found her sitting in a chair with her lips compressed tight and her hands clenched. She looked at me. "All right. I will. Send her up here."

"She can sleep in here with you, or in the room in front on this floor. You know how to ring for Fritz."

"All right."

I went down and told Squareface that Clara Fox wanted to speak to her, and shooed her up, and heard them exchanging greetings in the upper hall.

There was nothing in the office but a gob of silence; Wolfe was still in conference. I would have tried some bulldozing if I had thought he was merely dreaming of stuffed quail or pickled pigs' feet, but his lips were moving a little so I knew he was working. I fooled around my desk, went over Johnny's diagrams again in connection with an idea that had occurred to me, checked over Horstmann's reports and entered them in the records, reread the *Gazette* scoop on the affair at 55th Street, and aggravated myself into such a condition of uselessness that finally, at eleven o'clock sharp, I exploded:

"If this keeps up another ten minutes I'll get *Weltschmerz!*"

Wolfe opened his eyes. "Where in the name of heaven did you get that?"

I threw up my hands. He shut his eyes again.

The doorbell rang. I knew it couldn't

be Johnny Keems with another extra, because he was in the kitchen with Fritz, since I hadn't been able to prod an instruction from Wolfe to send him home again. It was probably Saul Panzer with the dope on Muir. But it wasn't; I knew that when the bell started again as I entered the hall. It kept on ringing, so I leisurely pulled the curtain for a look through the panel, and when I saw there were four of them, another quartet, I switched on the stoop light to make a good survey. One of them, in evening dress, was leaning on the bell button. I recognized the whole bunch. I turned and beat it back to the office.

"Who the devil is ringing that bell?" Wolfe demanded. "Why don't you —"

I interrupted, grinning. "That's Police Commissioner Hombert. With him are Inspector Cramer, District Attorney Skinner, and my old friend Purley Stebbins of the Homicide Squad. Is it too late for company?"

"Indeed." Wolfe sat up and rubbed his nose. "Bring them in."

16

They entered as if they owned the place. I tipped Purley a wink as he passed me, but he was too impressed by his surroundings to reciprocate, and I didn't blame him, as I knew he might get either a swell promotion or the opposite out of this by the time it was over. From the threshold I saw a big black limousine down at the curb, and back of it two other police cars containing city fellers. Well, well, I thought to myself as I closed the door, this looks pretty damned ominous. Cramer had asked me if Wolfe was in the office and I had waved him on, and now I brought up the rear of the procession.

I moved chairs around. Cramer introduced Hombert and Skinner, but Skinner and Wolfe had already met. At

Cramer's request I took Purley Stebbins to the kitchen and told him to play checkers with Johnny Keems. When I got back Hombert was shooting off his mouth about defiance of the law, and I got at my desk and ostentatiously opened my notebook. Cramer was looking more worried than I had ever seen him. District Attorney Skinner, already sunk in his chair as if he had been there all evening, had the wearied cynical expression of a man who had some drinks three hours ago and none since.

Hombert was practically yelling. ". . . and you're responsible for it! If you had turned those three people over to us last night this wouldn't have happened! Cramer tells me they were here in this office! Walsh was here! This afternoon we had him at headquarters and your man wouldn't point him out! You are directly and legally responsible for his death!" The Police Commissioner brought his fist down on the arm of his chair and glared. Cramer was looking at him and shaking his head faintly.

"This sudden onslaught is

overwhelming," Wolfe murmured. "If I am legally responsible for Mr. Walsh's death, arrest me. But please don't shout at me —"

"All right! You've asked for it!" Hombert turned to the inspector. "Put him under arrest!"

Cramer said quietly, "Yes, sir. What charge?"

"Any charge! Material witness! We'll see whether he'll talk or not!"

Cramer stood up. Wolfe said, "Perhaps I should warn you, Mr. Hombert. If I am arrested, I shall do no talking whatever. And if I do no talking, you have no possible chance of solving the problem you are confronted with." He wiggled a finger. "I don't shout, but I never say anything I don't mean. Proceed, Mr. Cramer."

Cramer stood still. Hombert looked at him, then looked grimly at Wolfe. "You'll talk or you'll rot!"

"Then I shall certainly rot." Wolfe's finger moved again. "Let me make a suggestion, Mr. Hombert. Why don't you go home and go to sleep and leave this affair to be handled by Mr. Cramer, an experienced policeman, and Mr. Skinner, an experienced lawyer? You probably have abilities of some sort, but they are obviously inappropriate to the present emergency. To talk of arresting me is childish. I have broken no law and I am a sufficiently respectable citizen not to be taken into custody merely for questioning. Confound it, sir, you can't go around losing your temper like this, it's outrageous! You are entangled in a serious difficulty, I am the only man alive who can possibly extricate you from it, and you come here and begin yelling inane threats at me! Is that sort of conduct likely to appeal either to my reason or my sympathy?''

Hombert glared at him, opened his mouth, closed it again, and looked at Cramer. District Attorney Skinner snickered. Cramer said to Hombert, "Didn't I tell you he was a nut? Let me handle him.''

Wolfe nodded solemnly. "That's an idea, Mr. Cramer. You handle me.''

Hombert, saying nothing, sat back and

folded his arms and goggled. Cramer looked at Wolfe. "So you know about Walsh."

Wolfe nodded. "From the *Gazette*. That was unfortunate, the reporter happening on the scene."

"You're telling me," Cramer observed grimly. "Of course the marquis isn't arrested. He can't be. Diplomatic immunity. Washington is raising hell because it got in the paper, as if there was any way in God's world of keeping it out of that lousy sheet once that reporter got away from there." He waved a disgusted hand. "That's that. The fact is, the Commissioner's right. You're responsible. I told you yesterday how important this was. I told you it was your duty as a citizen to help us protect the Marquis of Clivers."

Wolfe lifted his brows. "Aren't you a little confused, Mr. Cramer? Or am I? I understood you wished to protect Lord Clivers from injury. Was it he who was injured this evening?"

"Certainly it was," Hombert broke in. "This Walsh was blackmailing him!"

Cramer said, "Let me. Huh?"

"Did Lord Clivers say that?" Wolfe asked.

"No." Cramer grunted. "He's not saying anything, except that he knew Walsh a long time ago and went there to see him this evening by appointment and found him lying there dead. But we didn't come here to answer questions for you, we came to find out what you know. We could have you pulled in, but decided it was quicker to come. It's time to spill it. What's it all about?"

"I suppose so." Wolfe sighed. "Frankly, I think you're wrong; I believe that while you may have information that will help me, I have none that will help you. But we'll get to that later. My connection with this affair arises from my engagement to press a civil claim on behalf of two young women. Also, to defend one of them from a trumped up charge of larceny brought against her by an official of the Seaboard Products Corporation. Since I have succeeded in having the larceny charge withdrawn —"

District Attorney Skinner woke up. He

croaked in his deep bass, "Don't talk so much. What has that got to do with it? Come to the point."

Wolfe said patiently, "Interruptions can only waste time, by forcing me to begin my sentences over again. Since I have succeeded in having the larceny charge withdrawn, and since they cannot possibly be suspected of complicity in the murder of Mr. Walsh, I am willing to produce my clients, with the understanding that if I send for them to come here they will be questioned here only and will not be taken from this house. I will not have —"

"The hell you won't!" Hombert was ready to boil again. "You can't dictate to us —"

But the authority of Wolfe's tone and the assurance of his manner had made enough impression so that his raised palm brought Hombert to a halt. "I'm not dictating," he snapped. "Confound it, let us get on or we shall be all night. I was about to say, I will not have the lives of my clients placed in possible jeopardy by releasing them from my own protection.

Why should I? I can send for them and you can question them all you please —"

"All right, all right," Cramer agreed impatiently. "We won't take them, that's understood. How long will it take you to get them here?"

"One minute perhaps, if they are not in bed. Archie? If you please."

I arose grinning at Cramer's stare, stepped over Skinner's feet, and went up and knocked at the door of the south room.

"Come in."

I entered. The two clients were sitting in chairs, looking as if they were too miserable to go to bed. I said, "Egad, you look cheerful. Come on, buck up! Wolfe wants you down in the office. There are some men down there that want to ask you some questions."

Clara Fox straightened up. "Ask us . . . now?" Hilda Lindquist tightened her lips and began to nod her head for I told you so.

"Certainly." I made it matter of fact. "They were bound to, sooner or later. Don't worry, I'll be right there, and tell them anything they want to know. There's three of them. The dressed-up one with the big mouth is Police Commissioner Hombert, the one with the thin nose and ratty eyes is District Attorney Skinner, and the big guy who looks at you frank and friendly but may or may not mean it is Inspector Cramer."

"My God." Clara Fox brushed back her hair and stood up.

"All right," I grinned. "Let's go."

I opened the door, and followed them out and down.

The three visitors turned their heads to look at us as we entered the office. Skinner, seeing Clara Fox, got up first, then Hombert also made it to his feet and began shoving chairs around. I moved some up, while Wolfe pronounced names. He had rung for beer while I was gone, and got it poured. I saw there was no handkerchief in his pocket and went and got him one out of the drawer.

Cramer said, "So you're Clara Fox. Where were you this morning?"

She glanced at Wolfe. He nodded. She said, "I was here."

"Here in this house? All morning?"

"Yes, last night and all day."

Cramer handed Wolfe a glassy stare. "What did you do to Rowcliff, grease him?"

"No, sir." Wolfe shook his head. "Mr. Rowcliff did his best, but Miss Fox was not easily discoverable. I beg you to attach no blame to your men. It is necessary for you to know that three of us are prepared to state on oath that Miss Fox has been here constantly, to make it at once obvious that she is in no way involved in Mr. Walsh's death."

"I'll be damned. What about the other one?"

"Miss Lindquist came here at ten o'clock this evening. But she has been secluded in another part of the city. You may as well confine yourself to events previous to half-past six yesterday. May I make a suggestion? Begin by asking Miss Fox to tell you the story which she recited to me at that hour yesterday, in the presence of Miss Lindquist and Mr. Walsh."

"Why . . . all right." Cramer looked

at Clara Fox. "Go ahead."

She told the story. At first she was nervous and jerky, and I noticed that when she was inclined to stumble she glanced across at Wolfe as he leaned back, massive and motionless, with his fingers twined on his belly and his eyes nearly shut. She glanced at him and went ahead. They didn't interrupt her much with questions. She read the letter from her father, and when she finished and Cramer held out his hand for it, she glanced at Wolfe. Wolfe nodded, and she passed it over. Then she went on, with more detail even than she had told us. She spoke of her first letters with Harlan Scovil and Hilda Lindquist and her first meeting with Mike Walsh.

She got to the Marquis of Clivers and Walsh's recognition of him as he emerged from his hotel fifteen days back. From then on they were after her, not Cramer much, but Skinner and Hombert, and especially Skinner. He began to get slick, and of course, what he was after was obvious. He asked her trick questions, such as where had her mother been keeping the letter from her father when she suddenly produced it on her deathbed. His way of being clever was to stay quiet and courteous and go back to one thing and then abruptly forward to another, and then after a little suddenly dart back again. Clara Fox was no longer nervous, and she didn't get mad. I remembered how the day before she had stood cool and sweet in front of Perry's desk. All at once Skinner began asking her about the larceny charge. She answered; but after a dozen questions on that Wolfe suddenly stirred, opened his eyes, and wiggled a finger at the District Attorney.

"Mr. Skinner. Permit me. You're wasting time. The larceny charge is indeed pertinent to the main issue, but there is very little chance that you'll ever discover why. The fact is that the line you have taken from the beginning is absurd."

"Thanks," Skinner said drily. "If, as you say, it is pertinent, why absurd?"

"Because," Wolfe retorted, "you're running around in circles. You have a fixed idea that you're an instrument of justice, being a prosecuting attorney, and that it is your duty to corner everyone you see. That idea is not only dangerous nonsense, in the present case it is directly contrary to your real interest. Why is this distinguished company," Wolfe extended a finger and bent a wrist, "present in my house? Because $30,000 was mislaid and two men were murdered? Not at all. Because Lord Clivers has become unpleasantly involved, the fact has been made public, and you are seriously embarrassed. You have wasted thirty minutes trying to trap Miss Fox into a slip indicating that she and Mr. Walsh and Mr. Scovil and Miss Lindquist hatched a blackmailing plot against Lord Clivers; you have even hinted that the letter written by her father to her mother seventeen years ago, of which Mr. Cramer now has her typewritten copy in his pocket, was invented by her. Is it possible that you don't realize what your real predicament is?"

"Thanks," Skinner repeated, more drily still. "I'll get to you —"

"No doubt. But let me — no, confound it, I'm talking! Let me orient you a little.

Here's your predicament. An eminent personage, an envoy of Great Britain, has been discovered alone with a murdered man and the fact has been made public. Even if you wanted to you can't keep him in custody because of his diplomatic immunity. Why not, then, to avoid a lot of official and international fuss, just forget it and let him go? Because you don't dare; if he really did kill Mr. Walsh you are going to have to ask his government to surrender him to you, and fight to get him if necessary, or the newspapers will howl you out of office. You are sitting on dynamite, and so is Mr. Hombert, and you know it. I can imagine with what distaste you contemplate being forced into an effort to convict the Marquis of Clivers of murder. I see the complications; and the devil of it is that at this moment you don't at all know whether he did it or not. His story that he went to see Mr. Walsh and found him already dead may quite possibly be true.

"So, since an attempt to put Lord Clivers on trial for murder, and convict him, would not only create an international stink but might be disastrous for you personally, what should be your first and immediate concern? It seems obvious. You should swiftly and rigorously explore the possibility that he is not guilty. Is there someone else who wanted Harlan Scovil and Michael Walsh to die, and if so, who, and where is he? I know of only six people living who might help you in pursuing that inquiry. One of them is the murderer, another is an old man on a farm in Nebraska, and the other four are in this room. And, questioning one of them, what do you do? You put on an exhibition of your cunning at cross-examination in an effort to infer that she has tried to blackmail Lord Clivers, though he has had various opportunities to make such an accusation and has not done so. Again, you aim the weapon of your cunning, not at your own ignorance, but directly at Miss Fox, when you pounce on the larceny charge, though that accusation has been dismissed by the man who made it.

"Bah!" Wolfe looked around at them. "Do you wonder, gentlemen, that I have not taken you into my confidence in this affair? Do you wonder that I have no intention of doing so even now?"

Cramer grunted, gazing at a cigar he had pulled out of his pocket five minutes before. Skinner, scratching his ear, screwed up his mouth and looked sidewise at Clara Fox. Hombert let out a "Ha!" and slapped the arm of his chair. "So that's your game! You're not going to talk, eh? By God, you will talk!"

"Oh, I'll talk." Wolfe sighed. "You may know everything you are entitled to know. You are already aware that Mr. Scovil was in this room yesterday afternoon and got killed shortly after leaving it. Mr. Goodwin talked with him and will repeat the conversation if you wish it. You may hear everything from Miss Fox and Miss Lindquist that I have heard; and from Miss Fox regarding Mr. Walsh. You may know of the claim which I have presented to Lord Clivers on behalf of Miss Lindquist and her father, which he has offered to settle. But there are certain things you may not know, at least not from me; for instance, the details of a long conversation which I had with Lord Clivers when he called here this afternoon. He can tell you —"

"What's that?" Skinner sat up, croaking. Hombert goggled. Cramer, who had finally got his cigar lit, jerked it up with his lip so that the ash fell to the rug. Skinner went on, "What are you trying to hand us? Clivers called on you today?"

Wolfe nodded. "He was here over an hour. Perhaps I shouldn't say today, since it is nearly one o'clock Wednesday morning. Yes, Lord Clivers called. We drank eight bottles of beer, and he greatly admired that terrestrial globe you see there."

Without taking his cigar from his mouth, Cramer rumbled, "I'll be damned." Hombert still goggled. Skinner stared, and at length observed, "I've never heard of your being a plain liar, Wolfe, but you're dishing it up."

"Dishing it up?" Wolfe looked at me. "Does that mean lying, Archie?"

"Naw," I grinned, "it's just rhetoric."

"Indeed." Wolfe reached to push the button, and leaned back. "So you see, gentlemen, I not only have superior knowledge in this affair, I have it from a superior source. Lord Clivers gave me much interesting information, which of course I cannot consider myself free to reveal." He turned his eyes on the Police Commissioner. "I understand, Mr. Hombert, that Mr. Devore, Mr. Cramer and you were all in communication with him, protecting him, following the death of Mr. Scovil. It's too bad he didn't see fit to take you into his confidence. Maybe he will do so now, if you approach him properly."

Hombert sputtered, "I don't believe this. We'll check up on this."

"Do so." Wolfe opened the bottle and filled his glass. "Will you have beer, gentlemen? No? Water? Whiskey? Miss Fox? Miss Lindquist? —You haven't asked Miss Lindquist anything. Must she sit here all night?"

Skinner said, "I could use a good stiff highball. Listen, Wolfe, are you telling this straight?"

"Of course I am. —Fritz, serve what is required. —Why would I be so foolish as to invent such a tale? Let me suggest that the ladies be permitted to retire.''

''Well . . .'' Skinner looked at Hombert. Hombert, tight-lipped, shrugged his shoulders. Skinner turned and asked abruptly:

''Your name is Hilda Lindquist?''

Her strong square face looked a little startled at the suddenness of it, then was lifted by her chin. ''Yes.''

''You heard everything Clara Fox said. Do you agree with it?''

She stared. ''What do you mean, agree with it?''

''I mean, as far as you know, is it true?''

''Certainly it's true.''

''Where do you live?''

''Plainview, Nebraska. Near there.''

''When did you get to New York?''

''Last Thursday. Thursday afternoon.''

''All right. That's all. But understand, you're not to leave the city —''

Wolfe put in, ''My clients will remain in this house until I have cleared up this matter.''

''See that they do.'' Skinner grabbed

his drink. "So you're going to clear it up. God bless you. If I had your nerve I'd own Manhattan Island." He drank.

The clients got up and went. I escorted them to the hall, and while I was out there the doorbell rang. It was Saul Panzer. I went to the kitchen with him and got his report, which didn't take long. Johnny Keems was there with his chair tipped back against the wall, half asleep, and Purley Stebbins was in a corner, reading a newspaper. I snared myself a glass of milk, took a couple of sips, and carried the rest to the office.

Hombert and Cramer had highballs and Fritz was arranging another one for Skinner. I said to Wolfe: "Saul's back. The subject left his office a few minutes before six and showed up at his apartment about a quarter after seven and dressed for dinner. Saul hasn't been able to trace him in between. Shall he keep after it tonight?"

"No. Send him home. Here at eight in the morning."

"Johnny too?"

"Yes. —No, wait." Wolfe turned "Mr.

Cramer. Perhaps I can simplify something for you. I know how thorough you are. Doubtless you have discovered that there are various ways of getting into that place on 55th Street, and I suppose you have had them all explored. You may even have learned that there was a man there this afternoon, investigating them."

Cramer was staring at him. "Now, somebody tell me, how did you know that? Yeah, we learned it, and we've got a good description, and there are twenty men looking for him . . ."

Wolfe nodded. "I thought I might save you some trouble. I should have mentioned it before. The man's out in the kitchen. He was up there for me."

Cramer went pop-eyed. "But good God! That was before Walsh was killed!" He put his drink down. "Now what kind of a —"

"We wanted to see Walsh, and knew you would have a man posted at the entrance. He was there to find a way. He left a few minutes after six and was here from six-thirty until eight o'clock. You may talk with him if you wish, but it will be a waste of time. My word for it."

Cramer looked at him, and then at me. He picked up his drink. "To hell with it."

Wolfe said, "Send Johnny home."

Cramer said, "And tell Stebbins to go out front and tell Rowcliff to cancel that alarm and call those men in."

I went to perform those errands, and after letting the trio out I left the door open a crack and told Purley to shut it when he came back in. The enemy was inside anyhow, so there was no point in maintaining the barricade.

Back in the office, Skinner and Hombert were bombarding Wolfe. It had got now to where it was funny. Clivers was the bird they had been busy protecting, and the one they were trying to get out of hanging a murder onto, and here they begging Wolfe to spill what Clivers had disclosed to him over eight bottles of beer! I sat down and grinned at Cramer, and darned if he didn't have decency enough to wink back at me. I thought that called for another highball, and went and got it for him.

Skinner, with an open palm outstretched,

was actually wheedling. "But, my God, can't we work together on it? I'll admit we went at it wrong, but how did we know Clivers was here this afternoon? He won't tell us a damn thing, and as far as I personally am concerned I'd like to kick his rump clear across the Atlantic Ocean. And I'll admit we can't coerce you into telling us this vital information you say you got from Clivers, but we can ask for it, and we do. You know who I am. I'm not a bad friend to have in this county, especially for a man in your business. What's Clivers to you anyhow, why the devil should you cover him up?"

"This is bewildering," Wolfe murmured. "Last night Mr. Cramer told me I should help him to protect a distinguished foreign guest, and now you demand the opposite!"

"All right, have your fun," Skinner croaked. "But tell us this, at least. Did Clivers say anything to indicate that he had it ready for Mike Walsh?"

Wolfe's eyelids flickered, and after a moment he turned to me. "Your notebook, Archie. You will find a place where I asked Lord Clivers, 'Don't you believe him?' I was referring to Mr. Walsh. Please read Lord Clivers' reply."

I had the notebook and was thumbing it. I looked too far front, and flipped back. Finally I had it, and read it out:

"Clivers: 'I don't believe anybody. I know damn well I'm a liar. I'm a diplomat. Look here. You can forget about Walsh. I'll deal with him myself. I have to keep this thing clear, at least as long as I'm in this country. I'll deal with Walsh. Scovil is dead, God rest his soul. Let the police do what they can with that. As for the Lindquists . . .' "

Wolfe stopped me with a finger. "That will do, Archie. Put the notebook away."

"He will not put it away!" Hombert was beating up the arm of his chair again. "With that in it? We want —"

He stopped to glare at Skinner, who had tapped a toe on his shin. Skinner was ready to melt with sweetness; his tone sounded like Romeo in the balcony scene. "Listen, Wolfe, play with us. Let us have that. Your man can type it, or he can dictate from his notes and I'll bring a man in to take it. Clivers is to sail for Europe Sunday. If we don't get this thing on ice there's going to be trouble."

Wolfe closed his eyes, and after a moment opened them again. They were all gazing at him, Cramer slowly chewing his cigar, Hombert holding in an explosion, Skinner looking innocent and friendly. Wolfe said, "Will you make a bargain with me, Mr. Skinner? Let me ask a few questions. Then, after considering the replies, I shall do what I can for you. I think it is more than likely you will find me helpful."

Skinner frowned. "What kind of questions?"

"You will hear them."

A pause. "All right. Shoot."

Wolfe turned abruptly to the inspector. "Mr. Cramer. You had a man following Mr. Walsh from the time you released him this afternoon, and that man was on post at the entrance of the boarding on 55th Street. I'd like to know what it was that caused him to cross the street and enter the enclosure, as reported in the

Gazette. Did he hear a shot?''

''No.'' Cramer took his cigar from his mouth. ''The man's out in the kitchen. Do you want to hear it from him?''

''I merely want to hear it.''

''Well, I can tell you. Stebbins was away from his post for a few minutes, he's admitted it. There was a taxi collision at the corner of Madison, and he had to go and look it over, which was bright of him. He says he was away only two minutes, but he may have been gone ten, you know how that is. Anyhow, he finally strolled back, on the south side of 55th, and looking across at the entrance of the boarding he saw the door slowly opening, and the face of a man looked out and it wasn't Walsh. There were pedestrians going by, and the face went back in and the door closed. Stebbins got behind a parked car. In a minute the face looked out again, and there was a man walking by, and the face disappeared again. Stebbins thought it was time to investigate and crossed the street and went in, and it was just lousy luck that that damn newspaper cockroach happened to see him. It was Clivers all right, and Walsh's body was there on the ground —"

"I know." Wolfe sighed. "It was lying in front of the telephone. So Mr. Stebbins heard no shot."

"No. Of course, he was down at the corner and there was a lot of noise."

"To be sure. Was the weapon on Lord Clivers' person?"

"No." Cramer sounded savage. "That's one of the nice details. We can't find any gun, except one in Walsh's pocket that hadn't been fired. There's a squad of men still up there, combing it. Also there's about a thousand hollow steel shafts sticking up from the base construction, and it might have been dropped down one of those."

"So it might," Wolfe murmured. "Well . . . no shot heard, and no gun found." He looked around at them. "I can't help observing, gentlemen, that that news relieves me enormously. Moreover, I think you have a right to know that Mr. Goodwin and I heard the shot."

They stared at him. Skinner demanded, "You what? What the hell are you talking about?''

Wolfe turned to me. "Tell them, Archie."

I let them have my open countenance. "This evening," I said, and corrected it, " —last evening — Mr. Wolfe and I were in this office. At two minutes before seven o'clock the phone rang, and it happened that we both took off our receivers. A voice said, 'Nero Wolfe!' It sounded far off but very excited — it sounded — well, unnatural. I said, 'Yes, talking,' and the voice said, 'I've got him, come up here, 55th Street, this is Mike Walsh, I've got him covered, come up.' The voice was cut off by the sound of an explosion, very loud, as if a gun had been shot close to the telephone. I called Walsh's name a few times, but there was no answer. We sent a phone call to police headquarters right away."

I looked around respectfully for approval. Skinner looked concentrated, Hombert looked about ready to bust, and Cramer looked disgusted. The inspector, I could see, didn't have far to go to get good and sore. He burst out at Wolfe,

"What else have you got? First you tell me the man I've got the whole force looking for, thinking I've got a hot one, is one of your boy scouts acting as advance agent. Now you tell me that the phone call we're trying to trace about a shot being heard, and you can't trace a local call anyway with these damn dials, now you tell me you made that too." He stuck his cigar in his mouth and bit it nearly in two.

"But Mr. Cramer," Wolfe protested, "is it my fault if destiny likes this address? Did we not notify you at once? Did I not even restrain Mr. Goodwin from hastening to the scene, because I knew you would not want him to intrude?"

Cramer opened his mouth but was speechless. Skinner said, "You heard that shot on the phone at two minutes to seven. That checks. It was five after when Stebbins found Clivers there." He looked around sort of helpless, like a man who has picked up something he didn't want. "That seems to clinch it." He growled at Wolfe, "What makes you so relieved about not finding the gun and Stebbins not hearing the shot, if you heard it yourself?''

''In due time, Mr. Skinner.'' Wolfe's forefinger was gently tapping on the arm of his chair, and I wondered what he was impatient about. ''If you don't mind, let me get on. The paper says that Mr. Stebbins felt Lord Clivers for a weapon. Did he find one?''

''No,'' Cramer grunted. ''He got talkative enough to tell us that he always carried a pistol, but not with evening dress.''

''But since Lord Clivers had not left the enclosure and since no weapon can be found, how could he possibly have been the murderer?''

''We'll find it,'' Cramer asserted gloomily. ''There's a million places in there to hide a gun, and we'll have to get into those shafts somehow. Or he might have thrown it over the fence. We'll find it. He did it, damn it. You've ruined the only outside leads I had.''

Wolfe wagged his head at him. ''Cheer up, Mr. Cramer. Tell me this, please. Since Mr. Stebbins followed Mr. Walsh all

355

afternoon, I presume you know their itinerary. What was it?"

Skinner growled, "Don't start stalling, Wolfe. Let's get —"

"I'm not stalling, sir. An excellent word. Mr. Cramer?"

The inspector dropped his cigar in the tray. "Well, Walsh stopped at a lunch counter on Franklin near Broadway and ate. He kept looking around, but Stebbins thinks he didn't wise up. Then he took a surface car north and got off at 27th Street and walked west. He went in the Seaboard Building and took the elevator and got off at the 32nd floor and went into the executive offices of the Seaboard Products Corporation. Stebbins waited out in the hall. Walsh was in there nearly an hour. He took the elevator down again, and Stebbins didn't want to take the same one and nearly lost him. He walked east and went into a drug store and used a telephone in a booth. Then he took the subway and went to a boarding-house in East 64th Street, where he lived, and he left again a little after half-past five and walked to his job at 55th street. He got there a little before six.''

Wolfe had leaned back and closed his eyes. They all looked at him. Cramer got out another cigar and bit off the end and fingered his tongue for the shreds. Hombert demanded, ''Well, are you asleep?''

Wolfe didn't move, but he spoke. ''About that visit Mr. Walsh made at the Seaboard Products Corporation. Do you know who he saw there?''

''No, how could I? Stebbins didn't go in. Even if there had been any reason — the office was closed by the time I got Stebbins's report. What difference does it make?''

''Not much.'' Wolfe's tone was mild, but to me, who knew it so well, there was a thrill in it. ''No, not much. There are cases when a conjecture is almost as good as a fact — even, sometimes, better.'' Suddenly he opened his eyes, sat up, and got brisk. ''That's all, gentlemen. It is past two o'clock, and Mr. Goodwin is yawning. You will hear from me tomorrow — today, rather.''

Skinner shook his head wearily. ''Oh,

no no no. Honest to God, Wolfe, you're the worst I've ever seen for trying to put over fast ones. There's a lot to do yet. Could I have another highball?"

Wolfe sighed. "Must we start yapping again?" He wiggled a finger at the District Attorney. "I offered you a bargain, sir. I said if I could get replies to a few questions I would consider them and would then do what I could for you. Do you think I can consider them properly at this time of night? I assure you I cannot. I am not quibbling. I have gone much further than you gentlemen along the path to the solution of this puzzle, and I am confronted by one difficulty which must be solved before anything can be done. When it will be solved I cannot say. I may light on it ten minutes from now, while I am undressing for bed, or it may require extended investigation and labor. Confound it, do you realize it will be dawn in less then four hours? It was past three when I retired last night." He put his hands on the edge of his desk and pushed his chair back, arose to his feet, and pulled at the corners of his vest where a wide band of canary yellow shirt puffed out. "Daylight will serve us better. No more tonight, short of the rack and the thumbscrew. You will hear from me."

Cramer got up too, saying to Hombert, "He's always like this. You might as well stick pins in a rhinoceros."

17

When, about a quarter after nine Wednesday morning, I went up to the plant rooms with a message, I thought that Wolfe's genius had at last bubbled over and he had gone nuts for good. He was in the potting room, standing by the bench, with a piece of board about four inches wide and ten inches long in each hand. He paid no attention to me when I entered. He held his hands two feet apart and then swiftly brought them together, flat sides of the two pieces of board meeting with a loud clap. He did that several times. He shook his head and threw one of the boards down and began hitting things with the other one, the top of the bench, one of its legs and then another one, the seat of the chair, the palm of his hand, a pile of wrapping paper. He kept shaking his head. Finally, deciding to admit I was there, he tossed the board down and turned his eyes on me with ferocious hostility.

"Well, sir?" he demanded.

I said in a resigned tone, "Cramer phoned again. That's three times. He says that District Attorney Skinner got tight after he left here and is now at his office with a hangover, cutting off people's heads. As far as that's concerned, I've had four hours sleep two nights in a row and I've got a headache. He says that the publisher of the *Gazette* told the Secretary of State to go to hell over long distance. He wants to know if we have seen the morning papers. He says that two men from Washington are in Hombert's office with copies of cables from London. He says that Hombert saw Clivers at his hotel half-an-hour ago and asked him about his visit to our office yesterday afternoon, and Clivers said it was a private matter and it will be a nice day if it don't rain. He says you have got to open up or he will open you. In addition to that, Miss Fox and Miss Lindquist are having a dogfight because their nerves are going back on them. In addition to that, Fritz is on the warpath because Saul and Johnny hang out in the kitchen too much and Johnny ate up some tambo shells he was going to put mushrooms into for lunch. In addition to that, I can't get you to tell me whether I am to go to the Hotel Portland to look at Clivers' documents which came on the *Berengaria*. In addition to that . . ."

I stopped for breath. Wolfe said, "You badger me. Those are all trivialities. Look at me —" he picked up the board and threw it down again " —I am sacrificing my hours of pleasure in an effort to straighten out the only tangle that remains in this knot, and you harass me with these futilities. Did the Secretary of State go to hell? If so, tell the others to join him there."

"Yeah, sure. I'm telling you, they're all going to be around here again. I can't hold them off."

"Lock the door. Keep them out. I will not be hounded!"

He turned away, definitely. I threw up

my hands and beat it. On my way downstairs I stopped a second at the door of the south room, and heard the voices of the two clients still at it. In the lower hall I listened at the kitchen door and perceived that Fritz was still shrill with fury. The place was a madhouse.

Wolfe had been impossible from the time I first went to his room around seven o'clock, because he hadn't taken his phone when I buzzed him, to report the first call from Cramer. I had never seen him so actively unfriendly, but I didn't really mind that, knowing he was only peeved at himself on account of his genius not working right. What got me on edge was first, I had a headache; second, Fritz and the clients had to unload their troubles on me; and third, I didn't like all the cussings from outsiders on the telephone. It had been going on for over two hours and it was keeping up.

After taking another aspirin and doing a few morning chores around the office, I sat down at my desk and got out the plant records and entered some items from Horstmann's reports of the day before, and went over some bills and so on. There were circulars and lists from both Richardt and Hoehn in the morning mail, also a couple of catalogues from England, and I glanced over them and laid them aside. There was a phone call from Harry Foster of the *Gazette,* who had found out somehow that we were supposed to know something, and I kidded him and backed him off. Then, a little after ten o'clock, the phone rang again, and the first thing I knew I was talking to the Marquis of Clivers himself. I had half a mind to get Wolfe on, but decided to take the message instead, and after I rang off I gathered up the catalogues and circulars and reports and slipped a rubber band around them and proceeded upstairs.

Wolfe was standing at one side of the third room, frowning at a row of seedling hybrids in their second year. He looked plenty forbidding, and Horstmann, whom I had passed in the tropical room, had had the appearance of having been crushed to earth.

I sailed into the storm. I flipped the rubber band on my little bundle and said,

"Here's those lists from Richardt and also some from Hoehn, and some catalogues from England. Do you want them or shall I leave them in the potting room? And Clivers just called on the telephone. He says those papers came, and if you want to go and look at them, or send me, okay. He didn't say anything about his little mix-up with the police last night, and of course I was too polite —"

I stopped because Wolfe wasn't listening. His lips had suddenly pushed out a full half-an-inch, and he had glued his eyes on the bundle in my hand. He stood that way a long while and I shut my mouth and stared at him.

Finally he murmured, "That's it. Confound you, Archie, did you know it? Is that why you brought it here?"

I asked courteously, "Have you gone cuckoo?"

He ignored me. "But of course not. It's your fate again." He closed his eyes and sighed a deep sigh, and murmured, "Rubber Coleman. The Rubber Band. Of course." He opened his eyes and flashed them at me. "Saul is downstairs? Send him up at once."

"What about Clivers?"

He went imperious. "Wait in the office. Send Saul."

Knowing there was no use pursuing any inquiries, I hopped back down to the kitchen door and beckoned Saul out into the hall. He stuck his nose up at me and I told him:

"Wolfe wants you upstairs. For God's sake watch your step, because he has just found the buried treasure and you know what to expect when he's like that. If he requests anything grotesque, consult me."

I went back to my desk, but of course plant records were out. I lit a cigarette, and took my pistol out of the drawer and looked it over and put it back again, and kicked over my wastebasket and let it lay.

There were steps on the stairs, and Saul's voice came from the door: "Let me out, Archie. I've got work to do."

"Let yourself out. What are you afraid of?"

I stuck my hands in my pockets and

stretched out my legs and sat on my shoulder blades and scowled. Ten minutes after Saul had left the phone rang. I uttered a couple of expletives as I reached for it, thinking it was one of the pack with another howl, but Saul Panzer's voice was in my ear:

"Archie? Connect me with Mr. Wolfe."

I thought, now that was quick work, and plugged and buzzed. Wolfe's voice sounded:

"Nero Wolfe."

"Yes, sir. This is Saul. I'm ready."

"Good. Archie? You don't need to take this."

I hung up with a bang and a snort. My powers of dissimulation were being saved from strain again. But that kind of thing didn't really get me sore, for I knew perfectly well why Wolfe didn't always point out to me the hole he was getting ready to crawl through: he knew that half the time I'd be back at him with damn good proof that it couldn't be done, which would only have been a nuisance, since he intended to do it anyway. No guy who knows he's right because he's too conceited to be wrong can be expected to go into conference about it.

Five minutes after that phone call from Saul the fun began. I got a ring from Wolfe upstairs:

"Try for Lord Clivers."

I got the Hotel Portland and got through to him, and Wolfe spoke: "Good morning, sir. I received your message . . . Yes, so I understand . . . No, he can't go . . . If you will be so good — one moment — a very important development has taken place, and I don't like to discuss details on the telephone. You may remember that on the phone yesterday afternoon Mr. Walsh spoke to you regarding a certain person whom he had just seen . . .Yes, he is both dangerous and desperate; moreover, he is cornered, and there is only one person open to you that can possibly prevent the fullest and most distasteful publicity on the whole affair . . . I know that, that's why I want you to come to my office at once . . . No, sir, take my word for it, it won't do, I should have to expose him immediately and publicly . . . Yes, sir . . . Good.

That's a sensible man. Be sure to bring those papers along. I'll expect you in fifteen minutes . . .''

Clivers rang off, but Wolfe stayed on.

"Archie. Try for Mr. Muir."

I got the Seaboard Products Corporation, and Miss Barish, and then Muir, and buzzed Wolfe.

"Mr. Muir? Good morning, sir. This is Nero Wolfe. . . . One moment, sir, I beg you. I have learned, to my great discomfiture, that I did an act of injustice yesterday, and I wish to rectify it . . . Yes, yes, quite so, I understand . . . Yes, indeed. I prefer not to discuss it on the telephone, but I am sure you will find yourself as satisfied as you deserve to be if you will come to my office at half-past eleven this morning, and bring Mr. Perry with you . . . No, I'm sorry, I can't do that. Miss Fox will be here . . . Yes, she is here now . . . No, half-past eleven, not before, and it will be necessary to have Mr. Perry present . . . Oh, surely not, he has shown a most active interest . . . Yes, it's only a short distance . . .''

I heard Muir's click off, and said into

my transmitter, "That will bring that old goat trotting up here without stopping either for Perry or his hat. Why didn't you —"

"Thanks, Archie. Try for Mr. Cramer."

I got headquarters, and Cramer's extension and his clerk. Then the inspector. Wolfe got on:

"Good morning, Mr. Cramer . . . Yes, indeed, I received your message, but I have been occupied to good purpose . . . So I understand, but could I help that? Can you be at my office at half-past eleven? I shall be ready for you at that time . . . The fact is, I do not intend merely to give you information, I hope to deliver a finished case . . . I can't help that either; do you think I have the Moerae running errands for me? . . . Certainly, if they wish to come, bring them, though I think it would be well if Mr. Hombert went back to diapers . . . Yes, eleven-thirty . . ."

Cramer was off. I said. "Shall I try for the Cabinet?"

"No, thanks." Wolfe was purring. "When Lord Clivers arrives, bring him up here at once."

18

I let Saul Panzer in when he came. There was no longer any reason why I shouldn't relinquish the job of answering the door, which normally belonged to Fritz, but it seemed tactful to give him time to cool off a little; and besides, if I left him to his own devices in the kitchen a while longer without interruption, there was a chance that he would bounce a stewpan on Johnny's bean, which would have done them both good.

So I let Saul in and parked him in the front room, and also, a little later, I opened up for the Marquis of Clivers. Whereupon I experienced a delightful surprise, for he had his nephew along. Apparently there was no wedding on today; Horrocks looked sturdy and wholesome in a sack suit that hung like a dream, and I got so interested looking at it that I almost forgot it was him inside of it. I suggested him towards the office and said to Clivers:

"Mr. Wolfe would like to see you upstairs. Three flights. Climb, or elevator?"

He was looking concentrated and sour. He said climb, and I took him up to the plant rooms and showed him Wolfe and left him there.

When I got back down Horrocks was still standing in the hall.

"If you want to wait," I said, "there's a place in the office to hold the back of your lap. You know, chair."

"The back of my lap?" He stared, and by gum, he worked at it till he got it. "Oh, quite. Thanks awfully. But I . . . I say, you know, Miss Fox got quite a wetting. Didn't she?"

"Yeah, she was good and damp."

"And I suppose she is still here, what?"

It was merely a question of which would be less irritating, to let him go on and circle around it for a while, or cut the knot for him and hand him the pieces.

Deciding for the latter, I said, "Wait here," and mounted the stairs again. They seemed to have quieted down in the south room. I knocked and went in and told Clara Fox:

"That young diplomat is down below and wants to see you and I'm going to send him up. Keep him in here. We're going to be busy in the office, and it gives me the spirit of 'seventy-six to look at him."

She made a dive for her vanity case, and I descended to the hall again and told Horrocks he knew the way.

It was ten after eleven. There was nothing for me to do but sit down and suck my finger. There was one thing I would have liked to remind Wolfe of before the party began, but I didn't myself know how important it was, and anyway, I had no idea how he intended to stage it. There was even a chance that this was to be only a dress rehearsal, a preliminary, to see what a little panic would do, but that wouldn't be like him. The only hint he condescended to give me was to ring me on the house phone and tell me he would come down with Clivers after the others had arrived, and until then I was to say nothing of Clivers' presence. I went in to see if Saul was talking, but he wasn't, so I went back and sat down and felt my pulse.

The two contingents, official and Seaboard, showed up within three minutes of each other. I let them in. The official came first. I took them to the office, where I had chairs pulled up. Skinner looked bilious, Hombert harassed, and Cramer moderately grim. When they saw Wolfe wasn't in the office they started to get exasperated, but I silenced them with a few well-chosen phrases, and then the bell rang again and I went for the second batch.

Muir and Perry were together. Perry smiled a tight smile at me and told me good morning, but Muir wasn't having any amenities; I saw his hand tremble a little as he hung his hat up, and he could have gone from that right on into permanent palsy without any tears wasted as far as I was concerned. I nodded them ahead.

They stopped dead inside the office door, at sight of the trio already there. Muir looked astonished and furious; Perry seemed surprised, looking from one to the other, and then turned to me:

"I thought . . . Wolfe said eleven-thirty, so I understood from Muir . . . if these gentlemen . . ."

"It's all right." I grinned at him. "Mr. Wolfe has arranged for a little conference. Have chairs. Do you know Mr. Hombert, the Police Commissioner? Inspector Cramer? Mr. Ramsey Muir. Mr. Anthony D. Perry."

I got to the house phone on my desk and buzzed the plant rooms. Wolfe answered, and I told him, "All here." The two bunches of eminent visitors were putting on a first-class exhibition of bad manners; neither had expected to see the other. Cramer looked around at them, slowly from one face to another, and then looked at me with a gleam in his eyes. Hombert was grumbling something to Perry. Skinner turned and croaked at me, "What kind of damn nonsense is this?" I just shook my head at him, and then I heard the creak of the elevator, and a moment later the door of the office opened and Wolfe entered with another visitor whom none of them had expected to see.

They approached. Wolfe stopped, and inclined his head. "Good morning, gentlemen. I believe some of you have met Lord Clivers. Not you, Mr. Perry? No. Mr. Muir. Mr. Skinner, our District Attorney. I want to thank all of you for being so punctual . . ."

I was seeing a few things. First, Clivers stood staring directly at Perry, reminding me of how Harlan Scovil had stared at him two days before, and Clivers had thrust his right hand into the side pocket of his coat and didn't take it out. Second, Perry was staring back, and his temples were moving and his eyes were small and hard. Third, Inspector Cramer had put his weight forward in his chair and his feet back under him, but he was sitting too far away, the other side of Skinner, to get anywhere quick.

I swiveled and opened a drawer unostentatiously and got out my automatic and laid it on the desk at my elbow. Hombert was starting to bellyache:

"I don't know, Wolfe, what kind of a high-handed procedure you think —"

Wolfe, who had moved around the desk and into his chair, put up a palm at him: "Please, Mr. Hombert. I think it is always advisable to take a short-cut when it is feasible. That's why I requested a favor of Lord Clivers." He looked at Clivers. "Be seated, sir. And tell us, have you ever met Mr. Perry before?"

Clivers, with his hand still in his pocket, lowered himself into his chair, which was between Hombert and me, without taking his eyes off of Perry. "I have," he said gruffly. "By gad, you were right. He's Coleman. Rubber Coleman."

Perry just looked at him.

Wolfe asked softly, "What about it, Mr. Perry?"

You could see from Perry's chin that his teeth were clamped. His eyes went suddenly from Clivers to Wolfe and stayed there; then he looked at me, and I returned it. His shoulders started going up, slowly up, high, as he took in a long breath, and then slowly they started down again. When they touched bottom he looked at Wolfe again and said:

"I'm not talking. Not just now. You go on."

Wolfe nodded. "I don't blame you, sir. It's a lot to give up, to surrender that old secret." He glanced around the circle. "You gentlemen may remember, from Miss Fox's story last night, that Rubber Coleman was the man who led that little band of rescuers forty years ago. That was Mr. Perry here. But you do not yet know that on account of that obligation Lord Clivers, in the year 1906, twenty-nine years ago, paid Coleman — Mr. Perry — the sum of one million dollars. Nor that this Coleman-Perry has never, to this day, distributed any of that sum as he agreed to do."

Cramer grunted and moved himself another inch forward. Skinner was sunk in his chair with his elbows on its arms and his finger-tips placed neatly together, his narrow eyes moving from Wolfe to Clivers to Perry and back again. Hombert was biting his lip and watching Clivers. Muir suddenly squeaked:

"What's all this about? What has this got to do —"

Wolfe snapped at him, "Shut up. You are here, sir, because that seemed the easiest way to bring Mr. Perry, and because I thought you should know the truth regarding your charge against Miss Fox. If you wish to leave, do so; if you stay, hold your tongue."

Clivers put in brusquely, "I didn't agree to this man's presence."

Wolfe nodded. "I think you may leave that to me. After all, Lord Clivers, it was you who originally started this, and if the hen has come home to roost and I am to pluck if for you, I must be permitted a voice in the method." He turned abruptly. "What about it, Mr. Perry? You've had a moment for reflection. You were Rubber Coleman, weren't you?"

"I'm not talking." Perry was gazing at him, and this time he didn't have to strain the words through his teeth. His lips compressed a little, his idea being that he was smiling. "Lord Clivers may quite possibly be mistaken." He tried the smile again. "It may even be that he will . . . will realize his mistake." He looked around. "You know me, Mr. Skinner. You too, Mr. Hombert. I am glad you are here. I have evidence to present to you that this man Wolfe is engaged in a malicious attempt to damage my reputation and that of my vice-president and the firm I direct. Mr. Muir will bear me out." He turned small hard eyes on Wolfe. "I'll give you rope. All you want. Go on."

Wolfe nodded admiringly. "Superlative." He leaned back and surveyed the group. "Gentlemen, I must ask you to listen, and bear with me. You will reach my conclusion only if I describe my progress toward it. I'll make it as brief as possible.

"It began some forty-five hours ago, when Mr. Perry called here and asked me to investigate a theft of $30,000 from the drawer of Mr. Muir's desk. Mr. Goodwin called at the Seaboard office and asked questions. He was there from 4:45 until 5:55, and for a period of 35 minutes, from 5:20 until 5:55, he saw neither Mr. Perry nor Mr. Muir, because they had gone to a conference in the directors' room. The case seemed to have undesirable features, and we decided not to handle it. I find I shall need some beer.''

He reached to push the button, and leaned back again. ''You know of Harlan Scovil's visit to this office Monday afternoon. Well, he saw Mr. Perry here. He not only saw him, he stared at him. You know of the phone call, at 5:26, which summoned Mr. Scovil to his death. Monday night, in addition to these things, I also knew the story which Miss Fox had related to us in the presence of Mr. Walsh and Miss Lindquist; and when, having engaged myself in Miss Fox's interest, it became necessary to consider the murder of Harlan Scovil, I scanned the possibilities as they presented themselves at that moment.

''Assuming, until disproven, that Harlan Scovil's murder was connected with the Rubber Band affair, the first possibility was of course Lord Clivers himself, but Tuesday morning he was eliminated, when I learned that the murderer was alone in the automobile. An article in Sunday's *Times,* which Mr. Goodwin had kindly read to me, stated that Lord Clivers did not know how to drive a car, and on Tuesday, yesterday, I corroborated that through an agent in London, at the same time acquiring various bits of information regarding Lord Clivers. The second possibility was Michael Walsh. I had talked with him and formed a certain judgment of him, and no motive was apparent, but he remained a possibility. The same applied to Miss Lindquist. Miss Fox was definitely out of it, because I had upon consideration accepted her as a client."

Somebody burst out, "Ha!" Hombert ventured a comment, while Wolfe poured beer and gulped, but it went unheeded. Wolfe wiped his lips and went on:

"Among the known possibilities, the most promising one was Anthony D. Perry. On account of the phone call which took Mr. Scovil to the street to die, it was practically certain that his murderer had known he was in this office; and because, so far as I was aware, Mr.

Perry was the only person who had known that, it seemed at least worth while to accept it as a conjecture. Through *Metropolitan Biographies* and also through inquiries by one of my men, I got at least negative support for the conjecture; and I got positive support by talking over long distance to Nebraska, with Miss Lindquist's father. He remembered with considerable accuracy the appearance of the face and figure of Rubber Coleman, and while of course there could be no real identification by a telephone talk after forty years, still it was support. I asked Mr. Lindquist, in fact, for descriptions of all the men concerned in that affair, thinking there might be some complication more involved than this most obvious one, but it was his description of Rubber Coleman which most nearly approximated that of Mr. Perry. The next step —"

"Wait a minute, Wolfe." Skinner's croak was imperative. "You can't do this. Not this way. If you've got a case, I'm the District Attorney. If you haven't —"

Perry cut in. "Let him alone! Let him

hang himself.''

Hombert muttered something to Cramer, and the Inspector rumbled back. Clivers spoke up: "I'm concerned in this. Let Wolfe talk." He used a finger of his left hand to point at Perry because his right hand was still in his coat pocket. "That man is Rubber Coleman. Wolfe learned that, didn't he? What the devil have the rest of you done, except annoy me?"

Perry leveled his eyes at the marquis. "You're mistaken, Lord Clivers. You'll regret this."

Wolfe had taken advantage of the opportunity to finish his bottle and ring for another. Now he looked around. "You gentlemen may be curious why, if Mr. Perry is not Rubber Coleman, he does not express indignant wonderment at what I am talking about. Oh, he could explain that. Long ago, shortly after she entered Seaboard's employ, Miss Fox told him the story which you heard from her last night. He knows all about the Rubber Band, from her, and also about her efforts to find its surviving members. And by the way, as regards the identity — did Mr.

Walsh telephone you around five o'clock yesterday afternoon, Lord Clivers, and tell you he had just found Rubber Coleman?"

Clivers nodded. "He did."

"Yes." Wolfe looked at Cramer. "As you informed me, immediately after leaving the Seaboard office, where he had gone on account of his unfortunate suspicions regarding Miss Fox and myself after Harlan Scovil had been killed, Mr. Walsh sought a telephone. There — as can doubtless be verified by inquiry, along with multitudinous other details — he had seen Mr. Perry. It is a pity he did not inform me, since in that case he would still be alive; but what he did do was to phone Lord Clivers, with whom he had had a talk in the morning. He had called at the Hotel Portland and Lord Clivers had considered it advisable to see him, had informed him of the payment which had been made to Rubber Coleman long before, and had declared his intention of giving him a respectable sum of money. Now, learning from Mr. Walsh over the telephone that he had found Rubber Coleman, Lord Clivers saw that immediate and purposeful action was required if publicity was to be avoided; and he told Mr. Walsh that around seven o'clock that evening, on his way to a dinner engagement, he would stop in at the place Mr. Walsh was working, which was a short distance from his hotel. I have been told these details within the last hour. Is that correct, sir?"

Clivers nodded. "It is."

Wolfe looked at Perry, but Perry's eyes were fixed on Clivers. Wolfe said, "So, for the identity, we have Mr. Lindquist's description, Mr. Walsh's phone call, and Lord Clivers' present recognition. Why, after forty years, Mr. Scovil and Mr. Walsh should have recognized Rubber Coleman is, I think, easily explicable. On account of the circumstances, their minds were at the moment filled with vivid memories of that old event, and alert with suspicion. They might have passed Mr. Perry a hundred times on the street without a second glance at him, but in the situations in which they saw him recollection jumped for them." He looked again at the Seaboard president, and again asked, "What about it now, Mr. Perry? Won't you give us that?"

Perry moved his eyes at him. He spoke smoothly. "I'm still not talking. I'm listening." He suddenly, spasmodically, jerked forward, and there was a stir around the circle. Cramer's bulk tensed in his chair. Skinner's hands dropped. Clivers stiffened. I got my hand to my desk, on the gun. I don't think Perry noticed any of it, for his gaze stayed on Wolfe, and he jerked back again and set his jaw. He said not quite so smoothly, "You go on."

Wolfe shook his head. "You're a stubborn man, Mr. Perry. However — as I started to say, the next step for me, yesterday afternoon, was to get in touch with Mr. Walsh, persuade him of my good faith, show him a photograph of Mr. Perry, and substantiate my conjecture. That became doubly important and urgent after Lord Clivers called here and I learned of the payment that had been made to Coleman in 1906. I considered the idea of asking Lord Clivers for a description of Coleman, and even possibly showing him Perry's photograph, but rejected it. I was at that moment by no means convinced of his devotion to scruple, and even had I been, I would not have cared to alarm him further by showing him the imminence of Coleman's discovery — and the lid blown off the pot. First I needed Mr. Walsh, so I sent a man to 55th street to reconnoitre.

"Of course, I had found out other things. For instance, one of my men had visited the directors' room of the Seaboard Products Corporation and learned that it has a second door, into the public hall, through which Mr. Perry might easily have departed at 5:20 or thereabouts Monday afternoon on some errand, and returned some thirty minutes later, without Mr. Goodwin's knowledge. Questions to his business associates who were present might elicit answers. For another instance, Miss Fox had breakfast with me yesterday morning — and I assure you, Mr. Skinner, I did not waste the time in foolish queries as to where her mother used to keep letters sixteen years ago.

"Combining   information   with

conjecture, I get a fair picture of some of Mr. Perry's precautionary activities. In the spring of 1932 he saw an advertisement in a newspaper seeking knowledge of the whereabouts of Michael Walsh and Rubber Coleman. In a roundabout way he learned who had inserted it; and a month later Clara Fox was in the employ of the Seaboard Products Corporation. He could keep an eye on her, and did so. He cultivated her company, and earned a degree of her confidence. When she found Harlan Scovil, and later Hilda Lindquist, and still later Michael Walsh, he knew of it. He tried to convince her of the foolishness of her enterprise, but without success. Then suddenly, last Thursday, he learned she had found Lord Clivers, and he at once took measures to hamstring her. He may even then have considered murder and rejected it; at any rate, he decided that sending her to prison as a thief would completely discredit her and would be sufficient. He knew that her initiative was the only active force threatening him, and that with her removed there would be little danger.

An opportunity was providentially at hand. Friday afternoon he himself took that $30,000 from Mr. Muir's desk, and sent Miss Fox into that room with a cablegram to be copied. I don't know —"

Muir had popped up out of his chair and was squealing, "By God, I believe it! By God if I don't! And all the time you were plotting against her! You dirty sneak, you dirty —"

Cramer, agile on his feet, had a hand on Muir's shoulder. "All right, all right, you just sit down and we'll all believe it. Come on, now." He eased him down, Muir chattering.

Perry said contemptuously, bitingly, "So that's you, Muir." He whirled, and there was a quality in his movement that made me touch my gun again. "Wolfe, all this you're inventing, you'll eat it." He added slowly, "And it will finish you."

Wolfe shook his head. "Oh, no, sir, I assure you." He sighed. "To continue: I don't know how and when Mr. Perry concealed the money in Miss Fox's automobile, but one of my men has uncovered a possibility which the police can easily follow. At any rate, it is certain that he did. That is unimportant. Another thing that moved him to action was the fact that Clara Fox had told him that, having heard him speak favorably of the abilities of Nero Wolfe, she had decided to engage me in the Rubber Band enterprise. Apparently Mr. Perry did give my competence a high rating, for he took the trouble to come here himself to get me to act for the Seaboard Products Corporation, which would of course have prevented me from taking Miss Fox as a client.

"But he had an unpleasant surprise here. He was sitting in that chair, the one he is in now, when a man walked into the room and said, 'My name's Harlan Scovil.' And the man stared at Mr. Perry. We cannot know whether he definitely recognized him as Rubber Coleman or whether Mr. Perry merely suspected that he did. In any event, it was enough to convince Mr. Perry that something more drastic than a framed-up larceny charge was called for without delay; for obviously it would not do for any living person to have even the remotest suspicion that there was any connection between Anthony D. Perry, corporation president, bank director, multi-millionaire, and eminent citizen, and the Rubber Band. Lord Clivers tells me that forty years ago Rubber Coleman was headstrong, sharp of purpose, and quick on the trigger. Apparently he has retained those characteristics. He went to his office and at once phoned Mr. Goodwin to come there. At 5:20 he went to the directors' room. A moment later he excused himself to his associates, left by the door to the public hall, descended to the ground floor and telephoned Harlan Scovil, saying what we can only guess at but certainly arranging a rendezvous, went to the street and selected a parked automobile and took it, drove to where Scovil was approaching the rendezvous and shot him dead, abandoned the car on Ninth Avenue, and returned to the Seaboard Building and the directors' room. It was an action admirably quick-witted, direct and conclusive, with probably not one chance in a million of its being discovered but for the fact that Miss Fox had happened to pick me to collect a fantastic debt for her.''

Wolfe paused to open and pour beer. Skinner said, ''I hope you've got something, Wolfe. I hope to heaven you've got something, because if you haven't . . .''

Wolfe drank, and put his glass down. ''I know. I can see the open jaws of the waiting beasts.'' He thumbed at Perry. ''This one here in front. But let him wait a little longer. Let us go on to last evening. That is quite simple. We are not concerned with the details of how Mr. Walsh got to see Mr. Perry at his office yesterday afternoon; it is enough to know that he did, since he phoned Lord Clivers that he had found Rubber Coleman. Well, there was only one thing for Mr. Perry to do, and he did it. Shortly after half-past six o'clock he entered that building enclosure by one of the ways we know of — possibly he is a member of the Orient Club, another point for inquiry — crept up on old Mr. Walsh and shot him in the back of the head, probably muffling the sound of the shot by wrapping the gun in his overcoat or something else, moved the body to the vicinity of the telephone if it was not already there, left by the way he had come, and drove rapidly —"

"Wait a minute!" Cramer broke in, gruff. "How do you fit that? We know the exact time of that shot, two minutes to seven, when Walsh called you on the phone. And you heard the shot. We already know —"

"Please, Mr. Cramer." Wolfe was patient. "I'm not telling you what you already know; this, for you, is news. I was saying, Mr. Perry drove rapidly downtown and arrived at this office at exactly seven o'clock."

Hombert jerked up and snorted. Cramer stared at Wolfe, slowly shaking his head. Skinner, frowning, demanded, "Are you crazy, Wolfe? Yesterday you told us you heard the shot that killed Walsh, at 6:58. Now you say that Perry fired it, and then got to your office at seven o'clock." He snarled, "Well?"

"Precisely." Wolfe wiggled a finger at him. "Do you remember that last night I told you that I was confronted by a difficulty which had to be solved before anything could be done? That was it. You have just stated it. —Archie, please tell Saul to go ahead."

I got up and went and opened the door to the front room. Saul Panzer was sitting there. I called to him, "Hey, Mr. Wolfe says to go ahead." Saul made for the hall and I heard him going out the front door.

Wolfe was saying, "It was ingenious and daring for Mr. Perry to arrange for Mr. Goodwin and me to furnish his alibi. But of course, strictly speaking, it was not an alibi he had in mind; it was a chronology of events which would exclude from my mind any possibility of his connection with Mr. Walsh's death. Such a connection was not supposed to occur to anyone, and above all not to me; for it is fairly certain that up to the time of his arrival here today Mr. Perry felt satisfactorily assured that no one had the faintest suspicion of his interest in this affair. There had been two chances against him: Harlan Scovil might have spoken to Mr. Goodwin between the time that Mr. Perry left here Monday afternoon and the time he phoned to summon Mr. Goodwin to his office; or Mr. Walsh might have communicated with me between five and six yesterday. But he thought not, for there was no indication of it from us; and he had proceeded to kill both of them as soon as he could reasonably manage it. So he arranged —"

Skinner growled, "Get on. He may not have had an alibi in mind, but he seems to have one. What about it?"

"As I say, sir, that was my difficulty. It will be resolved for you shortly. I thought it better — ah! Get it, Archie."

It was the phone. I swiveled and took it, and found myself exchanging greetings with Mr. Panzer. I told Wolfe, "Saul."

He nodded, and got brisk. "Give Mr. Skinner your chair. If you would please take that receiver, Mr. Skinner? I want you to hear something. And you, Mr. Cramer, take mine — here — the cord isn't long enough, I'm afraid you'll have to stand. Kindly keep the receiver fairly snug on your ear. Now, Mr. Skinner, speak into the transmitter, 'Ready.' That one word will be enough."

Skinner, at my phone, croaked, "Ready." The next development was funny. He gave a jump, and turned to glare at Wolfe, while Cramer, at Wolfe's phone, jerked a little too, and yelled into the transmitter, "Hey! Hey, you!"

Wolfe said, "Hang up, gentlemen, and be seated. —Mr. Skinner, please! That demonstration was really necessary. What you heard was Saul Panzer in a telephone booth at the druggist's on the next corner. There, of course, the instrument is attached to the wall. What he did was this."

Wolfe reached into his pocket and took out a big rubber band. He removed the receiver from his French phone, looped the band over the transmitter end, stretched it out, and let it flip. He replaced the receiver.

"That's all," he announced. "That was the shot Mr. Goodwin and I heard over the telephone. The band must be three-quarters of an inch wide, and thick, as

I learned from experiments this morning. On this instrument, of course, it is nothing; but on the transmitter of a pay-station phone, with the impact and jar and vibration simultaneous, the effect is startling. Didn't you find it so, Mr. Skinner?"

"I'll be damned," Cramer muttered. "I will be damned."

Skinner said, "It's amazing. I'd have sworn it was a gun."

"Yes." Wolfe's eyes, half shut, were on Perry. "I must congratulate you, sir. Not only efficient, but appropriate. Rubber Coleman. The Rubber Band. I fancy that was how the idea happened to occur to you. Most ingenious, and ludicrously simple. I wish you would tell us what old friend or employee you got to help you try it out, for surely you took that precaution. It would save Mr. Cramer a lot of trouble."

Wolfe was over one hurdle, anyway. He had Skinner and Hombert and Cramer with him, sewed up. When he had begun talking they had kept their eyes mostly on him, with only occasional glances at

398

Perry; then, as he had uncovered one point after another, they had gradually looked more at Perry; and by now, while still listening to Wolfe, they weren't bothering to look at him much. Their gaze was on Perry, and stayed there, and, for that matter, so was mine and Muir's and Clivers'. Perry was obviously expecting too much of himself. He had waited too long for a convenient spot to open up with indignation or defiance or a counter-attack, and no doubt Wolfe's little act with the rubber band had been a complete surprise to him. He was by no means ready to break down and have a good cry, because he wasn't that kind of a dog, but you could see he was stretched too tight. Just as none of us could take our eyes off of him, he couldn't take his off of Wolfe. From where I sat I could see his temples moving, plain.

He didn't say anything.

Skinner's bass rumbled, "You've made up a good story, Wolfe. I've got a suggestion. How about leaving your man here to entertain Perry for a while and the rest of us go somewhere for a little talk?

I need to ask some questions."

Wolfe shook his head. "Not at this moment, sir, if you please. Patience; my reasons will appear. First, is the chronology clear to all of you? At or about 6:35 Mr. Perry killed Mr. Walsh, leaving his body near the telephone, and immediately drove downtown, stopping, perhaps, at the same drug store where Saul Panzer just now demonstrated for us. I think that likely, for that store has a side entrance through which the phone booths can be approached with little exposure to observation. From there he phoned here, disguising his voice, and snapping his rubber band. Two minutes later he was at my door, having established the moment at which Michael Walsh was killed. There was of course the risk that by accident the body had been discovered in the twenty minutes which had elapsed, but it was slight, and in any event there was nothing to point to him. As it happened, he had great luck, for not only was the body not discovered prematurely, it was discovered at precisely the proper moment, and by Lord Clivers himself! I think it highly improbable that Mr. Perry knew that Lord Clivers was expected there at that hour, or indeed at all; that was coincidence. How he must have preened himself last evening — for we are all vainer of our luck than of our merits — when he learned the news! The happy smile of Providence! Isn't that so, Mr. Perry?"

Perry smiled into Wolfe's face — a thin tight smile, but he made a go of it. He said, "I'm still listening . . . but it strikes me you're about through. As Mr. Skinner says, you've made up a good story." He stopped, and his jaw worked a little, then he went on: "Of course you don't expect me to reply to it, but I'm going to, only not with words. You're in a plot to blackmail Lord Clivers, but that's his business. I'm going back to my office and get my lawyer, and I'm going to come down on you for slander and for conspiracy, and also your man Goodwin. I am also going to swear out a warrant against Clara Fox, and this time there'll be no nonsense about withdrawing it." He clamped his jaw, and loosened it again. "You're done, Wolfe. I'm telling you,

you're done."

Wolfe looked at the District Attorney. "I am aware, Mr. Skinner, that I have exasperated you, but in the end I think you will agree that my procedure was well-advised. First, on account of the undesirable publicity in connection with Lord Clivers, and the fact that he is soon to sail for home, prompt action was essential. Second, there was the advantage of showing Mr. Perry all at once how many holes he will have to plug up, for he is bound to get frantic about it and make a fool of himself. He was really sanguine enough to expect to keep his connection with this completely concealed. His leaving the directors' room Monday afternoon and returning; his access to Clara Fox's car for concealing the money, which is now being investigated by one of my men, Orrie Cather; the visit to him by Michael Walsh; his entrance into, and exit from, the building enclosure last evening; his overcoat, perhaps, which he wrapped around his pistol; his entering the corner drug store to telephone; all these and a dozen other details are capable of inquiry;

and, finding himself confronted by so many problems all requiring immediate attention, he is sure to put his foot in it."

Skinner grunted in disgust. "Do you mean to say you've given us all you've got? And now you're letting him know it?"

"But I've got all that's necessary." Wolfe sighed. "For, since we are all convinced that Mr. Perry did kill Harlan Scovil and Michael Walsh, it is of no consequence whether he can be legally convicted and executed."

Cramer muttered, "Uh-huh, you're nuts." Skinner and Hombert stared, speechless.

"Because," Wolfe went on, "he is rendered incapable of further mischief anyway; and even if you regard the criminal law as an instrument of barbarous vengeance, he is going to pay. What is it that he has been trying so desperately to preserve, with all his ruthless cunning? His position in society, his high repute among his fellow men, his nimbus as a master biped. Well, he will lose all that, which should be enough for any law." He extended his hand. "May I have those papers, Lord Clivers?"

Clivers reached to his breast pocket and pulled out an envelope, and I got it and handed it to Wolfe. Wolfe opened the flap and extracted some pieces of paper, and unfolded them, with the usual nicety of his fingers.

"I have here," he said, "a document dated Silver City, Nevada, June 2, 1895, in which George Rowley agrees to make a certain future compensation for services rendered. It is signed by him, and attested by Michael Walsh and Rubber Coleman as witnesses. I also have another, same date, headed PLEDGE OF THE RUBBER BAND, containing an agreement signed by various persons. I also have one dated London, England, August 11, 1906, which is a receipt for two hundred thousand, seven hundred sixty-one pounds, signed by Rubber Coleman, Gilbert Fox, Harlan Scovil, Turtle-back, Victor Lindquist and Michael Walsh. After the 'Turtle-back,' in parentheses, appears the name William Mollen. I also have a check for the same amount, dated September 19, drawn to the order of James N. Coleman and endorsed by him for payment."

Wolfe looked around at them. "The point here is, gentlemen, that none of those men except Coleman ever saw that receipt. He forged the names of all the others." He whirled suddenly to Perry, and his voice was a whip. "Well, sir? Is that slander?"

Perry held himself. But his voice was squeezed in his throat. "It is. They signed it."

"Ha! They signed it? So at last we have it that you're Rubber Coleman?"

"Certainly I'm Coleman. They signed it, and they got their share."

"Oh, no." Wolfe pointed a finger at him and held it there. "You've made a bad mistake, sir; you didn't kill enough men. Victor Lindquist is still alive and in possession of his faculties. I talked to him yesterday on the telephone, and I warned him against any tricks that might be tried. His testimony, with the corroboration we already have, will be ample for an English court. Slander? Pfui!" He turned to the others. "So you see, it isn't really so important to convict Mr. Perry of murder. He is now past sixty. I don't know the English penalty for forgery, but certainly he will be well over seventy when he emerges from jail, discredited, broken, a pitiable relic —"

Wolfe told me later that his idea was to work Perry into a state where he would then and there sign checks for Clara Fox and Victor Lindquist, and Walsh's and Scovil's heirs if any, for their share of the million dollars. I don't know. Anyhow, the checks didn't get signed, because dead men can't write even their names.

It happened like lightning, a bunch of reflexes. Perry jerked out a gun and turned it on Wolfe and pulled the trigger. Hombert yelled and Cramer jumped. I could never have got across in time to topple him, and anyway, as I say, it was reflex. I grabbed my gun and let him have it, but then Cramer was there and I quit. There was a lot of noise, Perry was down, sunk in his chair, and they were pawing him. I dived around the desk for Wolfe, who was sitting there looking surprised for once in his life, feeling with his right hand at his upper left arm.

Him protesting, I pulled his coat open and the sleeve off, and the spot of blood on the outside of the arm of the canary yellow shirt looked better to me than any orchid. I stuck my finger in the hole the bullet had made and ripped the sleeve and took a look, and then grinned into the fat devil's face. "Just the meat, and not much of that. You don't use that arm much anyhow."

I heard Cramer behind me, "Dead as a doornail," and turned to see the major casualty. They had let it come on out of the chair and stretched it on the floor. The inspector was kneeling by it, and the others standing, and Clivers and Skinner were busy putting out a fire. Clivers was pulling and rubbing at the bottom front of one side of his coat, where the bullet and flame had gone through when he pulled the trigger with his hand still in his pocket, and Skinner was helping him. He must have plugged Perry one-tenth of a second before I did.

Cramer stood up. He said heavily,

"One in the right shoulder, and one clear through him, through the heart. Well, he asked for it."

I said, "The shoulder was mine. I was high."

"Surely not, Archie." It was behind me, Wolfe murmuring. We looked at him; he was sopping blood off of his arm with his handkerchief. "Surely not. Do you want Lord Clivers' picture in the *Gazette* again? We must protect him. You can stand the responsibility of a justifiable homicide. You can — what do you call it, Mr. Cramer? — take the rap."

19

"Five thousand pounds," Clivers said. "To be paid at once, and to be returned to me if and when recovery is made from Coleman's estate. That's fair. I don't say it's generous. Who the devil can afford to be generous nowadays?"

Wolfe shook his head. "I see I'll have to get you on the wing. You dart like a humming-bird from two thousand to ten to seven to five. We'll take the ten, under the conditions you suggest."

Clara Fox put in, "I don't want anything. I've told you that. I won't take anything."

It was nearly three o'clock and we were all in the office. There had been six of us at lunch, which had meant another pick-me-up. Muir had gone, sped on his way by a pronouncement from Wolfe to the effect that he was a scabrous jackass, without having seen Clara Fox. Cramer and Hombert and Skinner had departed, after accepting Wolfe's suggestion for protecting the marquis from further publicity, and I had agreed to it. Doc Vollmer had come and fixed up Wolfe's arm and had gone again. What was left of Rubber Coleman-Anthony D. Perry had been taken away under Cramer's supervision, and the office floor looked bare because the big red and yellow rug where Perry had sat and where they had stretched him out was down in the basement, waiting for the cleaners to call. The bolt was back on the front door and I was acting as hallboy again, because reporters were still buzzing around the entrance like flies on the screen on a cloudy day.

Wolfe said, "You're still my client, Miss Fox. You are under no compulsion to take my advice, but it is my duty to offer it. First, take what belongs to you; your renunciation would not resurrect Mr. Scovil or Mr. Walsh, nor even Mr. Perry. Almost certainly, a large sum can be collected from Mr. Perry's estate. Second, remember that I have earned a fee and you will have to pay it. Third, abandon for good your career as an adventuress; you're much too soft-hearted for it."

Clara Fox glanced at Francis Horrocks, who was sitting there looking at her with that sickening sweet expression that you occasionally see in public and at the movies. It was a relief to see him glance at Wolfe and get his mind on something else for a brief moment. He blurted out:

"I say, you know, if she doesn't want to take money from that chap's estate, she doesn't have to. It's her own affair, what? Now, if my uncle paid your fee . . . it's all the same . . . ."

"Shut up, Francis." Clivers was impatient. "How the devil is it all the same? Let's get this settled. I've already missed one engagement and shall soon be late for another. Look here, seven thousand."

Hilda Lindquist said, "I'll take what I can get. It doesn't belong to me, it's my father's." Her square face wasn't exactly cheerful, but I wouldn't say she looked wretched. She leveled her eyes at Clivers. "If you had been half way careful when you paid that money twenty-nine years ago, father would have got his share then, when mother was still alive and my brother hadn't died."

Clivers didn't bother with her. He looked at Wolfe. "Let's get on. Eight thousand."

"Come, come, sir." Wolfe wiggled a finger at him. "Make it dollars. Fifty thousand. The exchange favors you. There is a strong probability that you'll get it back when Perry's estate is settled; besides, it might be argued that you should pay my fee instead of Miss Fox. There is no telling how this might have turned out for you but for my intervention."

"Bah." Clivers snorted. "Even up there, I saved your life. I shot him."

"Oh, no. Read the newspapers. Mr. Goodwin shot him."

Clivers looked at me, suddenly exploded with his three short blasts, haw-haw-haw. "So you did, eh? Goodwin's your name? Damned fine shooting!" He turned to Wolfe. "All right. Draw up a paper and send it to my hotel, and you'll get a check." He got up from his chair, glancing down at the mess he had made of the front of his coat. "I'll have to go there now and change. A fine piece of cloth ruined. I'm sorry not to see more of your orchids. You, Francis! Come on."

Horrocks was murmuring something in a molasses tone to Clara Fox and she was taking it in and nodding at him. He finished, and got up. "Right-o." He moved across and stuck out his paw at Wolfe. "You know, I want to say, it was devilish clever, the way you watered Miss Fox yesterday morning and they never suspected. It was the face you put on that stumped them, what?"

"No doubt." Wolfe got his hand back again. "Since you gentlemen are sailing Saturday, I suppose we shan't see you again. *Bon voyage.*"

"Thanks," Clivers grunted. "At least for myself. My nephew isn't sailing. He has spent a fortune on cables and got himself transferred to the Washington embassy. He's going to carve out a career. He had better, because I'm damned if he'll get my title for another two decades. Come on, Francis."

I glanced at Clara Fox, and my dreams went short on ideals then and there. If I ever saw a woman look smug and self-satisfied . . .

20

At twenty minutes to four, with Wolfe and me alone in the office, the door opened and Fritz came marching in. Clamped under his left arm was the poker-dart board; in his right hand was the box of javelins. He put the box down on Wolfe's desk, crossed to the far wall and hung up the board, backed off and squinted at it, straightened it up, turned to Wolfe and did his little bow, and departed.

Wolfe emptied his glass of beer, arose from his chair, and began fingering the darts, sorting out the yellow ones.

He looked at me. "I suppose this is foolhardy," he murmured, "with this bullet-wound, to start my blood pumping."

"Sure," I agreed. "You ought to be in bed. They may have to amputate."

"Indeed." He frowned at me. "Of course, you wouldn't know much about it. As far as my memory serves, you have never been shot by a high-calibre revolver at close range."

"The lord help me." I threw up my hands. "Is that going to be the tune? Are you actually going to have the nerve to brag about that little scratch? Now, if Hombert's foot hadn't jostled his chair and he had hit what he aimed at . . ."

"But he didn't." Wolfe moved to the fifteen-foot mark. He looked me over. "Archie. If you would care to join me at this . . ."

I shook my head positively. "Nothing doing. You'll keep beefing about your bullet-wound, and anyway I can't afford it. You'll probably be luckier than ever."

He put a dignified stare on me. "A dime a game."

"No."

"A nickel."

"No. Not even for matches."

He stood silent, and after a minute of that heaved a deep sigh. "Your salary is raised ten dollars a week, beginning last Monday."

I lifted the brows. "Fifteen."

"Ten is enough."

I shook my head. "Fifteen."

He sighed again. "Confound you! All right. Fifteen."

I arose and went to the desk to get the red darts.

The publishers hope that this Large Print Book has brought you pleasurable reading. Each title is designed to make the text as easy to see as possible. G. K. Hall Large Print Books are available from your library and your local bookstore. Or you can receive information on upcoming and current Large Print Books by mail and order directly from the publisher. Just send your name and address to:

G. K. Hall & Co.
70 Lincoln Street
Boston, Mass. 02111